BEAST OF '77

REMASTERED EDITION
BOOK I OF III

SHAWN A. JENKINS

BEAST OF '77 REMASTERED EDITION
BOOK I OF III

iUniverse books may be ordered through booksellers or by contacting:

iUniverse
1663 Liberty Drive
Bloomington, IN 47403
www.iuniverse.com
1-800-Authors (1-800-288-4677)

ISBN: 978-1-5320-5243-9 (sc)
ISBN: 978-1-5320-5244-6 (e)

Print information available on the last page.

iUniverse rev. date: 06/19/2018

Circa 1977, twas a year I recall...with a lovely fondness.
The Unknown...

FOREWORD

November 26th 1976

"Don't forget the man's arm. It's lying over there."
Detective Wilson pointed while surveying the living room
from a distant corner with a queasy appearance attached to his
dark, middle-aged face.

Wrapped in his black *London Fog* winter coat, the stocky
Wilson meticulously scratched his heavy mustache as though
he were entangled in some sort of deep thought.

The mangled and tattered front door was still hanging
wide open to allow his fellow officers to enter and exit at
will. The bitter cold morning wind swept its way into the foul
smelling house where four motionless bodies laid on the floor.

Some officers, as they entered, would pause to watch the
detective stand in his safe corner as though he were trying to
avoid work. Truth be told, it was the ungodly stench of the
house that kept the veteran lawman in place. The odor was
that of both bloody bodies and marijuana hanging profusely
in the air.

From left to right on the carpeted floor laid a menagerie
of carnage. Three horribly mutilated black males and their
appendages and intestines strewn all over the floor, and one

other person, who appeared to still be intact, sprawled out in all his skinny nakedness.

Wilson watched in somber angst as the coroners lifted arms, severed heads and legs into black *Hefty* bags as though they were scooping up leaves from off the ground.

"Hey, Wilson," a young, white police officer called out from the front door. "The captain wants an update on the situation!"

Detective Wilson slightly shifted his eyes away from the macabre scene on the floor to look at the officer as he approached him.

"Situation," Wilson questioned with a grunt in his dry throat. "Tell 'em to come down here. I've got a situation for him."

The young officer stepped up beside the detective and peered down at the floor where Wilson was staring. From where Wilson was standing it was hard for his eyes to take in everything all at once. So much blood and mayhem contained in one area. The smell was overwhelming to the degree that his breathing had become stifled.

"Have you ever seen anything like this before, Detective?"

Wilson rolled his eyes in agitation before saying, "Dawson, why do you even ask such a question?"

Dawson sucked in his gut and modestly asked, "Just what exactly do you think did this?"

Gingerly, Wilson turned his pudgy body around to a destroyed closet door and said, "Well, it looks as though our Jamaican friends that were all over the floor a while ago may have had some kind of animal locked up in this here closet. It must've got out and tore the poor bastards apart."

"Poor," Dawson asked with a grimace. "Detective, look at the table, it's lined with coke and pot. It looks to me like these guys had it coming to them."

"Perhaps," Wilson shrugged while still examining the closet door.

"And what about this one," Dawson pointed down where the naked man was lying. "There's not a scratch on him."

Wilson reached into the closet and picked up a pair of torn *Levi* blue jeans that was lying on the floor. He then dug into the back pocket and pulled out a wallet.

Wilson gazed at the photo on the driver's license and said, "That looks like him, alright."

"But what about his face," Dawson inquired. "Looks like he was beaten up."

Wilson knelt down to view the young black man's swollen features. "Not a single scratch on him. How then did his clothes end up in that closet? Was he locked in there along with the animal?" Wilson irritably grumbled.

Dawson took his flashlight from out of his holster and inspected the closet even closer. He saw nothing but jackets, shoeboxes and shards of long, black hair that was layered all over the floor.

"Detective, take a look at this."

Wilson stood back up and stepped over to where Dawson was standing. "What is it, son?"

"This." Dawson pointed as he stooped down to pick up the thick fuzz."

"What is it, a dust bunny?"

"I'm afraid not, Detective. It looks like fur."

"Fur from what, for God's sake?"

"It's hard to say, given what it did to these fellows."

"Could it be a black bear?"

"In these parts, sir," Dawson smugly replied. "It's highly unlikely."

"Don't stand there and beat around the bush, boy. It is likely that a bear, or something like a bear, got into this house, killed the three men and then escaped out the front door. And if it's escaped this house, then this city has a helluva problem on its hands; something a whole lot worse than some kidnapper."

"It was strong enough to tear a hole not only through the closet door, but also the front door as well." Dawson added. "But, Detective, I can assure you that this was no bear."

"How can you be sure of that?"

"Look at the size of the closet. It's the same size as my mother's linen closet. It's impossible that a full grown bear could fit inside there."

"But a full grown bear could eat three full grown men up like appetizers."

"It's a possibility, but judging from the bullet holes in the walls, it seemed as if the guys were able to pull off a few rounds before meeting their maker. Those guns on the floor are nine millimeters; three men with three guns weren't able to take down a full grown bear."

"Wait a minute." Wilson inhaled. "I'm guessing that those voodoo motherfuckers probably stole a bear from the zoo, brought it home and the damn thing went crazy and killed them. Hell, if an animal is mad enough it could withstand a shotgun blast. Who knows what went on in here last night? For all we know, they could have fed the bear some of that coke before it went on its rampage. These Jamaicans are half out of their mind anyways."

"You can say that again."

"Take that fur down to the station and give it to forensics. We'll see what they come up with."

"Forensics," Dawson griped. "I hate going down to the basement to see those guys. They talk your ear off."

"What are you complaining about? You don't have to fill out the paperwork on this mess." Wilson offhandedly replied while holding in a hearty belch that was trying to bring up his wife's macaroni and cheese from the Thanksgiving feast from the night before.

"Well, at least that poor guy is still alive." Dawson commented as he and Wilson watched the paramedics lift the naked man onto a gurney.

"Alive…and still in one piece," Wilson said. "Helluva way to spend the holidays."

"Just what are you going to tell the captain when you speak to him, sir?"

Wilson glanced over at the curious young man, and with a glare of conceit in his eyes, he confidently exclaimed, "Are you kidding? It won't matter what I say to the old man. When I get home tonight, my wife and I are gonna plan our vacation to Hawaii. I'd like to see him stop that."

As both men began for the disheveled front door, Wilson couldn't help but to pause and look back once more at the gory sight that was once a living room. Blood plastered all over the carpet, walls and the dining table. It all appeared as though someone had gone crazy and splashed red paint everywhere in reckless abandon.

"Happy Thanksgiving, fellas," Wilson haplessly stated before exiting the home.

CHAPTER 1

FEBRUARY 1977

"I KNOW SHE'S YOUR sister, but we've been planning this vacation for months now, Julie." Young Doctor Levin abrasively griped over the black telephone that was seated uncomfortably in his lap.

The bright morning sun shined into the intelligent looking office where he was waiting for his superior to arrive. Large books on tall shelves lined the sizeable, cozy room, along with multiple honors and pictures of five little Hindu girls and an older woman of identical origin.

"Julie, listen, maybe Justine can stay at your mother's place. She's got plenty of room. You and I just moved into that house."

Levin straightened his brown, *Sears* purchased tie while trying in earnest to keep his glasses on his face and the phone from slipping off his lap. His conversation with his wife was as important as the meeting he was patiently awaiting. He realized that it was rude to use his senior's phone without asking, but it was a matter of life and death as far as he was concerned. Every so often he would glance at the door to see if it would suddenly blow open at a moment's notice.

"Honey, I can't help it that Dan left Justine, that's not our problem."

Just then, like a rushing wind, the door swung open revealing behind it a medium sized Hindu man in his early sixties with thick, black eyeglasses and a collection of manila folders in hand.

"Uh, honey, my meeting is about to begin, so we'll talk when I get home tonight. Love you, too." Levin frantically said as he quickly hung up the phone and carefully placed it back on his colleague's desk. "Good morning, Doctor Sanyupta." He extended a sweaty right hand as he sat up.

"Good morning, Doctor. How are you?" Sanyupta, dressed in a white lab coat, graciously smiled in his broken English as he shook the young man's hand back.

"Doing well, sir," Levin himself smiled from ear to ear.

"Please have a seat, Doctor." Sanyupta said as he sat himself down behind his oak-lined desk and placed his folders down neatly beside him. "I understand that you are pressed for time this morning, so I will try and make this as short and sweet as possible."

"Very well," Levin replied as he sat back down and crossed his legs.

"I trust that your journey here to Ashlandview was a pleasant one?"

"It was." Levin continued to cheese. "I got lost around I-70, but after a few turns here and there, I was back on track again."

"Yes, the road to this facility is riddled with twists and turns, I am afraid."

"Among other things," Levin cracked while holding his knocking knees in place.

Sanyupta only sat back and squared his eyes at the man as to say the comment flew right past him. "Yes." Sanyupta sighed. "Well, as I said, I will try not to take up too much of your time. Today we have two of our residents that will be departing from the facility." Sanyupta explained while picking up one of the folders and opening it.

Levin sat up and tried to catch a glimpse of the photo inside the folder.

"First, we have Shannon Carter. White female, age thirty four," Sanyupta said. "Shannon has been with us for four years and seven months as of today. Six years ago, Shannon was raped by her father. One night while he was sleeping, Shannon used a pair of her mother's sewing scissors and stabbed her father twenty-seven times in the neck."

Gradually, Levin sat back in his seat and swallowed. Not only was he flabbergasted by the woman's heinous action, but also by the calm, unflinching manner in which Doctor Sanyupta used in explaining her situation."

"The courts, given the nature of what led her to commit the murder, chose to place Shannon in multiple institutions. She bounced around from one facility to the next, until she arrived here. Like many of our new residents, Shannon was quite reluctant to comply at first."

"That is until your treatments came into play?" Levin proudly chimed in.

"Well, Sanyupta paused, "do not be so hasty to congratulate me just yet, my friend. First I had to convince Shannon that I was not here to judge her; I was here to help her. It was a long, frustrating road, but eventually, through time, she and I began to see eye to eye. Once she felt comfortable receiving my treatments, her obstinacy ceased. Just make sure you do not mention her father...in any sense of the word."

Levin only nodded his head in approval as though Sanyupta was waiting for it.

"Next, we have Isaac Mercer." The doctor said as he whipped out another folder. "Black male, age twenty. Isaac has been with us now since the beginning of December. I am not sure if you recall the incident that took place last November, where three men were found mutilated inside their own home."

"I do recall that." Levin pondered. "Police say that it was some mad dogs that killed those men."

"Well, a lot of people have their own personal theories on that sordid situation. But Isaac was the sole survivor the attack. When he came home from the hospital, he began to have hallucinations and periods of blackouts. His violent paranoia became so intense that his father suggested that he be brought here for observation. At first, Isaac refused to sit in on the sessions, but seeing the results that my treatments have had on the others first hand, he decided to give it a try."

"So after only two and a half months he's ready to leave?"

"Believe it or not," Sanyupta responded. "Isaac's recovery is nothing short of miraculous. He is like a brand new man. I am quite sure that his father will be proud of his son's progress."

"So let me see if I have this straight, Isaac's paranoia stems from perhaps a guilt of surviving the attack? From what I read in the paper, that was a pretty nasty discovery inside that house."

"Uh no, I am afraid that it is more complex than that, Doctor Levin." Sanyupta sat back in his chair. "You see, Isaac believes that he is a werewolf." He plainly and seriously clarified without batting a single eyelash.

Doctor Levin sat up again in his suddenly uncomfortable seat and cracked a tense smirk at Sanyupta.

CHAPTER 2

"Good morning. I'm Helen *Lewis with Action Seven News. We are pre-empting our regularly scheduled programming to bring you this live report. I'm here on the campus of Cypress State Community College where yet another kidnapping has just taken place here just twenty minutes ago. Twenty-two year old Gloria Cohen was abducted right here, in front of this vending machine by the elusive B.O.D. Kidnapper According to eyewitnesses, Gloria, who is a psychology major here at the college, left one of her classes. Her schoolmates say that she stops here every day to purchase a candy bar and a soda. One moment everything is fine, and then the next moment, Gloria is heard screaming while being snatched away by a large man wearing a blue ski mask. This man grabbed Gloria, tossed her into a blue Ford van and took off down Charleston Street. Members of the Cypress State basketball team chased after the van, but to no avail, as the vehicle sped away down the road. Gloria's abduction makes this the sixteenth kidnapping by the same individual. We got a chance to speak with some of Gloria's classmates. Sir, can you tell us just what took place here?"*

"I don't know...it all happened so fast. One second, Gloria was by the vending machine, then you turn your head for one moment, and she's gone. Just like that. Where are the police when something like this happens? What are our parents paying takes for when the cops aren't even around to protect people?"

"Okay, obviously a very distraught young man, indeed. Ma'am, were you able to describe the individual that snatched Gloria away?"

"He was wearing a blue ski mask and black gloves! He just picked her up like a baby and threw her into the van! He was tall! I don't know, maybe six-foot four or five! I can't believe this is happening! Gloria is such a nice person! Who would do such a thing?"

"Well, as you can see, tensions are high here at Cypress State. We will keep you apprised of this tragic situation as it unfolds. For Action Seven News, I'm Helen Lewis. We now send you back to The Jokers Wild."

Isaac Mercer. Six foot. Dark brown skin. Low cut hair; a pair of brown jeans, and amber eyes that shined like shards of crystal in the dark.

One by one, Isaac neatly placed articles of clothing into his blue suitcase while listening to the disorderly commotion outside his room.

They were the white noises that he would be taking home with him. Sounds of disturbed patients screaming and moaning for no apparent reason other than the want of attention.

From his room he could smell the cafeteria preparing lunch for the day; macaroni and cheese, tapioca, and his favorite, beef stew.

As he placed his last pair of *Fruit of the Loom* underwear into the suitcase, Isaac paused and glanced over at the picture of his mother that was sitting on the nightstand next to his made bed. He reached over, picked up the frame and glared deeply into the woman's smiling face. Almost instantly, Isaac himself began to smirk as though she would be waiting for him the moment he walked out of the building.

Gently, Isaac packed the frame into his suitcase before reaching over and taking the photo of his longtime girlfriend and young son. His body could hardly contain itself from the overwhelming feeling it had in knowing that in only an hour's time he would be seeing them once again.

Isaac couldn't count how many times he had masturbated to his lady's image before falling asleep at night, or just the thought of holding his little boy in his arms as though he were a newborn all over again. It all made his body jitter with unbridled elation.

"Hey, man." A muscular, bearded black man came into Isaac's room with a brown paper bag in hand.

"Hey, what's up?" Isaac smiled as he gave the man their daily, five point "ghetto" hand shake.

"Not much, just thought I'd stop by and give you this before you left." The orderly remarked as he handed Isaac the bag.

Isaac took the bag and reached inside to find a carton of oatmeal cream pies. He snickered and said, "Thanks, brother. I'm gonna need these for that long trip home."

"I sure as hell ain't gonna miss sneaking those things to you at two in the morning!" The orderly laughed out loud.

"I hear you, man!" Isaac laughed back. "Listen, I really appreciate everything you've done for me since I was here."

"That's my job, my man." He shrugged. "You just make sure you take care of that woman and son of yours."

"Will do," Isaac said as he slapped hands with the man once again. "You gonna come and meet my dad before we leave out?"

"Sorry, my man, I gotta go clean Mr. Reynolds' bed." The orderly sighed. "You know how that dude can get after he eats cornbread. But you state loose, Merc."

"I will. You do the same." Isaac grinned as he watched the man exit the bedroom, leaving the door opened behind him.

As Isaac turned around he found himself suddenly paralyzed by his own reflection in the mirror that was mounted on the closet door. He couldn't explain why the image seized him so violently at that moment, or why he even spun around so quickly to begin with.

Skittishly, he approached the mirror and stared deeply into his own strange looking eyes, the same eyes he had been carrying with him since last November. He then took his right hand and gipped his left forearm. He squeezed and rubbed the appendage as though it were bothering him.

Once he was through massaging his arm, he slowly opened the creaking closet door and vigilantly looked inside. From left to right all he could see was empty space, ready for the next patient's arrival.

The odor or feces began to whisper into Isaac's room like the air was carrying it straight to him personally. He shut the closet door and tossed a few last items into his stuffed suitcase before hoisting it off the bed and carrying on out the room.

"Ahh, Isaac my friend." Doctor Sanyupta called out as both he and Doctor Levin rounded the corner. "I see you are ready to leave us today, young man." He graciously smiled.

"I sure am." Isaac humbly and bashfully grinned.

"Before you leave I would like for you to meet Doctor Jeremiah Levin. He will be taking my place for the next two months while I practice over in Asia."

"How are you, Isaac?" Levin greeted with a smile and a handshake.

"Doing good." Isaac responded in kind.

"Doctor Levin will be meeting with you at his office in Ligon in a few days. Anything you need you will take it to him."

"Okay." Isaac simply replied.

"I am very proud of you, young man." Sanyupta beamed. "You're recovery here has been nothing short of phenomenal. You are now on the road to a bright future."

All Isaac could do was stand in the middle of the hallway floor and blush. Suddenly, the heavy weight of his suitcase seemed almost inconsequential.

"Well, we must be on our way. Goodbye, Isaac." Sanyupta said while shaking Isaac's hand.

"Goodbye, sir."

"So long, Isaac," Levin said as he shook Isaac's hand once more before following in behind Sanyupta down the hallway.

Isaac watched as both men turned down a noisy corridor full of the boisterous sounds of men and women groaning and crying for someone to assist them.

Isaac turned and began walking in the opposite direction. The door up ahead, just mere feet away, seemed like crossing an ocean as the rackets increased with every room that he passed by. Isaac twisted the knob, pushed open the door and then shut it behind him.

Like the flick of a light switch, the enchanting harmonies of *Glen Miller's, 'Moon Love'* cooed into his warm ears from the speaker up above his head.

At the front desk stood a late fiftyish, portly black man who was writing on a notebook pad. Instantly, the man looked up and noticed Isaac standing at the doorway. A delighted beam shined under his full mustache.

He dropped his pen that he was using, and without saying a word, the large gentleman grabbed Isaac into his arms and hugged the life out of him.

"How are you, boy?" The man smiled, rubbing his mustache.

"I'm alright, dad." Isaac modestly replied as he dropped his suitcase to the floor, straightened his white undershirt and stepped back to examine his father from afar. "Uh, oh, looks like you've been losin' some weight there."

Embarrassed, Isaac's father waved his right hand and said, "Cut that mess out, boy. Any weight I've lost is in my head. C'mon and let's go home." The man chuckled while handing Isaac a grey winter coat.

Isaac put on the coat, picked up his suitcase and followed in behind his father. "Is it real cold out?"

"You better believe it is. Zip up so you won't catch your death out here." Father replied, holding the door open for his son.

The second Isaac stepped out of the warm confines of Ashlandview, his entire body surged with shocking electricity. It was well below ten degrees that cloudy morning, but Isaac could feel nothing inside of him except serene and affectionate warmth. Ashlandview wasn't a prison, but no one ever called it home.

The customary odors of urine, stale vegetables and soiled linen were all replaced with the aroma of a cold winter breeze that would have any other person running for shelter; but to Isaac, it felt fresh and brand new, like the start of a new year.

Unlike most of the other patients, Isaac's stay at Ashlandview was short. Over the time he was there the young man had been inundated with stories from other residents and orderlies about how horrible it was to be inside for only one week.

Dissimilar from his father, Isaac wasn't much of a praying man, but he made sure to thank God every day for pulling through.

Both men stepped over sheets of ice and snow on their way to a brown, 1972 *Ford Pinto* that was parked next to a large, white laundry truck.

"I thought you were gonna get a brand new car, dad." Isaac mentioned as he climbed in on the passenger's side.

"Shucks," the elder Merger sniggered, "I'm still trying to

recover from all that Christmas shopping I did. How do you expect me to get a brand new anything, son?"

"I figured God would make a way for you." Isaac offhandedly jibed.

"You know better than to test the Lord," Isaac's father rebuked before cutting on the rickety ignition and pulling out of the parking lot.

From Ashlandview to home was a forty-five minute trip, Isaac realized that his father had a lot of questions to ask, notably inquiries about his condition. Isaac wasn't looking forward to any of them, but he braced himself nonetheless, like an oncoming accident waiting to take place.

"So, did you see that *Superbowl* last month?" Father asked as he cut on the car's heater.

"Yes, sir, Oakland sure put a whoopin' on those Vikings." Isaac *smiled*. Minnesota ain't never gonna win a title. Everybody up in that place was goin' crazy. Even Sanyupta had money on that game."

"What?" Father frowned. "What does he need money for? He's a doctor."

"Dad, it was all just for fun. Isaac respectfully chided his father.

"I see." Isaac's father relented while worriedly glancing over at his son's face. "Did they ever find out what was wrong with your eyes?"

As though he were put on the spot, Isaac immediately directed his attention to the window beside him and said from out of the side of his mouth, "Uh, Doctor Sanyupta said that it may have something to do with trauma. Almost like hysterical blindness, but without the blindness. If that makes any sense."

"Hysterical blindness, huh," the man shrugged in disbelief. "Well, I've heard of hysterical blindness, but I ain't never heard of someone's eye color just up and changing overnight like yours did. And you're not even blind. You've been that way since the beginning of last November."

"C'mon, dad," Isaac moaned. "I told you last month, it's nothing big. It'll go away soon."

Isaac's father sighed. Isaac figured that the man was trying to conjure up another series of questions to hurl his way.

"I heard the weatherman say that we were gonna get some more snow soon." Isaac said.

"Yeah, maybe six or seven inches by the end of the week. But you know how these weather folks are, they say snow and we end up getting rain. Hey, did you happen to catch previews for that new movie series coming to TV, about the slaves?"

"The only thing we ever saw on TV in that place was these stupid singing shows. If I see another episode of *Hee Haw* I'm gonna snap." Isaac giggled.

Isaac's father joined in laughing. "You think that's bad? All last week they showed nothing but the *Donny and Marie Show* for twenty-four hours. Now that's torture!"

Unexpectedly, Isaac's melancholy mood began to diminish, right along with the frost that had gathered on the windshield.

"It wasn't so bad in there." Isaac exhaled. We got three squares a day. We really didn't have to worry about much, expect Doctor Sanyupta's treatment sessions."

"Treatment sessions," Mr. Mercer grimaced. "What kind of treatments are we talking about?"

"Do you remember a couple of years ago, you and Deacon Hawthorne went to see that *Jack Nicholson* movie?"

Mr. Mercer pondered and then squinted his eyes, "You mean that cuckoo movie?"

"Yes, sir," Isaac said.

"Okay, I remember."

"Well, Doctor Sanyupta's treatment sessions were sorta like that. No one got electrocuted or smothered with pillows. We just sat around, talked about our feelings and mediated like a bunch of monks." Isaac explained. "There was this one woman named Shannon. She killed her dad with some scissors years ago and acted like nothing ever happened. But after a few sessions, she started to open up, and before you knew it, she was okay."

"I see." Mr. Mercer sighed. "So, do you think you're okay now?"

Isaac hesitated at first to reply; it was as if he were waiting for something to interrupt him. "I think so. Although I'm not too crazy about going back to church, or the old neighborhood again."

"Why on earth not," Mr. Mercer asked.

"C'mon, dad," Isaac whined, "everyone knows where I went and why I went there. It's embarrassing. I'd rather say that I went to the Penn than to a mental hospital."

"Don't say that, son. Only me, Lynnette and the good Lord know where you've been. What's done is done. God wants you to move forward with your life. He's given you a brand new slate, now its time to start writing a new chapter in your life."

Isaac listened intently to his father speak words that before going away were torturous to him. But sitting there in the same car alongside his father and away from the institution, the man's speech never sounded so relieving.

"Lynn and Isaiah can't wait to see you again, and as far as folks in the church and neighborhood are concerned, everyone thinks that you went to see your Aunt Doris down in Columbus for the past few months. And that's another thing, I wanna see you and Lynn in church for a change. It's time you start showing your family how a man comes back from adversity. Proverbs 23:18 says: *surely there is a future, and your hope will not be cut off.*"

Isaac glanced over at his dad and noticed the man's eyes watering up. He had never seen his father cry outwards, but for the very first time, the man that he knew as the strongest human being alive was sitting in the driver's seat, silently weeping.

"Hey, dad, if you had to do it all over again, sending me away…would you?"

Mr. Mercer wiped his eyes and said, "Son, you weren't exactly yourself a few months back. As much as it killed me to do so, I did what I thought was right. You have to understand, before then, I've never seen you behave that way. Can you believe that Deacon Hawthorne actually wanted me to perform, of all things, one of those exorcisms on you?"

Isaac looked up and cracked a whimsical smirk before asking, "You mean like the movie?"

"I'm dead serious, man." Mr. Mercer chuckled. "I kept on telling the brother that the Lord will know what to do. Whatever is wrong with Isaac, God will make a way. He always does in the end."

Isaac once more lowered his head in shame. Every so often he would peek at his uncanny eyes in the rearview mirror beside him as though he were expecting something sinister to occur out of nowhere.

He then closed his tired eyelids and slumped deep into his seat, listening carefully as the car's loud engine hummed along the endless highway that led homeward.

CHAPTER 3

MR. MERCER STOPPED THE car in front of a shabby, one floor, white and black house and said, "I won't be able to come and pick you up till around eight tonight."

"That's cool, I'll just catch the bus home." Isaac nonchalantly responded while fixing his hair in the rearview mirror.

Mr. Mercer then began to fiddle with the car keys that were still lodged in the ignition until he was able to unhinge a rusty, gold key and hand it to Isaac.

"You be careful coming home."

"Yes, sir," Isaac replied as he grabbed the key that was still tightly gripped inside his father's large hand.

Without looking at each other, both men's hands grasped the others for a few moments. There were no words exchanged during the event, just heavy breathing and longing silence. Isaac's own hand was becoming increasingly sore with his father's paw gripping his, but the young man held on, and he held on some more.

"See you at home, boy." Mr. Mercer said as he released Isaac's sweaty hand.

Isaac took the key and got out of the car. With water in his eyes he watched as his dad pulled away back onto the main road before carrying on towards the house ahead of him.

He didn't even want to ponder on how his father felt at that point, Isaac knew that it would only cause him to shatter right there on the sidewalk.

The neighborhood was a rundown excuse for a community. On both sides of the street sat six houses, four of the six on Isaac's side were boarded up, while the others were completely in shambles; all forgotten by a city that in and of itself was in the thralls of ruination.

Just as Isaac was about to step up onto the dilapidated porch, loud music could be heard clashing down the street. It was a dark green *Volkswagen Beetle* proudly playing *Rose Royce's, 'Car Wash'* for everyone to hear.

For Isaac, it wasn't the song that caught his attention, nor was it the volume at which it was playing, but rather the vehicle's color that seemed to mesmerize the man. Only his drooling eyes watched as the car tooled down the road. Its green tint flashed in his face like an explosion.

Isaac stood on the porch and waited for the car to clear the street before turning and knocking on the front door. Suddenly, all he could see was the color green in front of him.

Standing there on the porch, Isaac could hear footsteps march their way to the door. He immediately wiped his sweaty palms on his jeans and waited ever so impatiently for the door to swing open.

Abruptly, the door opened to reveal a young, short, brown skinned woman with hair rolled up in pink curlers. The young lady's face instantly became mortified and nervously excited at the sight of Isaac.

"Isaac." She stuttered as though he were the last person in the world that she was expecting to see standing on the other side of the door. "I…I thought you wouldn't be here till tomorrow."

Smiling from ear to ear, Isaac said, "I wanted to surprise you."

Isaac then stepped through the door and hugged the woman with such force that he could hear her bones pop a bit.

Quaintly, the woman unhinged herself from Isaac's grip before looking into his face and asking with a serious expression, "They still haven't figured out what's wrong with your eyes?"

Isaac drew back surprised, and with a confused glare on his face he remarked, "I get home after two whole months and you ask me about my eyes?"

"I'm sorry, I guess I still haven't gotten used to them." She humbly replied. "I sure wish I knew that you would be here today. I would've done something with this crazy hair of mine. How did you get here from the hospital?"

Relaxing himself a bit, Isaac said, "Dad brought me." He then moved in and passionately kissed the woman on the lips. "Damn, you look fine."

"Negro, please, my hair is a mess, and I got a hole in my jeans." She callously waved off.

"You don't see me complaining, do you?"

"You sure look like you've lost a lot of weight." The woman studied Isaac from top to bottom. "Are you still in pain?"

"A little bit...here and there." Isaac carefully answered. "But, hey, I didn't come here to talk about me, Lynn. Where's that boy of mine at?"

"He's in there asleep." Lynn pointed behind her.

Isaac stood in the middle of the living room, only three inches away from Lynn, and stared her thin body up and down with both intense passion and empathy in his abnormal eyes. He could sense just by her shaky tone that his very presence was unsettling to her.

"Isaac...I—"

Just then, a small, chubby-legged little boy clothed in a dark blue *Batman* t-shirt and diapers came waddling out of the hallway and into the warm living room. His bleary-eyed self nearly bumped into the hot kerosene heater that was positioned up against the wall.

Immediately, Isaac rushed over and scooped the sleepy toddler into his arms as though he were handling a pot of gold. He excitedly kissed the boy's soft cheeks and forehead while rubbing his thick head of hair.

"He's been such a good little boy since daddy's been gone." Lynn said while standing next to Isaac and caressing the child's cheeks.

Isaac sat himself and Isaiah down onto the couch and tried to wake his son from his hazy blindness.

"Wassup, little man? How you been doin'?" Isaac jovially laughed.

"Say, 'I've been a good little boy, daddy.' Lynn mocked as she sat down next to Isaac.

Gradually, the child opened his brown eyes and gazed strangely upon his father as if he were looking at a total stranger.

Isaac continued to play with the baby until Isaiah began to anxiously wrestle out of his dad's hold and reach for his mother.

Isaac's entire body went completely numb at that moment. "Damn, Lynn, he wouldn't even let me hold 'em for two seconds."

Cradling the baby in her arms, Lynn patiently replied, "Well, he hasn't seen you for two months, Isaac. You have to give him time to get used to you all over again."

"Maybe if you would've brought him along when you came to visit me back in December, then he probably wouldn't act like that." Isaac pouted as if Lynnette were his greatest nemesis.

Lynn looked over at Isaac with a stale glaze in her eyes and said, "Isaac, I told you that I don't want our son to see his father in a place like that."

A few moments of blistering silence passed before Isaac

spitefully turned his head and asked, "So, how have you two been doin'?"

Sighing, Lynn responded, "We've been okay. Got behind on the electric bill again last month. Mr. Harris said if it happens again then we'll have to find another place to live."

"Another place," Isaac gasped. "But you're only renting this shithole! How can he treat you like that?"

Rolling her eyes, Lynn said, "Isaac, I don't make the rules, I just follow them. Your father has been helping me, but...I'm tired of other people helping me out. If it's not your father then it's mine. If not my dad then it's my mother and sisters. I need my man to help me." She urgently explained while pensively eyeballing Isaac.

"Does your family know where I was these past two months?"

"No, Isaac." Lynn irritably groaned. "I haven't told anyone else."

"Look, I'll see if I can get my old job back at the—"

"At where," Lynn contemptuously interjected. "Down at Larry's garage, where they also sell drugs after hours? Isaac, if your father knew all of that was going on there, he would have a fit."

"But he doesn't know!" Isaac intolerantly yelled.

"Shh, baby, it's alright." Lynn softly said into Isaiah's ears as she tried to console the startled baby that was beginning to sob.

Isaac shot up from off the couch and began to wander about the small living room that was full of nothing but two wooden chairs and a fireplace with pictures placed on the mantle above.

"Did Mr. Harris ever fix the backdoor?"

"No, he said that he'd have to replace the entire thing."

Out of agitation, Isaac rolled his eyes and stormed into the smoldering kitchen where he noticed a pot of greens boiling on the stove. He bypassed the cooking food that was making his stomach grumble to reach the backdoor.

The second he grabbed the door's knob Isaac tried with all his might to twist and turn the rusty thing only to discover that it was practically welded shut.

"It probably just needs some *WD-40*!" He proclaimed while making his way back into the living room. "These landlords will do anything to escape doing their job."

"Well, let's just forget about." Lynn sighed. "Since we've been here I haven't needed to use the backdoor for anything."

Sitting back down on the couch, Isaac smirked at Lynn, "I see you cookin' up some greens without me."

Grinning back, Lynn said, "Well,

if someone had told me that they were coming home today then I would have made more."

"Later for you, girl, I'll go home and get some food then." Isaac playfully leaned over and kissed Lynn on the cheek. "I wanna take us out tomorrow."

"Yeah, you wanna see a movie or something?"

"What's playing?"

"There's this one movie called *Fun with Dick and Jane* that looks kinda funny."

"Who's in it?"

"*Jane Fonda.*"

Isaac simply glanced over and twisted his lips as to say that the idea was ludicrous.

"Okay then, turkey, do you have any plans?" Lynn jokingly shoved Isaac's shoulder.

"Instead of spending $2.20 a head for a movie ticket just so we can see *Jane Fonda's* skinny ass, let's all three of us go to *Jimmy's* and have pizza."

Lynnette approvingly shook her head and said, "Okay that sounds good. But I wanna hurry and get back before eight, because I wanna see this movie that's coming on about the slaves."

"Dad was talkin' about that in the car. What in the world is so important about this movie?" Isaac tossed up his hands.

Appearing surprised, Lynn replied, "You mean you haven't heard about it? It's called *Roots*. It's supposed to be really good. It's got *James* from *Good Times* and *O.J. Simpson* in it." She eagerly explained.

Isaac disapprovingly sighed before uttering, "Lynn, the last thing I wanna see is more depression. I just got out of the nut house."

"Don't call it that." Lynn put her hand on Isaac's lap. "You were just…a little tightly wound, after what you went through in that house and all."

Isaac turned his head in the other direction and began to blush as though the subject were too devastating to discuss.

"Isaac, I just want you to know that if you want to talk about what happened at the house, or back at Ashlandview, I'm here for you." Lynn compassionately clarified.

Isaac looked over to see his son gazing wildly back at him as if his father's image were slowly becoming more and more familiar.

"Well, let me get lunch together so Isaiah can eat." Lynn feebly exhaled as she got up, with child in tow, from off the couch.

Isaac sat and watched as Lynnette carried on into the kitchen. In all aspects, he wasn't in any sort of mood to watch a movie or go out and face other people, but the desire to reconnect with his family was so overwhelming that Isaac would have shed blood just to complete such a valiant mission.

Isaac realized the damage that he caused months earlier to both Lynnette and his father, and above all else he was bound and determined to make amends, even if it meant having to swallow chunks of pride along the way.

Just being inside the house alongside his girlfriend and son caused the young man to gulp deeply until he felt it hit the pit of his churning stomach. On one hand he was overjoyed, on the other, the front door was only a mere five feet away from where he was seated.

Distraught, Isaac stood up and began for the bathroom, but before he could even round the corner, he stopped in the hallway and caught his somber reflection in the small mirror hanging on the wall next to the clothes hamper.

It seemed that every time he happened to stare upon his own likeness all he could see staring back at him was an insidious man, someone that he hated more than anything in the world. There was absolutely nothing within his image that made him content.

He poked and pulled at his face before rubbing his arms up and down, just as he did back at Ashlandview, checking for any more pain that may suddenly arise without notice.

It was a relentless, tedious habit that he repeated five times a day, every day.

CHAPTER 4

THAT EVENING, ISAAC STOOD at his father's bedroom door with a fist pick lodged in his thick hair, silently watching as the well-disciplined man studied his bible, as he did every evening prior to falling asleep.

Forever it amazed Isaac at how deep and methodical his dad would sink himself into his lessons, even to the point where the man would become totally oblivious to another person standing near him.

Isaac examined his father up and down as though he were an age old masterpiece that was clothed in a pair of striped pajama bottoms and a white *Fruit of the Loom* undershirt. His drooping cheeks and sullen eyes gave the impression that whatever he was reading upon in his great book was something very serious, yet somber.

Mr. Mercer then sighed and took off his reading glasses before slowly closing his book and staring off straight ahead at the bare, white wall for ten seconds. Once the ten seconds had passed, the man gradually looked up at Isaac and slightly grinned as if he were awakening from a stupor.

"Hey." Mr. Mercer yawned as he placed his bible on the bed next to him. "I didn't see you there."

Humbly grinning with his hands in his pockets, Isaac

said, "You never do, dad. I just stopped by to see how you were doin.'"

"Aww, shoot, I'm just getting ready to fall asleep." Mr. Mercer gleefully smiled while stretching his chunky arms outwards. "It's been a long day. A long, good day, son."

"You know, I was just thinkin' to myself, perhaps I'll go and find a job."

"You goin' back to the garage?"

"Uh…no, sir," Isaac began to squirm. "I was thinkin' about maybe another line of work. Maybe…cleaning."

Almost immediately, Mr. Mercer's eyes grew two sizes larger with joy at his son's remark. "Cleaning, huh? And what brought this on? I thought you liked working down at the garage with Larry and Marvell. You three have been buddies for years."

"Yeah, I know, but…I wanna do something on my own for a change."

"Well, I can put in a good word for you with Mr. Wallace. Maybe he can put you with me at the federal building downtown. We can go in together every afternoon. That is if you don't mind getting off at eight every evening."

"That's cool. I figure it's time for me to start something new. Like you said this morning, 'start a brand new slate.'"

Mr. Mercer smiled favorably at his boy and asked, "So, what was it like to see Isaiah after all this time?"

"Okay, I guess." Isaac huffed.

"Just okay," Mr. Mercer questioned in awe. "I figured you'd be over there all night."

"Yeah, me too, but he acts like he doesn't even know me." Isaac griped. "Lynn says that I just need to give him time to readjust to me all over again. Man, if only she had brought him along when she came to visit, then he wouldn't be actin' like this."

"Sometimes we act in the best interest of those we love."

Mr. Mercer patiently explained. "Lynnette did what she thought was right for your son. You can't be mad at her for that. Proverbs 14:29 says that whoever is patient has great understanding, but one who is quick-tempered displays folly."

Isaac swallowed heavily at his father's words and asked, "So does that mean I'm supposed to forgive Lynn, even when she keeps my boy away from me?"

"It means put it behind you and be thankful for what you have now. God hates an unforgiving heart."

Isaac humbly shook his head and then said, "I was planning on taking us three down to *Jimmy's* tomorrow for dinner."

"Oh yeah," Mr. Mercer yawned.

"Yes, sir, just a little something to get us all back together again."

Without saying another word, Mr. Mercer reached over to his nightstand drawer and pulled out a black wallet. He then took out a bill and handed it to Isaac.

Isaac took the money and gazed seriously at the numeral 20 as if he had never laid eyes on such a large amount of money before in his life.

"For real," Isaac marveled.

With a grin and a shrug, Mr. Mercer said, "Why not? You can pay me back when you get your first paycheck."

Isaac stuffed the bill into his pants pocket and watched as his father began to tuck himself into his covers.

There was so much he wanted to tell the man on the way home from Ashlandview, but the shock of leaving the place was still laying heavy on his soul.

"Hey, dad," Isaac stuttered, trying not to allow his voice to crack in mid-sentence, "I just wanted to say that I'm...sorry for everything I did."

Mr. Mercer raised himself up from out of the bed and stroked his face while looking up at his child with consoling eyes.

With a heavy sigh, the man said, "Son, what happened has happened. Neither God nor I want you to live the rest of your life full of regret. I realize that what took place back in November with your friends getting killed really tore you apart, but they're in the good Lord's hands now. You're here, and you have to move on, not just for your sake, but also for Lynnette and Isaiah. You've always been a good boy, now go and be a good man."

With that, Mr. Mercer cut off his lamp while Isaac, with tears welling up in his eyes gently whispered, "Goodnight, dad."

Isaac turned and carefully shut his father's bedroom door before venturing out into the darkened hallway.

Wearing only a long John shirt and a pair of grew sweatpants, Isaac went into the living room and turned on the television. The full moon outside shined brightly into the room like a fog lamp in the darkness.

He flicked on the lamp and picked up the TV's remote control to flip the channels. Isaac recalled his dad saying that it was a good day. The young man wanted more than anything to put the past behind him. It seemed as though that all the important people that he had hurt had pretty much forgiven him, which in turn set him at ease.

Isaac tossed the remote down onto the couch and stepped over to the mantle where a wide mirror was mounted, along with an assortment of *Kodak* pictures that sat side by side above the fireplace. Isaac picked up the frame of himself, before his eyes changed their color. From the photo to the mirror and back again he gazed.

The person he saw in the picture was someone he missed the most, while the man in the mirror was someone that he realized would not go away anytime soon, no matter how much and how hard he prayed.

The longer he peered into the mirror that was the angrier

his stomach seemed to grow. Isaac placed the frame back onto the mantle and made his way into the kitchen.

11:10 p.m., *Jiffypop* popcorn cooked on the stove that Isaac was standing over. He watched and waited as the metallic package ballooned in both size and smell over the course of three and a half minutes.

11:16 p.m., Isaac watched television while gobbling down every kernel of buttery popcorn that his wide mouth could inhale, along with the oatmeal cream pies that were given to him earlier in the day.

11:21 p.m., from one channel to the next he flipped and flipped; from the eleven o' clock news, to a *Bewitched* rerun, and all the way to an interview with President *Jimmy Carter.*

Isaac wasn't sleepy, which was odd considering that he had been awake since four that morning awaiting his release from the institution.

For him, being away from such a protected environment like a mental hospital meant that all of the things that he wanted to do while he was interned there could at last come to fruition, but sitting there in the lonely living room, gawking at a television screen and listening to the furnace roar from out of the nearby register wasn't exactly what he had in mind for a homecoming.

Isaac envisioned a girlfriend that was no longer leery of her man's behavior. He longed for a son that would embrace his dad the moment he walked through the door, but when all of his so called hopes and aspirations fell through, there remained only an empty feeling in the pit of his gut.

He was bored and let down, and watching a President babble on and on wasn't going to alleviate his condition one bit.

12:33 a.m., Isaac got up, went to the bathroom and shaved. The young man detested even the slightest stubble on his face. With every meticulous stoke of the blade Isaac made sure that not one shard of hair was left behind. Even if it meant cutting close to the grain, nothing was missed.

Deeper and more carefully he shaved, until at last, like many times in the past, he nicked himself, this time just beside his left nostril.

"Shit!" He screeched, making sure that his father was nowhere near to hear him.

Isaac reached over and ripped off a piece of toilet paper before patting the open wound that was beginning to drip into the sink below.

At first, Isaac ignored the blood, as he usually did in past instances; it was just his own blood. But the more he tried to soak up the substance that was all the more his nostrils began to flare. Suddenly, the blood had a scent that seemed to burn his nose hairs every time he inhaled.

Without notice, everything around Isaac began to drop into slow motion. The man felt as light as a feather at that moment.

Just then, the bathroom light started to flicker off and on. Isaac looked up and twisted the hot bulb to make sure it was screwed in tight. He then looked down at his bloody fingers. His mind went completely blank at the sight. It was as if he had never witnessed such a gruesome occurrence before.

There was no fear, angst or even a slight hint of shock, just subtle curiosity and a strong aroma that caused his once settled stomach to rumble all over again.

The light flickered again, but by then Isaac gave it no attention, he was entirely too mesmerized by his messy hands.

Minutes passed by before, like an oncoming, rushing wind, a bald, naked black man unexpectedly stumbled into the bathroom with his head hung low to where his youthful face could not be seen.

The very second Isaac looked up his eyes immediately caught sight of the uncanny figure. Out of sheer fright he stumbled back into the shower curtain, nearly tearing the plastic off the rod.

"C'mon, man." Isaac pitifully whimpered, too scared to scream out loud.

The intruder said nothing. With his head still hanging, he simply dragged himself back out of the bathroom and into the dark hallway.

Breathing heavily, Isaac began to cry before getting back to his feet and reluctantly following in behind the slow marching phantom.

Isaac trailed him all the way to the living room where the television set was still on. Isaac watched as the man dropped himself down onto the sofa. The man sat there, apparently waiting for Isaac's petrified self to join him.

Isaac stood next to the television, staring down at the nude figure. He wanted to see the man's face, just to make sure that he resembled a human, if not at one time in its existence.

The phantom then raised his right hand, and just like that, the television and the lamp went out simultaneously, leaving the entire living room completely black.

Out of fear, Isaac began to turn and run, but the phantom only held up his right index finger in a forceful manner, as to tell the young man not to move.

Isaac paused directly in the middle of the floor, seemingly entranced by the intruder's potent motion. He then slowly walked over and sat down in the chair that was placed in front of the couch.

Piece by piece Isaac began to take off his own clothes until he was stark naked. His mind was stagnant as his eyes shined away in the darkness. No words left his tight lips. Isaac remained still while his eyes stared straight ahead at the specter across from him.

2:37 a.m.: Mr. Mercer awoke to a scratchy throat that early morning. It was usual, which was why he always had a glass of water seated on his nightstand beside him.

He reached over and swallowed half of the cool drink before placing the cup back onto the table.

As he rolled back over in the bed, out of the corner of his foggy left eye was a twinkle which resembled two, tiny lights staring back at him from the side of the bed.

Mr. Mercer squeezed his eyes enough to where he could make out a round shape behind the lights. Panicked and out of breath, the man grabbed a hold of his covers and gasped for air while squinting some more until the silhouette rose up and began lurking itself around the bed.

"Isaac…is that you, son?" He stammered, holding the covers as tight as he could.

As Isaac casually stumbled towards the door, he slurred, "Em llik." (Kill me)

Mr. Mercer watched as his son crept out the already opened door before watching the door itself slam shut without Isaac even grabbing a hold of the knob.

The man laid there in his bed, drowning in his own pool of sweat and breathing heavier than he had done so in years.

CHAPTER 5

JIMMY'S ROLLER RINK: ON Just about any and every night the establishment was an energetic madhouse of young, black men and women skating, playing video games and frequent hookups.

The insane rumblings of roller skates scraping across every square inch of the floor could be heard clear outside the building, along with the loud melodies of *Junior Walker & The All Stars', 'Shotgun',* booming in the speakers above the rink, as part of the club's weekly retro night.

Isaac eagerly stood in line behind four people, waiting not only for his turn to order but also to return to his table where both Lynnette and Isaiah were seated.

From the concession stand he had a bird's eye view of both of them nodding their heads to the music. To him, it still felt strange to be amongst their presence after so long. Two months away seemed more like two years.

With each person that was in front of him ordering food and drinks that was all the more Isaac wanted to just throw up his hands in frustration and take his tiny family elsewhere, until eventually it was his turn to approach the counter. With only ten dollars left in his pocket, he ordered two *Pepsi's* and a small bucket of popcorn.

Once he was through at the counter, Isaac attempted the

arduous task of trekking his way back across the room while ducking and dodging skaters left and right.

The instant he was able to reach the table in one piece, Isaiah looked up, and almost instantly his bright eyes bubbled at the sight of the red and white container of popcorn that his father brought with him.

"Man, he ain't never gonna let his old man get some!" Isaac elatedly remarked as he sat down across from Lynnette and the baby.

Sipping on her cup of soda, Lynnette explained, "The boy loves him some popcorn." She then sat her cup down on the table and said, "It was nice of your father to give us some money to go out. Lord knows he's already done so much for us as it is."

"Yeah, well, that's gonna change real soon." Isaac adamantly stated.

"How do you mean?"

"Dad is gonna put in a good word for me at his cleaning company so I can get put on."

"For real," Lynnette beamed. "You mean to say that you're not going back to Larry's again?"

"Nope, I'm done with that fool."

"Thank God." Lynnette graciously exhaled. "Sooner or later he was gonna end up getting himself killed or you in the process."

As Isaac fiddled with his straw's wrapper, every so often his eyes would shift from the table in front of him to Lynnette's curly hair that was wrapped in a green scarf in the back, and her large, sparkling green earrings. He was aware of just how uncomfortable she would become whenever he stared at her, but he wanted to grab her attention.

"What are you looking at?" Lynnette blushed as if everyone in the rink were gawking at her all at once.

"Just the most beautiful girl in the place," he slyly smirked.

Lynnette rolled her eyes and smiled, "Please, you need your eyes checked."

"I can see things just fine."

"I bet you can." Lynnette murmured. "So, what did you end up doing last night when you got home?"

"Nothing much," Isaac shrugged. "Just watched some TV. When I woke up this morning, I was laying at the foot of my bed. For the life of me I can't remember what I did after I watched TV."

"You sure you weren't watching that nasty *Benny Hill Show* again?" She joked.

"Huh, so you wanna jive a brother?" Isaac laughed out loud. "For your information, while I was away I was actually reading a lot about mental health issues and all the stuff doctors are doing to help folks."

Lynnette dropped her head before asking, "It's not like it is in the movies, is it? Where they give people shock therapy and all that?"

"No, it's not like that." Isaac waved his hand. "Actually, the only bad thing about Ashlandview was the food. My first night there they served hotdogs for supper. I ended up having the runs for almost an entire week after eating their food."

"That's real nice to know right after I just got through eating a Coney dog myself, Isaac." Lynnette grimaced before taking another sip of soda. "I know you don't like talking about it, but I was just curious, that's all. I just don't want you to hate me for not bringing Isaiah along when I came to visit."

"I'm not mad. I thought about it, and you were right, it wasn't a good place to bring a child. All the folks in there yelling and screaming like they're…crazy. But I'll tell you this, I really enjoyed your poems. They helped me through some lonely nights. I'm glad that you never gave that up."

"I have a friend that I go to *Cypress State* with, and she says that my poetry is good enough to be published. She knows someone who may be able to send it off to an editor. Who knows, maybe I can get a book deal." Lynnette proudly blushed.

"Damn right, girl!" Isaac proclaimed excitedly. "I knew you could do it!"

Lynnette's once prideful expression immediately sank within a matter of two seconds. She stared at Isaac with a serious glare on her face and said, "This is really important to me; my poetry and becoming a nurse, Isaac. All three of my sisters got pregnant in high school and dropped out. Now, all they do is sit at home, collect welfare and watch *The Price Is Right* every day. I swore that I would never end up like them." Lynn's voice began to tremble. "It's hard, Isaac. It's damn hard for me to do this all on my own. I'm sick and tired of getting up at five a.m. every morning, feeding a baby, getting a baby ready for the sitter, running off to school, then off to work, just to come home and start all over again, when I should have my man there every step of the way."

Isaac couldn't tear his jittery eyes away from Lynnette at that second. He had heard the same scorching speech over and over again from her, except right then, the words were actually bleeding through to the bone.

Isaac stared a bit more at Lynnette's shaky face before he sat back in his leather seat and said, "I never did tell you what my father did years ago, did I?"

Lynnette scrunched up her face and asked, "What, he wasn't always a janitor?"

"No. You see, back in the day, he was a pimp and a drug dealer."

Lynnette only started to snigger while rolling her disbelieving eyes. "Yeah right, not Mr. Merc."

"The one and only," Isaac replied.

"Are you serious?" Lynnette lit up. "What happened?"

"Well, he and his crew used to run 89th and Forest Blvd

back then. Until one day, he saw this woman coming out of church one Sunday. He wanted to get with her so bad. He'd start rappin' about how much he would take care of her, and how pretty she was. But this woman, being a church going woman and all, wasn't gonna have anything to do with him. But dad kept on and on until finally, this same woman broke down and told him that if he changed his ways, stop pimping and selling drugs, then maybe, just maybe, she'd have a cup of coffee with him. So anyways, dad started to change, here and there. He gave up slanging the heroin and messing around with women. Two years later, he approached this woman again. Well, I figure she saw what an incredible transformation he had made in his life, and she kept her word about having coffee. So they went Downtown to Leonard's Café, had coffee, and they continued to do so for the next three years. They eventually got married, and nine months later I showed up."

Lynnette caressed Isaiah's head and modestly said, "I think I have a feeling where this story is headed."

Isaac sat up, reached his hands across the table and said, "Lynn, I know I fuc…messed up. But I'm trying real hard to change. All that stuff that happened last year, I wanna put it in the past. I wanna be there for you two. I hate seeing you work your ass off all the time. I want us to get married. I want you to be my wife and not my son's mom. I want all of the stuff that you want, even more. You gotta believe me." Isaac urged.

Isaac watched as Lynnette's eyes began to water, but he could sense that with such a large crowd looming about that she was hesitant to allow the tears to flow. She instead wiped her eyes and gazed upon Isaac's desperate conviction. Even Isaac, at that instant, was surprised at himself.

"Isaac…I want us to be together, too. But, I feel like I'm listening to a broken record. Do you know how much it hurt me to see you run out of the house like you did back on Thanksgiving?" She faintly sobbed. "And then all of the sudden wake up the next morning to find out that you're in the hospital? You and I have known each other since the sixth grade, Isaac. I thought we could talk to each other about anything."

Mortified, Isaac turned his head and looked the other way, too overwhelmed to stare into her tearful eyes a second longer.

"Uh, uh, you look at me." The young woman firmly commanded. "You always turn your head whenever someone tells you about yourself."

Isaac reluctantly did as ordered and redirected his attention back to Lynnette.

With an abrasive, yet vulnerable glaze written all over her face, Lynnette asked, "Do you promise to do better this time? Do you promise to control your temper and not run away every time we have a disagreement?"

It didn't take long for Isaac to respond to her ardent questions. Without mulling over it, he got up out of his seat, took three steps around the table and knelt down to one knee in front of Lynnette.

Everyone that passed by their direct vicinity paused, gasped and pointed at the young man who was in the midst of making the so called ultimate manly gesture.

With a plunging stomach, Isaac looked straight into Lynnette's eyes and said, "I don't have a ring right now, but… will you be my wife?"

With popcorn balled up in his tiny right hand, Isaiah glanced up at his overly blushing mother who appeared more thunderstruck than anything else.

There was no verbal response from the young woman, only a quaint smile and a simple nod yes before reaching down and hugging Isaac's sweaty neck.

All the female bystanders gave their collective "Aww's" before letting out a chorus of jubilant applause at the young couple's happiness.

"You see that, folks? Everyone falls in love at *Jimmy's!*" Jimmy Clark, the owner of the rink, loudly and delightedly announced over the P.A. system.

The cheers went on and on as *Marvin Gaye's, 'You're all I need'* began playing on the speakers.

Amidst all the adoring accolades Isaac continued to hold his woman's body, not wanting to let go.

"Isn't this better than sitting home and watching a movie about slaves?" He teased into her ear.

Isaac could feel Lynnette's body jiggle with laughter. Still, the woman had no words to utter. Isaac only hugged her tighter.

CHAPTER 6

WITH A HEAD FULL of irate bluster, Isaac blasted out of the small, white building in front of his father like a madman on a mission. The second he reached his dad's car, he slammed his fists on the roof as hard as he could.

"Isaac, hitting things isn't gonna make the situation any easier." Mr. Mercer rationally explained as he walked around to the driver's side and got in.

Isaac waited until his dad unlocked the other door before he jumped inside and slammed the door behind him.

"What does he mean," 'I don't have any experience?' "What kind of experience do you need to clean toilets?" He yelled while wiping sweat from off his forehead. "Ain't this about a blip?"

"You gotta understand something, son, there's a lot more to being a janitor than just cleaning toilets. Besides, Mr. Wallace already has a full staff. He said that he'll give you a call when something opens up again." Mr. Mercer calmly clarified before cutting on the ignition and pulling away onto the street.

"Yeah right, and when something does open up, that jive turkey will probably forget all about my black ass!"

"Cut that out!" Mr. Mercer scolded. "God never once promised any of us an easy life. Times are tough for everyone right now. People are losing jobs left and right. Gas is drying up. It's our hardships that make us stronger people. You'll find something. Besides, you've got a wedding to plan."

Isaac just turned his head in disgust and remarked, "What good is a wedding when the husband doesn't even have a job? I promised Lynn that I would help her out. Now what?"

"Now, you trust in the Lord. You have to allow him to take control of the situation."

Isaac rolled his eyes in silent frustration at his father's constant religious intervention. To him, it was like dousing a cup of acid on an already gaping wound.

As they drove along the decaying side streets of *Cypress*, it suddenly donned on Isaac as to just where he was at that moment.

He had been away for only two months, but yet, it was those two months that seemed to make all the startling difference in the world when it came to his ugly urban surroundings.

Once tall, busy downtown buildings had tragically succumbed to the plight of an economic slump. Crippled and dilapidated structures layered almost every corner of the vicinity. Most businesses, which had been around since the turn of the century, had become mere shadows of a more vibrant and industrious yesterday; a bittersweet reminder of a once thriving metropolis known as *Cypress, Ohio.*

As they passed by a *Dairy Queen*, Isaac caught himself fondly recalling a childhood memory where he was holding his mother's hand as they both walked down the strip to the restaurant on hot summer days.

The mini-mall that was located just across the road from where his father would take him every other weekend to buy comic books was by then only a convenient store that had a *store closing* sign posted on the front window.

Those and many other institutions had been shut down for months and years, and still Isaac could not seem to get it into his head that time had passed him by seemingly overnight.

Every so often he would glance over at his father, who by then needed his glasses to drive even in the daytime, hunched over the steering wheel as though seeing the road ahead of him was a million dollar challenge. The mightiest man in the world had the striking appearance of a feeble senior citizen who looked as though he were ready to fall asleep at a moment's notice.

All Isaac could do was soak in every remembrance, past and present, sigh and shut his eyes. The feeling of hopelessness squeezed the life out of him.

Mr. Mercer began to giggle to himself before saying, "I feel like a woman every time I think about you and Lynn getting married."

Isaac snapped out of his disparaging trance and muttered, "Whaddya mean?"

"I just wanna plan everything, from the invitations, right down to the kind of tux you'll be wearing. Your mama sure would be happy to see you getting married. Yes, sir, that woman sure loved her some weddings."

Isaac's sorrowful mood wasn't dissipating, but just for a few glimmering seconds, just seeing his father's gushing face seemed to relieve a tiny measure of pressure enough for him to breath.

As they tooled along, unexpectedly, out of the corner of his eye, Isaac took notice of the *Tri-State Savings & Loan* bank building to his right that they were speeding by. His head had to take a double spin backwards just to make sure he wasn't seeing things.

"Do you think I can find a job soon, dad?"

"Sure you can." Mr. Mercer exhaled. "There's still plenty of work out there, you just have to keep on looking."

Isaac relented. He held back as much as he possibly could, fighting the temptation like a wild, rampaging animal...but it was too much to stomach.

"Dad…can you let me out here?" He sheepishly uttered.

"Right here, at this stop light?"

"Yes, sir, I think I saw a help wanted sign back there."

"Well, do you want me to turn around and wait until you fill out an application?"

"That's okay. Why don't you go home and get some rest? I'll catch the bus back."

Without any more words, Mr. Mercer pulled the car over. Isaac hopped out and began marching off in the opposite direction down the cold sidewalk.

He wanted something, anything to either distract or stop him altogether from going back, but the closer he neared his destination, that was all the more he realized that it was inevitable for him to do what he had to.

He cut down a corner and felt the harsh winter wind slap his fidgety face. Isaac stopped in front of the bank building before looking to his immediate left where he eyed a broke-down garage that had its closed sign facing the outside window.

He stepped over to the garage, ignored the sign and entered through the surprisingly unlocked front door, allowing the tiny clashing bells above his head to ring.

"We're fuckin' closed!" A loud, angry voice yelled from the noisy back where *Stevie Wonder's, 'I Wish'* was blaring on a stereo.

Isaac apprehensively entered the darkened garage accidentally knocking over an empty gas can along the way. The instant he approached an ajar door he braced himself and barged his way through to spot one young, skinny, light skinned, shirtless man seated at a table snorting lines of what looked to be cocaine, and a large, heavily bearded black man pointing a .45 handgun directly at his face.

"I said we're fuckin' closed, motherfucker!" The shirtless man hollered as he looked up to see Isaac shuddering at the doorway.

In a deep, coarse tone, the large man, with a black knit hat on his head, announced, "Look who it is, Larry, the prodigal son."

Wiping the powder away from his nose, Larry slurred, "What the fuck? Put your piece away, Marvell. Can't you see we got company?"

Isaac inched a bit closer to Larry, but not too much to where he was within arm's reach. He made sure to keep his jittery eyes poked at the backdoor.

"How'd you get in here, man?" Larry asked.

"The front door was unlocked."

From out of a nearby corner came trotting a female Doberman pincher who skittishly shuffled past Isaac on her way to a nearby tool table where she eventually cowered underneath.

Isaac began to move towards the dog only to have the animal whimper and whine the closer he approached.

"It's okay, Queen, it's only Isaac." Larry assured his pet while stumbling towards Isaac. "She's still afraid of you, brother," he grinned. "So, what brings you back here after all this time?"

"I, uh, I just came by to see how things were going." Isaac stuttered while maintaining a vigilant eye on Marvell, who in turn had both of his eyes locked on him while flipping through hundred dollar bills.

"Going?" Larry exclaimed. "Shit, things are goin' real will, my nigga. Look around you, business is boomin'!" Larry proclaimed with outstretched arms. "*Jimmy The Peanut* is already lookin' after us colored folks. Before you know it, *Larry's Garage* will be the only mechanic racket in town."

As Isaac reached for a stool behind him, Marvell brazenly snatched it away before placing it beside him instead, not once taking his eyes off of the scared, young man.

"Don't mind Marvell, someone just stiffed him yesterday

for a couple of hundred. You know how he gets whenever someone holds out on him." Larry clarified as he wandered back to his table. "Hey, Marv, turn on something for the lucky man!"

"Lucky? Whaddya mean, lucky?" Isaac questioned.

"You getting' married, aint' you?"

"How'd you find out about that, man?"

"This is ain't *L.A.* or *New York*." Larry tossed up his hands. "It doesn't take long for news to travel in *Cypress*."

"No...not really," Isaac bowed his head.

"So, you and that fine ass Lynn are finally tying the knot, huh? Man, if that were my woman I'd be smiling from ear to ear. What's with the sour puss, brother man?"

Isaac reached back into the furthest corner of his brain to try and remember why he even bothered to show up at all.

Larry then boldly stepped into Isaac's face and asked, "What, did you come back to get your job?"

"No." Isaac stammered. "I just came back to see how you were doing."

Both Larry and Marvell began to laugh out loud at Isaac's seemingly innocent response, as though they were expecting it all along.

"C'mon, Isaac, you can tell me. Why are you back here?" Larry persisted on, only in a more serious tone.

Isaac's hands became increasingly sweaty as he glanced down at the equally frightened dog under the tool table ahead of him. It was already warm inside the garage, so it was no surprise to Isaac that he would be sweating buckets while two dangerous men were surrounding him.

"I know why you're here." Larry sniffed. "You wanna give me some jive about how sorry you are that you just up and left the way you did. Is that it, Isaac? You wanna apologize for acting like a fool the way you did?"

Marvell got up from off his seat, strolled over to the table where Larry was snorting cocaine and picked up a *Phillips* wrench. He then began to toss the tool back and forth in his large hands as if it were a football he was playing with.

Staring deep into Isaac's face, Larry questioned, "Where did you go, Isaac?"

"Whaddya mean?" Isaac stuttered while smelling Larry's noxious breath.

"You gonna stand there and bullshit me like that, man? You've been gone since December. You see, I got it in my head that you was up to no good back in November. If you wanted in on the operation, why didn't you just say so?" He grabbed Isaac by the shoulders.

"What operation, man?" Isaac nearly lost his breath.

"C'mon, Isaac, you didn't have to go behind my back, you could've trusted me, I'm your best friend."

"Larry, I don't know what you're talkin' about, man." Isaac began to squirm. "Okay, you want the truth? Fine. I did come back here for a job. I need one bad, man!"

"Fuck a job!" Larry screamed as he pounded his right fist on the table beside him. "You make a deal with those Jamaican motherfuckers, and you leave us out of it?"

"Jamaicans," Isaac turned up his nose.

"Those nigga's deal with more heroin than American's do! And you leave us out of the deal? Then what happens? You pissed off the wrong person, and they let their dogs loose on your black asses. All you had to do was let Marvell and me know, we could've dealt with them. We all could have made some serious loot. Ya dig?"

"Larry," Isaac hysterically panted, "you know I ain't never dealt with that shit! We've known each other since the fifth grade, man! Why would I double cross you after all these years?"

"Because you're a dumb ass nigga, that's why." Marvell sniggered.

"Fuck you, motherfucker! Ain't nobody asked your black ass!" Isaac irately retaliated.

Just like that, Marvell balled up his right fist and punched Isaac square in the forehead, sending him crashing to the floor. Both Larry and Marvell knelt down and grabbed Isaac's body while the cowering dog whimpered even louder from behind.

"Shut the fuck up, Queen!" Larry yelled before turning his attention back to Isaac. "You see, I think I got this all figured out after all this time. You deal with the Jamaicans, behind our backs no less. Get fucked up on some of their ganga shit. Start acting all crazy. Your eyes get all fucked up. Then, out of the blue, you just vanish into black air." Larry steadily explained while holding Isaac's shaking legs still. "I think you was with the fuzz these past few months, tellin' them everything about our little operation here. Wait a minute… you're probably wired right now."

"C'mon, Larry," Isaac beseeched. "It wasn't anything like that! I didn't have anything to do with those Jamaican cats!"

"Shit, whoever you hired to kill those dudes sure did a helluva job. They made sure to spare your black ass." Larry snickered. "I'm surprised you're even walking around out there. Don't you know that there's a kidnapper on the loose? He snatches up cute little white girls and pretty little colored boys like you."

"He probably takes 'em back to his pad and fucks them up in the ass!" Marvell howled before ripping open Isaac's coat and white button down shirt.

At that painstaking instant, all Isaac could think of was his father's beaming face back in the car, and just how proud he was of him.

The cold, hard wrench that Marvell was pressing against Isaac's face felt like ice sinking into his flesh. All he could see in front of him was a glimpse of Queen staring back in fearful trepidation. He watched the dog's frightful eyes shift up and down right before his own blood that was seeping from his wounded forehead began to drip down his face and blind his vision.

"I say we tear out this nigga's tongue and break his legs." Marvell insidiously grimaced. "We'll see how well he walks down the aisle in crutches. I wanna hear him try and say I do!"

All of the sudden, Isaac's eyesight grew dim. The words that the men were screaming were becoming more distant and foreign, like they were speaking a different language altogether.

"Yeah, maybe I can drop by and see how Lynn is doin'." Larry jumped in. "I never told you, I would pass by her house every now and then just to make sure that the electric was still on." He laughed as he took the wrench from Marvell and bashed Isaac's right leg with it as hard as he could.

But instead of screaming or even wincing in pain, to the shock of both Larry and Marvell, Isaac did something completely unexpected. He shut his eyes and began to hum.

"Dog llik." *(Kill God)* Isaac moaned in a coarse tone before surprisingly snatching the wrench from out of Larry's startled hand and somehow managing to power out from the clutches of both men.

Larry and Marvell stood to their feet and watched as Isaac, too, rose up. They looked on as he spoke more unfamiliar words, words that sounded as though they were coming from someone else's mouth rather than his own.

"This nigga is high again!" Marvell said as he stepped away, too alarmed to do anything at that instant.

With the wrench firmly gripped in his right hand, Isaac bumped up against one table and into another, nearly falling to the floor in the process. Queen helplessly yelped from underneath the confines of her tool table.

Larry backed up, only enough to where he could gain a more precise view at what was taking place. He couldn't tell if what was happening was for real or just one of his own drug induced hallucinations.

Isaac's erratic movements looked more as if he were being pulled and pushed by an unseen force. The behavior lasted nearly two whole minutes before Isaac took the wrench that he was holding and cracked Marvell over the face with it, sending him reeling into the wall behind him. Isaac then lunged forward and struck Larry over the head.

"C'mon, Isaac, I was just playin'!" Larry dreadfully screamed while holding his hands up in merciful defense. "I didn't see your girl, man!"

Isaac's body turned around and began to beat Marvell over the head with the wrench until blood oozed out and onto the floor. From there he spun around and handed his childhood friend the same treatment.

"Eid uoy...eid uou, eid uoy!" *(You die, you die, you die)* Isaac viscously ranted on as he beat Larry over the head repeatedly until he could hear his skull crack wide open like a coconut.

Isaac then stood back and watched as Larry's unconscious body began to convulse right there on the cement floor in front of him. Isaac dropped the wrench, grabbed Larry by the neck and pulled him over to a corner where he proceeded to get down on all fours and lick up the blood that was seeping from out of his gaping head.

In the midst of his drinking feast, Isaac paused and turned to Queen, who by then had managed to sneak underneath Larry's tow truck.

Isaac's shiny eyes blinked in rapid sequence. He fed off of the animal's fear of him like a drug. It turned him on to see the dog cower like a pup.

"Ereh emoc." *(Come here)* Isaac grunted from his stomach. "Ereh emoc, uoy hctib! *(Come here, you bitch!)*

But the dog would not budge. It sat under the truck as Isaac, on all fours no less, began to crawl over towards its direction, hissing and grunting while shining his set of blood stained teeth along the way.

Soon, the sound of a fire engine blaring outside down the street sent Isaac scurrying back into another dark corner to where only his bright eyes could be seen.

He got to his feet and fled out the backdoor that led to the alley.

CHAPTER 7

LAKE LOGAN WENT ON for nearly eighty miles until it conjoined with *Lake Erie*. Isaac sat at the tip of the pier. The icy wind sliced right through his open coat and shirt and into his body like a rusty butcher knife.

His completely numb physique rocked back and forth on the ledge as though it were weightless. The waves fiercely crashed and jostled up and down as if they were distressed or angered.

Gripped strongly in the young man's right hand was a headless seagull. Its blood dripped down from out of its neck like water from a flowing faucet; being still a fresh kill.

Isaac's head hung low. His bottom lip was drooping, allowing the blood from the fowl to slowly funnel out of his gaping mouth.

His eyes were slightly opened, but there was no life in them whatsoever that harsh afternoon as the brutally cold waves splashed onto both his pair of dress shoes and the bottom portion of his Sunday pants, causing them to become more damp by the minute.

Behind Isaac, in a fifty yard distance, sat a bright green 1975 *Monte Carlo* with its engine humming. The windows were darkly tinted to where only the clandestine individual inside could see out.

The driver sat in the flashy vehicle and calmly watched the young, spellbound man down at the pier all by himself, appearing as if he were only inches away from being swept out into the violent current that was lashing out at him.

The driver in the green car just happened to be in the perfect position to possibly rear end Isaac directly into the water. But instead, the mysterious person put the car in reverse and simply drove away.

Isaac never budged an inch, unless the wind had nudged him. His eyelids didn't blink. It was as if his body was there, but his soul had remained back at the garage, along with his two former friends.

CHAPTER 8

DOCTOR LEVIN STOOD OVER his desk in his small, uncoordinated office while peering down at an x-ray of Isaac's skull and chatting over the phone with his ever so tenacious wife.

It didn't seem to bother him all too much that what he was staring at took center stage over what his wife was desperately trying to convey to him. He would catch only every other sentence that she was saying, and if she asked him to repeat what she had said he would find himself prevaricating the entire conversation right where he stood.

"I realize that, honey, but does your sister have to go to bed at eight? I have some very important colleagues stopping by tonight." Jeremiah wined while focusing his blue eyes closer in on the x-ray. "Just think what it would look like if they walked in and saw Justine sprawled out on the couch like a homeless woman."

For him, being a psychiatrist and not a medical doctor meant that he really had no idea as to what exactly he was looking at. In his eyes it was only a human skull.

"I know, Julie." He moaned. "We'll just have to take it step by step. "I'm a shrink, not a rabbi."

Levin shoved aside the one x-ray and pulled another set from out of a manila folder that was already lying on his paper burdened desk. He raised the images up to the light and closely studied all three sets. One was taken of Isaac's chest, the second of his arms and the last was of his legs and feet.

He wasn't a physician, but even he could see the hateful damage that had taken place in the x-rays. All of the sudden, his wife's incessant banter over the phone had become mere gibberish within the span of three minutes.

With a dry throat, Jeremiah said, "Uh, honey, let me call you back later. I've got a patient arriving soon. I love you, too." He mumbled as he hung up the phone without taking his eyes off of the disturbing images in front of him.

Without hesitating a second longer, he picked up the phone again and dialed a number. Levin waited as five dial tone's burped into his ears.

"Yes, this is Doctor Jeremiah Levin. I am partnered through the Ashlandview Psychiatric Center. I was wondering if I could speak with a Doctor Morgan Shields, please."

Levin waited for at least five of the longest minutes of his life for the anticipated doctor to answer while listening to *Barry Manilow's, 'I Write The Songs'*, over the line.

"This is Doctor Shields. To whom am I speaking?" The man seriously spoke.

"Yes," Levin coughed, "this is Doctor Jeri Levin. How are you today, sir?"

"Quite well, sir." He heavily exhaled, sounding as though his time were being wasted. *"What can I do for you?"*

"Well, I am here looking over a patient's x-rays, and if I'm not mistaken, you were the presiding physician when this young man was brought into your emergency room three months ago."

"I'm afraid you're going to have to be a bit more specific than that, Doctor Levin. Would this patient happen to have a name?"

"Yes, sir, it's Isaac Mercer. He was the young, black

male that was brought in following the animal attack on Thanksgiving."

At first there was a breathing pause over the phone, until Doctor Shields woke up and said, *"Now I remember. Yes, quite a bizarre tragedy if I recall. You don't exactly forget something like that, Doctor."*

"I can imagine. But you see, sir, I'm looking at Mr. Mercer's x-rays as we speak, and it seems as though there are some...abnormalities, concerning his bone structure." Levin gulped. "Doctor, if I may ask, was Isaac beaten before he was rushed in that morning? I'm seeing multiple bone fractures from head to toe. If I didn't know any better, I'd swear it looks as though his entire jaw was...stretched outwards? As ludicrous as that may sound."

"Yes, Doctor Levin, this young man was quite a puzzle to us all that morning. We all believed that he too was attacked by this so called animal, but there were absolutely no scars, or even a scratch on him. He was soaking in blood from head to toe. And yes, his bones had seemingly been broken."

"Had been," Levin questioned. "Can you elaborate?"

"It's still a mystery to myself, but it seems as though this young man's entire bone structure had been...reconfigured, and then restored all over again. If you notice in the x-rays that I took that morning, certain joints seemed to have, pardon my illiteracy, come apart. His muscles also went through a tremendous amount of trauma as well. It looked as if he had lifted weights for a whole week straight, non-stop. You could actually feel the soreness in them. He kept on crying that he needed Ben-Gay to rub all over himself." Doctor Shields flippantly carried on.

Levin sank himself into a long, drawn out trance the deeper he gazed at the three x-rays. If Doctor Shields had no clear cut explanation, then he too was completely dumbfounded.

"Are you still there, Doctor?" Shields asked.

"Yes, I'm still here, sir." Levin coughed himself back. "I apologize; I guess I got a little confused for a moment or two."

"Is Mr. Mercer alright?"

"Physically, yes," Jeremiah stated.

"I am forced to confess that I've never seen anything like it before in all my years. Most scientists could write novels on this kid. He's a modern marvel. Bones re-fusing themselves. Honestly, I was shocked just to see him walk out of this hospital at all."

"Yes, Doctor, it is a miracle." Levin muttered in a perturbed tone. "Well, sir, I do appreciate your time."

"The pleasure is all mine, Doctor. Good day."

Levin slowly hung up the phone and took out the previous x-ray of Isaac's once deformed skull. The slightly protruded jaw bone startled the man enough to where he had to push aside the image as though he were thoroughly repulsed by the very sight altogether.

He had to take a breath, just to clear his mind. The last thing he wanted was to drive himself mad before his patient arrived.

Right then, three knocks at the door interrupted Levin's irrational ramblings. As if he were trying to escape, he hastily shoved each of the x-rays into one folder before saying out loud, "Come in!"

From behind the door appeared Isaac.

CHAPTER 9

DRESSED IN HIS SLIGHTLY tattered grey winter coat, a *Cleveland Browns* knit hat and a Band-Aid in the center of his forehead, Isaac stepped inside and gladly shook Levin's hand.

"Hi, Isaac," Levin warmly greeted.

Rubbing his cold hands together, Isaac smiled back, "How ya doin', man"

"Well, why don't you have a seat?" Jeremiah said as he sat himself down behind his compact desk.

Isaac took off his coat and hat and laid them on the leather couch behind him. He then tried to caress some warmth into his arms. He was wearing a green *Izod* sweater and a faded pair of blue jeans, and even in all of his layers the young man still felt like a six foot tall ice pick.

"Can I bum a smoke off of you, my man?" Isaac anxiously asked.

"Sure." Levin strangely eyed Isaac as he opened a drawer within his desk and took out a pack of *Marlboro's*.

Isaac secured the cigarette from the doctor and waited until Levin whipped out a lighter to ignite the tip.

"I wasn't aware that you smoked." Levin curiously grinned.

Isaac sat down in the chair in front of the desk and stated, "I don't smoke in front of my father and kid. But anywhere else, I'm game."

"I understand." Levin nonchalantly waved his hand. "Everyone here seems to frown upon anyone who smokes anymore." He hopelessly sighed. "So, how are you doing these days?"

Gradually coming down from his cold fit, Isaac explained in between puffs, "Not bad. Been looking for a job. And I got engaged the other night."

"Congratulations!" Levin lit up. "When is the wedding?"

"My lady says she wants a spring wedding, so, I figure it'll be sometime around April or May."

"Super, just super," Levin graciously smiled.

Isaac stared pensively at the doctor while taking a long drag on his cigarette. He wasn't accustomed to being around such a young looking professional man. In a way, it put him at ease, it made him feel as though he didn't have to live up to a lofty, generational expectation that seemingly everyone over the age of forty had already set for him.

Studying Jeremiah with a keen eye, Isaac cunningly grinned, "You sure you're a psychiatrist and not some college kid trying to get extra credit from his professor or something?"

Levin just sat back. "I'm actually five years older than you. I received my bachelors from *Ohio State* when I turned twenty-three. I hope that meets your standards." He cracked a smile.

"Man, you must've been real smart back in high school. If it hadn't been for me smoking since the eighth grade I probably would've joined the football team. And who knows, maybe the *NFL*."

"My dad once told me that smoking was the poetry of liars. It hides the true you behind a façade of so called lethargy."

Isaac screwed up his face and giggled, "Your dad sounds like mine. I swear, that man can recite just about every verse out of the bible, and ninety-nine percent of the time I don't have a damn clue as to what he's talkin' about."

Jeremiah joined in on the humor while unhinging his

tie. "I have an uncle who happens to be a rabbit in *Utica, New York*. Till this day the man still gets me to recite verses out of the Tanakh."

"Does he have that real deep Jewish accent? You know, like he's gagging on something whenever he talks?" Isaac smirked.

"Yep, that's my uncle Jerome alright." Levin lightheartedly chuckled.

"Don't get me wrong, I love my dad to death, but you get tired of always hearing bible verses night and day. You would think after hearing it for twenty years that I'd have the whole bible memorized by now." Isaac joked while squashing the butt of his cigarette out in the glass ashtray on the desk.

"So tell me, how do you and your father get along?"

"We're cool, I guess." Isaac exhaled.

"Just cool," Jeremiah queried.

"Yeah, I mean, besides what happened back in November, me and him see eye to eye."

"You mean with what took place back at that house? Doctor Sanyupta never went into much detail back at *Ashlandview*."

"No, I mean me trying to hit my dad."

"Oh really," Levin panted. "What brought that on?"

"I don't know." Isaac sulked. "I wasn't exactly myself at the time. I swung at 'em, next thing I know, I wake up in my bed with a swollen jaw."

"It was that bad, huh?"

"Have you ever seen my father? The man isn't exactly a lightweight, if you catch my drift."

"How did you feel when your father brought you to *Ashlandview*, Isaac?"

Isaac sat back in his seat and rolled his eyes upwards as though he were ailing. "At first, I was pissed. I was pissed at a lot of things at the time. But when I finally came to and realized what I had done to both him and my lady, him sending me to that place made all the sense in the world."

Levin pointed his eyes down at his desk and said, "Doctor Sanyupta mentioned that your mother was deceased."

"Yeah, she died six years ago from a brain tumor."

"Would you say that her passing brought you and your father closer together?"

"I don't know, like I said, besides November, we always got along. If anything changed after my mom's death, it had to be that my dad stopped working so much. I think he slowed down so he could spend more time with me."

"You keep mentioning November." Levin insisted.

"Hold it right there." Isaac adamantly pointed. "I know what you're trying to do. Sanyupta did the same thing. So before you try and go back in time with me, understand, I can barely remember what happened yesterday, let alone three months ago."

"Really," Levin's eyes opened wide.

"Yeah, I keep on having these…blackouts. Sometimes I can't remember things. Hell, I can't even remember how I got this knot on my forehead." Isaac pointed to his skull.

Levin picked up his ballpoint pen and began to jot something down on a piece of white notebook paper in front of him.

"Doctor Sanyupta mentioned that you suffered from blackouts before. Have you seen a doctor about them? Are any of these blackouts preceded by headaches of any sort?"

"Look, I don't have the money to go see a doctor just so he can tell me to take some *Anacin*. If it weren't for the state paying for this visit I wouldn't be here now."

"I really want to get down to the root of these blackouts, Isaac, especially since they began after the incident in November."

Isaac squirmed about in his seat like an impatient five year old at that moment. He tried to cut his eyes away from the doctor's, but Levin was seemingly just as persistent in reaching his patient.

"The other night, I remember talking to my dad. Then I went and made some popcorn and watched some TV. After that, everything went dark. When I woke up the next morning, I was hanging out of my bed with the covers wrapped around my neck."

"I see." Levin murmured, still scribbling away on his pad. "Any headaches?"

"No, not really," Isaac shrugged. "And then there was yesterday. I remember waking up, eating breakfast, talking to Lynn on the phone and then my dad taking me down to his job to see if I could get on. Then, we got back in the car, my dad stopped at a red light, and...that's that." Isaac heavily pondered while staring endlessly at the brown carpeted floor.

"Doctor Sanyupta did mention that you would see... another person in your bedroom from time to time."

Isaac blushed before he turned his head and exhaled as if he were too ashamed to hear anything more come from the doctor's mouth.

"Isaac, look," Levin steadily spoke, extending his right hand outwards to Isaac, "it's just you and me in here. The only other person that knows about this is Sanyupta. I'm not trying to pry, I just want to make sure that you're okay."

Isaac looked up and coughed, acting as though he were trying to find the proper words to say at that stage.

"Look, ever since what happened back in November, I've been seeing this...thing. I'm not even gonna call it a person because I never see its face. It just comes out of nowhere, and then it just leaves. It never speaks. It just walks around. I don't know if it's a ghost or if it's all in my head." He bashfully explained. "Shit, I feel like *Ford*. I'm falling all over the fucking place."

"Isaac, I understand that you don't want to talk about what took place inside that house, but piece by piece, it'll start to come together for you. I mean, I heard when they first brought you to *Ashlanview* that you were a…for lack of a better term, a wreck. But after only a few weeks, you've made significant improvement. You're a totally different man."

Blushing, Isaac began to snicker to himself as if he were recalling something funny before he said, "I guess Sanyupta told you about what I thought I was."

Levin sat back and took off his glasses. "Uh, yeah," he modestly answered. "I'll admit that it's not exactly what I expected to hear from a man like yourself."

"What you really mean to say is that you've never heard a colored person sat that he was a…you know…that thing."

"I thought you people didn't like to be called colored." Levin haphazardly jibed while apparently waiting for a smile to make its way to Isaac's face.

Isaac glared oddly at the doctor before laughing. He got the joke, he was just awestruck at the sheer boldness of the person who was telling it.

"Isaac, look, I've been in this profession for two years now, and so far I've had three people tell me that they were vampires. One guy that swears he's *James Bond*. Another person tell me that he's the reincarnation of *Attila the Hun*, and a woman who believed that she was a ghost, even though she was about as alive as you and I are right now. What you think you are is the least of your problems. It's normal to have these thoughts. You saw three of your friends get killed. That would give anyone a jolt."

Isaac dropped his head and said, "Those cats weren't my friends. And as far as what happened back in November, let's just say, for now…I got caught up in something totally unexpected."

"Well, speaking of the unexpected, I happened across some

of your x-rays from your hospital visit after the incident. Isaac, I just have to know, were you beaten up that night? Because your x-rays revealed significant damage to your entire skeletal system. Extreme muscle strains. And even more amazing, it appeared as though your body healed within days." Levin explained, sounding astonished.

Isaac once again regressed into his vegetative state of silence. He was determined not to go back in time at all costs.

"I just can't even begin to imagine the utter pain and agony that you went through." Jeremiah nearly lost his breath.

"Well, all I can say is that…I wasn't beaten up. And you're damn right, it was painful." He gritted his teeth.

Just as it looked as if Levin were about to throw another barrage of inquiries at Isaac, he paused to examine the young man who suddenly took on the eerie appearance of someone who wasn't even in the same room alongside him.

Isaac sat in his seat, slumping closer and closer to the floor like he was about to melt right out of his chair. "I miss my mom." The young man uttered in a tone that seemed so distant.

"I beg your pardon?"

Sitting up, Isaac reiterated, "I said, I miss my mom. Sometimes she could be just like my dad, spitting bible verses left and right, but for a long time, she was my best friend. I was the one that pulled away from her. I got to that age when I thought I was too cool. Couldn't nobody tell me shit. I'll never forget the day before they took her to the hospital, she and I argued because I wasn't doing my homework. That was the last time I spoke to her before she passed. I always blamed myself for her dying."

With a look of syrupy sympathy in his blue eyes, Levin got up, sat down on the edge of his desk in front of Isaac and said, "Guilt binds us in all sorts of trouble, Isaac. This so called ghost that you see, this mythical creature that you think you are, it's all part of the culpability that you've been carrying all this time. It finally materialized when those men were killed in that house. Do you feel guilty that you were the only one that survived?"

Isaac's eyes shifted upwards to the doctor's face. "Guilt had nothing to do with what happened that night. Everything that I felt that night was real. I'm talking about a second chance. When I was laid up in *Ashlandview*, I got a chance to do a lot of thinking. I got a son. I look at a lot of brotha's out there now, fuckin' up, doin' things they're not supposed to be doin'. I swore that I'd be different. I want my son to look up to me like I look up to my dad. I want my fiancé to have a man that she can depend on. I swore to God and even my own mother that I would be different. God spared my life that night because he wanted to give me a second chance."

The more Isaac spoke, something inside of him began to twist and turn, much like a stomach ache, but on a less gut wrenching level. He felt a crucifixion taking place.

"I was wrong. I was wrong about everything, but now, I can change things." Isaac continued on. "What happened to me that night hasn't happened again since, and I wanna keep it that way."

Jeremiah, with a glare of confidence on his face, got up from off his desk and stuffed his hands into his pants pockets.

"So, is that it?" Isaac eagerly asked.

"Yeah…yeah, I think so." Levin smiled.

"So tell me, do you still think I'm crazy?" Isaac questioned while stepping over and picking up his coat, only to have several *Crayola* crayons fall from out of one of the pockets. Giggling while picking up the crayons, the man blushed, "My son and I were coloring together last night. That boy stuffed crayons any and everywhere he could, even in the toilet."

"Well, you're either crazy or you're the most rational man of the decade." Levin gladly remarked. "But I would like very much for you to see a doctor about those blackouts. That's something that could be potentially dangerous in the long run."

"I'll see what I can do, man." Isaac replied in a patronizing fashion before shaking the doctor's hand and heading for the door. "Oh, and be careful taking I-75 home this afternoon. There's a real big accident out there."

"Okay," Levin shrugged oddly, "but it's only 10:41."

Isaac cunningly smirked and asked, "Its Friday, aren't you people supposed to stop working by sunset?"

Jeremiah dropped his head and grinned back, saying, "Touché, my friend, touché."

"Ay ees. (See ya) Isaac spoke while walking out the door and heading towards the elevator.

However, the closer and closer he reached the doors, Isaac found it increasingly difficult to ignore his full bladder that possibly would not survive an hour long bus ride home.

Aware of the bus' strict schedule, the man turned and jogged back down the opposite end of the hallway that led to the men's bathroom.

The instant he stepped inside, Isaac didn't even bother to look around to see just who was in there along with him. He stormed his way into the first stall, locked the door and unzipped his pants. Immediately, the intense rush was a miraculous relief that he had been holding in for at least an hour. It was orgasmic enough to where Isaac had to close his eyes just to savor the moment.

The end was nearing. Just mere seconds away from finishing the last few drops, something from behind pulled Isaac backwards into the stall's door. A steady stream of urine sprayed all over both the stall and Isaac himself.

The young man sat there on the floor before going to his knees and swaying side to side in an entranced state of mind.

There was something lingering about inside his mouth, like a word that was hanging on the very tip of his tongue.

Isaac continued to bob from side to side while urine dripped from his midsection. He felt so sleepy all of the sudden; his eyes would hardly stay open.

Right then, someone walked into the bathroom. Immediately, Isaac stood to his feet and turned to face the stall door before groaning, "Tuo." (Out)

The person on the end of the stall was washing their hands. In Isaac's ears all he could hear was water, water that sounded as if it were a raging waterfall.

"Tuo," Isaac again moaned, nearly snarling as he scratched at the door with his own right hand.

"I'm sorry?" The man on the other end stammered. "Do you need help in there?"

"Tuo," he continued on.

A brief silence prevailed inside the bathroom before the man said out loud, "If you need help in there I can—

"Tuo," Isaac aimlessly rambled on.

Isaac could hear footsteps before what sounded like the bathroom's door being opened and shut echoed inside.

The stall's latch slid in the opposite direction. The door slowly swung open, allowing Isaac's half naked body to exit. With his pants still hanging down around his ankles, the young man caught a glimpse of his reflection in the mirror just a few feet ahead. He stumbled and plodded along the way while still mumbling his repetitive word.

The instant he reached the mirror, Isaac scraped his right hand across the glass and examined his face, as well as his bleeding forehead from where the *Band-Aid* was peeling off.

"Tuo...tuo...tuo...tuo."

Without looking, he reached into his coat pocket and pulled out coins, lint and crayons. However, out of all the items that spilled to the floor, the only one that remained stuck to his hand was a green crayon.

With the crayon, Isaac began to blindly scribble lines and peculiar childlike shapes on the mirror while uttering "tuo" over and over again.

The doodling went on seemingly for minutes until strange and uncoordinated lines began to take on a form; the form of words.

His fingers barely had a grip on the crayon that he was using; they were loose and limp as though he had forgotten how to use them.

On the mirror, in green *Crayola,* Isaac's hand wrote: Won tuo. (Out now)

CHAPTER 10

"WE PREEMPT HOLLYWOOD SQUARES *to bring you this Action Seven News, Special Report!"*

"Good Saturday evening. And welcome to this special, seven o'clock edition of Action News. I'm Paul Jensen. This evening, we take a more in depth look into the mind of a kidnapper. With me is Cypress police detective, Linus Bruin. Detective Bruin has been with the Cypress P.D. now for thirty-four years, and he is currently heading up the search for the Broad Open Daylight Kidnapper. Thank you for being with us this evening, Detective."

"Thank you, Paul; it's good to be here."

"Let's get down to business. Since September of '76, sixteen people have been, literally, snatched right off the streets and taken away. The latest of these abductions taking place just four days ago when Gloria Cohen was taken on her way to class at Cypress State Community College. Detective, what exactly are we dealing with here when it pertains to this individual?"

"Well, Paul, we're obviously dealing with an individual that has no fear of getting caught while snatching people right off the streets. Now, I'm no psychologist, but it almost seems that the suspect, if you'll excuse my tone, gets off, on committing these crimes not only during the daytime, but also where large associations of people just happen to be gathered. To him, it may be a very clever game that he enjoys playing."

"Detective, you mentioned getting off. I'm not sure if you and

I can get away with such terminology on broadcast TV, but, are we possibly dealing with a rapist? I mean, so far, the only people that the suspect has had any interest in abducting are young white females and young black males. Could there be a possible connection between the two, or are these abductions just random?"

"It's difficult to figure out the suspect's motives at this time, Paul. While it is possible to assume that the abductor may have, what we call, a fetish, we cannot bring ourselves to believe that these are just random kidnappings."

"C'mon, Detective, ten white females and six black males. It sounds to me like this person has an obsession if I've ever seen one."

"Like I said, Paul, we're not assuming anything at this point. Right now, we are more concentrated on the kidnapper's modes of transport. We have assessed that in each abduction, the suspect used a different color van. All Chevy's. Either this person is of great wealth or he must be stealing vans and then ditching them along the way."

"What leads, if any, do you have on the suspect?"

"So far we are going on the assumption that this person lives outside of town. Possibly westwards, near Cuyahoga Falls. One onlooker managed to catch a glimpse of his license place that read Summit County. As far as a description goes, all we have to go on is a stocky, well-built man that has a noticeable limp. No race has been established as of yet."

"Last night, a candlelight vigil was held in honor of Gloria on the campus of Cypress State. Are we to assume that these sixteen victims are all dead?"

"Paul, as hard as we at the Cypress Police Division like to hope above hope, we really do not want to toss salt on already open wounds. There is still a possibility that all sixteen of these people are still very much alive."

"What would you tell others out there to do if they are approached by an out of the ordinary individual?"

"Well, the best thing to do is stay within a group. Never travel alone if possible. Don't talk to strangers was probably some of the

best advice our parents ever gave us. Be aware of anything suspicious. Anything out of place. If you suspect something out of the ordinary, do not hesitate to contact the Cypress Police Department immediately. We are doing everything within our power to find not only the suspect, but also all sixteen victims. It is imperative to remember that screaming and yelling will possibly scare the individual away and save your life in the process."

"Good advice, Detective Bruin. Thank you for being with us this evening. Coming up next, the odd lives of The Cypress Zoo's first set of African lions. Can they adapt to our frigid environment? We'll talk to zoologist, Gary Ziggler, right after these messages."

CHAPTER 11

FROM AN AERIAL PERSPECTIVE, the scene inside the hallowed and raucous halls of *Saint John the Baptist Church* appeared at first glance to resemble an out of control gathering.

Both male and female black parishioners hooped and hollered at the powerful words that Mr. Mercer shouted as he stood firm behind his almighty wooden pulpit clear down in front of the church.

Outfitted in his customary black and red robe, Mercer preached with the fire of a man hell-bent on saving each and every soul that was seated in front of him. His arms flailed back and forth and up and down while his deep voice spewed words of God's love and forgiveness from one end of the old building to the other.

Old women sat in their pews, just waving their frail hands from side to side, too weak anymore to jump for joy, while old men nodded their heads and clapped their hands, assuring both the pastor and themselves that every word was soaking through just fine.

The younger crowd squirmed and fidgeted in their seats next to their parents, impatiently waiting for what they would consider an ordeal to be over a lot sooner than later.

Down clear in the front pew sat both Isaac and Lynnette, with Isaiah amazingly fast asleep in his mother's clapping arms.

Isaac sat glued to his pew, as he had been doing ever since he was smaller than his son, listening to every sentence that his father was shouting in his high stature.

The young man was in good spirits that Sunday Morning. He tapped his feet every time the organist hit a specific note that happened to coincide with one of the pastor's "highlight moments" in his all important message.

Every so often Isaac would turn and look over to his right to see Lynnette shouting the words "Amen and Praise God!" She, much like him, wasn't all too much into church going, save for Easter and Christmas.

There was a slight, proud smirk on the young man's face. A look of both peacefulness and warmth being amongst his familiar surroundings after being away for so long. No longer was he carrying the dreaded feelings of trepidation with him every time he dared think about what took place back in November. Sitting next to his family only made him realize what he truly missed, and ultimately nearly lost.

The louder his father preached on the book of *Galatians*, that was all the more rowdy the crowd's intensity seemed to increase. Though Isaac was not all too animated, he always found it within himself to be a curious bystander. The man glanced from side to side and from front to back as though he were inspecting the melee. He kept on and on until a stiff aroma ended up seizing him completely out of nowhere and all of the sudden.

He smelled the scent before, but never was it as breathtaking as it was that morning. The odor seared into his nostrils to the point where Isaac had to wipe his nose just to keep himself from sneezing.

He gawked around the church in the hopes of locating the area from which the stench was emanating, but the more his nose skulked about, the stronger the aroma seemed to grow.

Ever so gradually, he leaned over and sniffed Lynnette

while she wasn't noticing only to discover that she was only wearing her perfume which he had smelled all morning long.

He then turned to his left. Just three feet apart were another set of pews and a young, full-figured woman clothed in a black dress, black stockings and a black hat, clapping and cheering while joyfully jumping up and down in her seat.

At first glance, he smiled the interruption away, but Isaac was finding that the odor was far too powerful to be ignored, at least by him.

The more the woman's backside left her seat, the more Isaac's eyes began to drift away, as though he were becoming sleepy. His lips began to move; he was whispering the same words that his father was speaking, only Isaac's words were three seconds ahead of his dad's. It was as if he knew every part of the sermon, even though it was the very first time he had ever heard it in his life.

With his sullen eyes pointed directly at the large woman and his lips mimicking the pastor's, Isaac deeply inhaled. To anyone else who would have been able to smell it, it would have resembled a putrid stench, something to be discretely taken care of immediately by a member of the fairer sex, but to Isaac, it was utter bliss.

Isaac breathed in the strong odor that was soaking badly inside the overweight woman. Soon, and much to his own shock, everyone inside the church had vanished, everyone that is expect six people. Gone were his father, Lynnette, his son and the vast majority of the congregation, all that was left was six unfamiliar souls that sat in various other pews within the sanctuary.

Three young black men and three young white women, all of whom were clothed in blood soaked rags from head to toe. With drowsy eyes, Isaac studied each individual who had their heads pointed to the floor beneath them.

Isaac couldn't find the will to get up out of his seat, all

the man could do was continue to sit and watch the persons quietly remain in their places. The church itself was completely silent. A person could actually hear the other breathing, it was so quiet.

It was quiet enough for Isaac to hear what sounded like something moving across the carpeted floor towards him.

The young man turned around to see a tall figure clothed in a blood soaked white sheet standing right in front of him.

Isaac sat, but rather than become afraid, he just gawked at the individual as it stretched out its arms to him.

"The Lord is my Shepherd, I shall not want. He maketh me lie down in green pastures. He leadeth me beside still waters." All six of the young people gathered began chanting in unison.

Isaac spun around to see them all standing and reciting the 23rd Psalm in perfect synchronicity in all their bloody glory.

"Come home." The hooded figure in front of Isaac hissed before lunging at the man.

Isaac jumped back only to find Lynnette grabbing him by the back of his suit jacket and staring at him as though he had lost his mind. Isaac looked back at her with his amber eyes as though he was gazing at a total stranger all of the sudden. He was in shock to see her hand touching him.

Mr. Mercer had momentarily stopped preaching to take a long look at his son before he resumed his sermon.

The young man sat back and began to clap his hands along with the rest of the crowd. Everyone else in the congregation was seemingly ignoring Isaac; it was all part of the morning's entertainment as far they were concerned.

"Nema!" Isaac jubilantly said out loud to his father.

A half an hour later, church let out, with the usual after service cheer that went along with leaving after an extended

Sunday morning. Joyful faces smiling at one another and wishing love and peace for the following week ahead.

With half of the crowd inside and the other half out on the front steps, Isaac and Lynnette found themselves caught in between both streams of chaos. People glad to see them back in church again, and congratulating them on their engagement. Hugs, kisses and handshakes were traded back and forth while questions on Isaac's whereabouts were being evaded with artful precision by the young man who would have rather not have been snared into the subject in the first place.

Mr. Mercer, still dressed in his robe, came up beside Isaac and Lynnette and asked, "Hey, before you two head home, would you like to come with me and Deacon Hawthorne to *Don's* for supper?"

Both Lynnette and Isaac's faces lit up at that second with the visions of free food and hopeful leftovers to take home with them.

"We sure would, Pastor." Lynnette jovially smiled while putting on Isaiah's coat.

"Good." Mr. Mercer smiled back. "Let me get my clothes changed and I'll meet everyone outside."

"Man, I sure do miss *Don's* fried chicken." Isaac drooled. "Not as much as I miss momma's, but it's darn close."

Mr. Mercer happened to snag Isaac by the shoulder and whisper into his ear, "Son, I wanna see you before we leave."

Isaac shook a couple of more hands before following his dad back to his study that was located next to the restrooms in the back of the church.

The second Isaac stepped through the door, he immediately caught sight of his father taking off his robe and politely lancing it on a coat hanger that sat next to his desk where his bible, a portrait of Jesus looking upwards and a picture of his wife was placed.

"Have a seat, son." Mr. Mercer anxiously sighed while wiping sweat away from his brow.

Isaac sat himself down on a white stool in the middle of the floor and waited for his father to speak.

"Son, I wanted to talk to you about something, and—

"Dad, if this has anything to do with me not coming home last night, I can explain." Isaac hurriedly cut in. "I was at Lynn's house, and—

"No, it's not that." Mr. Mercer said as he leaned against the desk. "I wanted to talk to you about...the other night. I didn't want to bring it up the other day because you were so upset over not getting the job."

Isaac sat in his seat with his eyes focused directly at his father in a forceful, cold manner, dreadfully awaiting whatever was to come out of the man's mouth next.

"Son, what were you doing in my bedroom the other night around two a.m.?" Mr. Mercer suspiciously questioned.

Isaac thought to himself at first before saying, "Two a.m. Dad...I can hardly remember anything anymore. For the past few days, I've been having these blackouts."

"Blackouts," Mr. Mercer chocked. "Why didn't you tell me about this, boy?"

"Because, I didn't want to worry anyone. I did tell the psychiatrist back on Friday when I went to see him. He said to go to a doctor. I told him that I didn't have the money for that."

Frustrated, Mr. Mercer shot up from off the desk and said, "Isaac, this is very serious! You just can't take this so lightly!"

"I'm not taking it lightly, dad." Isaac vehemently protested. It's not like it happens every day."

"When was the last time it happened?"

"I dunno," Isaac shrugged, "I think back on Friday. But it was only for a few seconds."

"Son, I can't believe you're taking this so calmly. Don't you know how dangerous this sort of thing is?"

"I know, dad, and I'm sorry. For the life of me, I don't remember being in your room at two a.m. I remember you and I talking earlier that night, but—

At that very instant, Isaac heard a scratching racket at the door behind him. Immediately, he spun around and stared at the closed door.

"What is it, son?" Mr. Mercer questioned with folded arms and a concerned face.

The moment Isaac realized that he was the only person in the room that could hear the sound, he turned back around and shut his eyes for a few seconds in the hopes that the clawing noise would go away.

Isaac then opened his eyes, and just like that, the racket that was taking place on the other end of the door had ceased. Isaac looked to see his father with his back facing him.

"Son, I want you to—

"Why didn't you cry at mama's funeral?" Isaac abruptly asked.

Isaac could tell that the question had caught his father completely off guard, and in all rights, he himself couldn't comprehend why he had asked such a thing at the most inopportune moment.

Isaac sat and watched as his father slowly turned around to face him. The man's large hands were trembling while paleness engulfed his chubby face.

"I never told anyone before Friday, but before mama went to the hospital, she and I argued. The psychiatrist said that those delusions I was having last year may have come from guilt."

Mr. Mercer opened his mouth, but for the longest time nothing came out. "Son," he stuttered, "your mother and I knew that she was sick long before she went to the hospital. Neither of us wanted to upset you with it all."

Isaac remained stuck to his stool while listening to a man

that in his eyes appeared like someone who was creeping on the verge of a breakdown.

"Boy, for days leading up to your mama's death, I cried like a baby. By the time her funeral came around...I was all cried out. You didn't have anything to do with your mother dying. Is that what's been on your mind all these years?" He deeply frowned.

"Maybe," Isaac shamefully mumbled.

Mr. Mercer knelt down, placed his right hand on Isaac's shoulder and said, "Do you see what happens when we keep things away from each other? It's funny, I can talk to seventy-two people every Sunday about God, but I can't even tell my own son why I never cried at his mother's funeral. We learn something new every day." He timidly smirked.

Isaac then looked his father in the eye and uttered, "I don't want you to think that I hated you all these years, it's just something that came up back on Friday."

Mr. Mercer pulled Isaac close and kissed him on the cheek before softly saying, "I know you didn't, boy. I think this is the Lord's way of saying that everything is gonna be alright."

Feeling weightless, Isaac got to his feet. "I'll go start the car."

Mr. Mercer just pressed his lips together and nodded before rising and turning away towards the wall.

As Isaac began for the doorknob, he suddenly paused. He twisted the knob and ever so carefully pulled open the door before poking his head out into the hallway to make sure the coast was clear.

As Isaac rounded the corner that led to the front door of the church, the stiff aroma that he had caught earlier snatched him halfway down the aisle.

He clutched his aching stomach and listened as it rumbled as though it were about to explode. He looked back at the first pew where the large woman once sat. He was only four rows back from the stench, and yet, the odor was as prevalent and strong as if it were right there in front of his nose.

Isaac breathed in and out while gazing up at the rafters that looked as though they were rapidly closing in on him. A dominant sense of claustrophobia set in at that instant. The more he exhaled, the dizzier he became. He wanted ever so much to reach the front door but both of his legs weighed a ton each.

He grabbed one bench after another, trying his best to escape not only the aroma but also the clawing noise that he heard back in his father's study that had returned and was quickly gaining on him.

Suddenly, the scratching grew more angry and loud the closer he dared reach the front door, until at last, he was able to grab the final pew.

Isaac looked back to see nothing behind him but the old, empty church that he had grown up in, silently staring back at him.

Isaac clutched the door's handle and boldly pushed it wide open, allowing the cold, winter wind to enter the building before forcefully slamming it shut behind him.

CHAPTER 12

MR. MERCER DROVE DOWN the road at a steady pace while conversing back and forth with Deacon Hawthorne who was seated in the front while Lynnette, Isaac and Isaiah were all packed in the back seat of the car.

The deacon's bald, light skinned head bobbed up and down, agreeing with just about everything that Mr. Mercer was mentioning about the book of *Galatians,* while Isaac kept his attention solely at the passing scenery outside his window.

He had hardly said a single word ever since leaving church earlier; he didn't even acknowledge his own son when he reached out for him to be picked up into his arms.

Isaac's head was elsewhere that cloudy afternoon. Light flurries rained down from the sky, making it look like a complete whiteout, even though not one flake seemed to be sticking to the ground. With every building that passed, Isaac's stomach growled even more loud and irate.

"Uh oh," Deacon Hawthorne said, "sounds like someone didn't eat breakfast this morning."

"That boy always eats breakfast." Mr. Mercer giggled. "I can't imagine why he would be so hungry now."

Isaac could tell that his menacing silence was causing a bitter chill in the backseat. Even though he didn't want to look at her, Isaac could feel Lynnette's eyes pierce his flesh.

"Pastor Mercer," Lynnette all of the suddenly called out.

"Yes, ma'am," Mr. Mercer replied.

"Your son here told me a very interesting story about you the other night."

As if someone had clocked him over the head, Isaac awoke from his deep spell and stared peculiarly at Lynnette.

"He told me that you once were a pimp and a drug dealer before you became a pastor."

"Oh, did he now?" Mr. Mercer amazingly smiled.

"Yes, sir. Is it true? Because I'm having a very hard time believing that one myself."

"Yes, my dear, it's very true." Mr. Mercer appeared amused. "That was way back when Satan had his claws all over me. I was into a lot of mess back then. Then I met Mrs. Mercer, and well…let's just say that the Lord brings us special people to save our lives. And Isaac's mama was a very special person indeed."

"Amen, she surely was." Deacon Hawthorne nodded.

"I see," Lynnette grinned. "And then after all that, Isaac came along?"

"Yes…the end." Mr. Mercer laughed out loud.

Everyone inside the car, including Isaac, joined in on the chorus of laughter at the young man's expense.

"You all are some stone-cold, jive people." Isaac smirked. "You even got my own son laughing at me." He looked down and over at Isaiah who was grinning from ear to ear in his winter coat that had the hood down above his forehead.

"You know we're only foolin' with you, son." Mr. Mercer calmed down. "You're alright with me. But we'd better get some gas or else we won't make it to *Don's* at all."

As Mr. Mercer pulled into the *Texaco* station, little Isaiah chimed along with the ringing that the black, rubber hose made when the car rolled into the lot.

"Was that the baby doing that, too?" Deacon Hawthorne smiled as he looked at the child.

"Yes, sir," Lynnette replied. "He always does that every time we stop at the filling station. I think it's his favorite sound in the whole wide world."

"I'll pump for you, dad." Isaac said while zipping up his coat.

"Okay then." Mr. Mercer complied as he reached into his pocket, pulled out his wallet and handed Isaac a ten dollar bill." Go ahead and fill it up."

Isaac took the money and got out. As he marched his way into the blowing fury that was flying flurries towards the tiny cashier's hut, a homeless man, smoking a cigarette caught his attention. For some odd reason Isaac couldn't seem to take his eyes off of the man; it was like he was familiar with him. It was by sheer luck that he didn't bump into anyone along the way.

Isaac continued to walk before a face inexplicably flashed before his eyes. It was the face of a man, a light-skinned, young man that resembled an old, childhood friend. In his mouth he wanted to say a name, but his jaws seemed to be completely immobile.

"Hey, man, watch it!" A large black man warned as he and Isaac bumped into one another.

Isaac regained his senses and resumed his journey once more to the line where five other people were already standing, who instead of wanting to buy gasoline, only desired to purchase cartons and packs of cigarettes. Isaac, too, longed for a smoke, but at least he could wait until he got home.

Right in front of him was a young woman. She stood only a few inches shorter than Isaac. The lady was wearing an autumn orange and brown knit hat, a long, black leather coat that reached her knees and a pair of long, black leather boots.

Her long dreadlocks that sprouted from underneath her hat were yet another thing that snatched Isaac's already blundering attention for the day.

He waited behind the woman as she whispered at the clerk. Isaac impatiently rolled his eyes, thinking she too was in line for smokes.

The very instant the woman made her purchase she turned and eyeballed Isaac. Isaac looked back at the woman before nearly falling to the ground in devastating fear. She as well stopped dead in her tracks, as if someone had pointed a gun at her head.

Their bright, amber eyes stared into each other's fear-stricken faces. Nothing or no one could tear them apart from the other at that breathtaking moment; they were locked like two finely tuned targets.

"You're up next, Amigo." The cashier announced.

Isaac jumped back into the world and skittishly stepped forward to the counter while keeping his eyes on the woman who was racing back to her green *Monte Carlo* that was parked in the lot.

Forgetting why he even got out of his father's car to begin with, Isaac tore himself away from the counter and stormed back to the lot to watch the woman's vehicle rip out of the station and onto the road. He caught a mere glimpse of the license plate county name before racing back to his dad's car and jumping in.

"Did you pump already?" Mr. Mercer asked.

Sweating and breathing as if he had been running for miles, Isaac responded, "Uh…no, sir. They just shut down the pumps for a while. We gotta go to another station."

Sighing, Mr. Mercer said, "Well, we'd better hurry and find another station soon, or else we'll be pushing this old car home."

Ignoring every person inside the vehicle, Isaac held on to his door's handle as tight as he could. He would have given just about anything in the world at that second just to see the bright green *Monte Carlo* one more time; even if it meant giving his own life in the process.

CHAPTER 13

IT WAS COMPLETELY DARK inside Lynnette's bedroom that snowy evening as *The O'Jay's, 'Darlin', darlin', baby',* played on low volume on the *Panasonic* stereo that sat on the dresser next to the bed.

With the baby sleeping peacefully in his crib in a nearby corner and the kerosene heater blowing in their direction, both mother and father had to be especially quiet as not to awaken the child with their incessant moans of ecstasy.

Lynnette rubbed all over Isaac's head. He could tell just by the quivering of her naked body that she wanted so much to at least moan out loud.

Physically, Isaac was elated to be in the moment. The wider he opened Lynnette's pussy lips, the harder she grabbed his head. Just to hear her try and stifle the sounds only seemed to turn him on all the more as his lips did all the work. He loved how she would sensually caress his head and bury his face deeper into her pussy as though she were trying to smother him.

Emotionally, however, his mind was in a whole different place. For the remainder of the day, ever since running into the woman at the gas station, he was a man that did his best to evade everyone he loved. There were the gaps in his memory of the church service, along with his father telling him about his early morning visit inside his bedroom, which to Isaac could have only meant that his odd behavior had resurfaced.

Right then, Lynnette grabbed a hold of the bed's railing behind her, opened her mouth wide and let out a mute gasp the second she squirted all over Isaac's face.

Isaac raised his head slightly, closed his eyes and allowed the gooey substance to lacerate his mouth, the bridge of his nose and his eyelids. He then lowered his head again while trying to keep Lynnette's quivering body from squirming off the bed.

Isaac rose and watched as her entire naked body uncontrollably jolted up and down before coming to an eventual rest.

Isaac wiped his wet face clean before drawing close to Lynnette for a kiss, only to have the young lady subtly push him away.

"I'm sorry...I'm sorry." She whispered while pulling the covers onto her body.

Isaac wasn't upset at the gesture, he understood, but he was still horny, so he decided to attempt a new approach, something a bit more appealing. He pulled the covers away and proceeded to suck on her small breasts.

"Isaac...I have an early class in the morning." Lynnette winced while anxiously turning over and pulling the covers back onto her body.

Isaac laid there next to her feeling as though he had done something wrong. He wanted to get mad, but the anger was nowhere to be found inside of him. Next, he wanted to get up and walk away, but at the same time he didn't want to leave the presence of Lynnette's soft, warm body that made the entire bed feel so comfortable. So in the end, he chalked up his loses, wrapped his arm around her body and pulled her close to him.

"I'm sorry." He pitifully whispered into her ear.

Lynnette turned over. "I didn't mean to spoil the mood." She whispered back. "I guess I'm still not used to...the eyes."

"You didn't spoil anything, girl. Isaac replied as he kissed her on the forehead.

Lynnette wrapped her arms around Isaac's sweaty body and nestled herself deep into his hairy chest. As she lay there, Isaac could hear a sudden chuckle begin to bubble from out of her gut.

"What's so funny?" He glared strangely.

Lynnette looked into Isaac's eyes and said, "Isaac, if I asked you to be honest with me, would you?"

"I have before, haven't I?"

Lynnette sighed, "I don't know, you just seemed so distant today. It was like you didn't want to talk to anyone. You were even acting funny at *Don's*. You hardly touched your food. Is there something bothering you?"

"I just have these headaches every now and then." He shrugged. "It's nothing big."

"Isaac, I do believe in us. I don't know what you went through back at *Ashlandview,* but I want you to know that I was always thinking of you. I never wanted to see you leave."

"*Ashlandview* was cool. We got fed three times a day. Played a bunch of board games, watched TV and sat around in a circle and talked about our feelings. I even had one of the orderly's sneak oatmeal cream pies to me at night."

"You and your cream pies." She giggled.

"I can't help it, it's an addiction." Isaac sniggered back.

Lynnette rubbed her warm, clammy hands across Isaac's back at that moment. "Do you know what kind of wedding I want, Isaac?"

"What kind?"

"I want it to be down at the church. I want my nieces to be wearing purple dresses. I want Isaiah to be in a little tuxedo, carrying the ring down the aisle. I wanna see you dressed in that slick black and white tux that we saw last year at *Clancy's* department store Downtown."

Isaac laid and listened with attentive ears as Lynnette rattled on about her fantasy wedding. He wished she could have seen the ear to ear smile that was on his face right then. He wanted to bare his inner most joyous thoughts to her. For the first time since they had been together, he was excited about getting married.

"Isaac," Lynnette moaned into his face, "I want so much for us. What happened back in November is just a distant memory. The memories we make now are what will shape our future."

Isaac stared strangely at her and asked, "Is that from one of your poems, too?"

"Yeah, I just thought I'd slip it in at the right moment." She giggled.

Isaac, too, giggled along with her. "Do you remember when we were in the eleventh grade and we skipped school to go down to *Logan Park* to hang out?"

"Yep, and I also remember getting home that afternoon and having my ass torn apart by my father after the school reported us truant."

"But it was worth it though. We just walked around all day and did nothing but talk and make out."

"Yeah, it was a real nice day." Lynnette faintly uttered, creeping in and out of sleep.

Isaac looked down and took notice of her slurred speech. "It looks like we're gonna get a few feet of snow by morning. My dad doesn't have to go to work tomorrow, so I'm gonna take his car and look for a job."

"Can you take Isaiah to his aunt's house in the morning, too? Since I have that early class? And don't forget to buy some *Tylenol* nose drops for him; his cold is getting worse." Lynnette mumbled until cute little snores began to escape her mouth.

"Yeah, I can do that." Isaac whispered before kissing her on the cheek.

He laid there in bed for only a few more minutes before carefully climbing out and putting on his white undershirt that had the word *'Dynomite!'* printed across the front, along with a pair of long johns.

He then crept over and cut off the stereo before making his way to the door, stopping and looking back to mutter the words, "I don't want you to think I'm crazy, Lynn."

He found it incredibly difficult at best to tear himself away from the sight of the woman he loved lying serenely in her bed. It was like looking at a glowing figure. There was still someone left in the world that loved and trusted him all over again.

Isaac turned and stepped out of the warm confines of the bedroom and into the cool hallway. As he made his way out into the living room, unbeknownst to Isaac, his mysterious phantom snuck behind him from out of nowhere and crept down the other end of the hallway, as quiet and stealth as a mouse.

Isaac stood in front of the living room window and gazed out into the pink sky where huge snowflakes fell hard onto the already snow covered ground. By then, the entire neighborhood was glazed in a finely coated mixture of both snow and light rain.

All day long he tortured himself by pondering on the woman back at the gas station. He was even thinking about her while eating Lynnette out. It had become something of a recurring nightmare to him.

Her green *Monte Carlo* roaring away into traffic kept on beating into his head like a thousand drums all at once. Her eyes…her bright, amber eyes caused his stomach to gurgle and turn over, as if he were becoming sick.

He lied to Lynnette when he told her about the headaches. He hated doing so, but it was all he could think of without having her worry about him. All of the sudden, ever since leaving *Ashlandview,* everything he had chalked up to paranoia and superstition had all come rushing back at him like a raging tsunami.

Rapidly, the coldness in the living room had become a mere afterthought; Isaac had his fear to keep him warm for the remainder of the evening.

In a few months he would be getting married. The very next day, he would be leaving town. All Isaac could hope for was a possible safe return.

A pathetic belly chuckle coughed up into his throat. Everything was real, he thought to himself.

CHAPTER 14

LATE AFTERNOON,
THE FOLLOWING DAY

ISAAC DIDN'T LIE WHEN he told Lynnette that he would be going job hunting. He had been up since five a.m. racing from one end of *Cypress* to the other in his father's car in search of employment. If it wasn't *Dairy Queen* then it was other shops or even the local car wash scene. When he had exhausted every ounce of patience and ink in his pen from filling out countless job applications, he fled town.

It took him well over an hour to reach *Summit County*. His slow timing wasn't due to the snow covered roads, the city cleanup crews did a fairly decent job in removing a lot of the snow that had fallen overnight, it was his fear that caused a lackadaisical right foot to barely touch the gas.

The brooding expression on his exhausted face would have suggested that he would have rather been anywhere else in the world at that stage than to be on the long road that he found himself traveling upon.

The bright sun caused its rays to glare off the white blanket of snow that covered the vast farmland he was passing by. The strong shimmer would have caused anyone else to pull down the visor to shield their eyes, but instead, Isaac chose to allow the warmness to soothe his emotionally battered skin, hoping to gain a measure of calm from the breath of God in the process.

Just up ahead, a few yards to the left, Isaac caught sight of a small diner with a rotating sign on top of the roof that read 'Scats'. Right then, Isaac's stomach began to grumble all over again, just as it had been doing all day, off and on.

He pulled his father's car into the full parking lot, parked and glanced over to his right to see the same green *Monte Carlo* sitting only two spaces down.

He turned off the vehicle's ignition and listened as it putted and sputtered for at least a minute before finally shutting down. Then, with about as much determination as he could assemble, Isaac loosened his black Sunday tie, climbed out and marched towards the diner's front door as though he were heading straight for an old west showdown of sorts. He unzipped his stuffy coat and snatched out the bottom half of his white, button down dress shirt for more comfort.

The instant he opened the door, *The Eagles', 'Hotel California'* could be heard playing on the cheap stereo system that was mounted on a table in a corner behind the lunch counter. The aromas of French fries and eggs pleasantly filled the entire restaurant.

"Just go ahead and have a seat anywhere, sweetheart, and I'll be with you in a moment!" A perky, young white woman said while carrying hot plates of food from one end of the diner to the other.

Isaac wasn't in search of a seat; his eyes were transfixed on the hungry characters that inhabited the busy establishment. From left to right sat nothing but white people of different ages, sexes and sizes, not one minority face could be found.

As Isaac began to lurch deeper into the diner it suddenly donned on him to look towards the women's bathroom. She was there; her car was still parked outside. She was the only person in the world that Isaac knew that drove a bright green *Monte Carlo.*

He stood at the counter, only a few feet away from the women's restroom. The young man patiently watched as two young white girls came out, laughing and giggling about a boy they both liked from school.

The longer he waited, the more some of the patrons started to gawk his way, wondering just what the peculiar black man was doing leaning near the women's bathroom.

Suddenly, after watching three more women step out, from behind the door a dark skinned black woman appeared, wiping her hands dry with a paper towel. At the snap of a finger, Isaac snatched her by her right arm and harshly whispered, "We need to talk."

The startled woman dropped her wet towel to the floor while looking up at Isaac as though he were bigger than life itself. Isaac could tell that she no more wanted to see him than he did her; but even she had to realize that their meeting was as inevitable as the coming of another day.

"I didn't know you were still here, Karyn." The young waitress smiled as she walked behind the counter. "Were you two going to have supper together?"

"Yeah, we're gonna have a seat for a moment." Isaac adamantly replied before practically dragging Karyn over to an empty booth and sitting down.

The two of them sat and stared each other down with cold, steel glares in their amber eyes, as if they wanted to explode all over the other at any second.

Karyn pressed her quivering lips together as tight as she could. In a disgraceful manner, she cut her eyes away from Isaac's firm face.

"Well," the waitress said as she approached the table with a pencil and pad in hand, "what can I get for you two?"

Without even looking in her direction, Isaac sternly responded, "Give us a moment. We still gotta think about it."

The waitress turned up her nose and simply walked away, leaving two frightened individuals awaiting the other's words to exit their throats.

"How did you find me?" Karyn stuttered in a raspy, Jamaican dialect while rapidly blinking her eyelids.

"I remembered that you lived in *Cuyahoga Falls*. I don't know, somehow I knew that you would be right here, at this place. Or did you forget about our little night together?"

"Don't sit there and give me that smug tone, Isaac." Karyn snapped before taking off her winter hat and slamming it down onto the table. "What do you want?"

Stunned by the very question itself, Isaac leaned forward and frowned, "What do I want? Bitch, look at my fuckin' eyes! Ever since you and I fucked, I've been going out of my damn mind. And don't you sit there and look at me like I'm crazy. Your ass never stuck around after that night at your friends' house."

Karyn sat back and lowered her sullen eyes as though she were distressed. "Isaac, do you really know what took place that night?"

"Hell yeah I know! You turned into a—

"Stop," Karyn forcefully pointed. "Before you even say another word, just stop, and listen to yourself. How do you know for sure what you saw that night? How do you know that same something is inside of you?"

It got under the young man's already burning skin to sit and listen as Karyn played everything off as paranoid delusion.

Isaac hopelessly giggled and said, "I figured it was all in my head at first. My own father sent me to a mental hospital because I was acting like fuckin' fool. Everyone, from my psychiatrist to my dad, convinced me that it was all in my head, and I believed it, too. That is until I ran into your ass yesterday.

Now…now I know what happened was for real. I know what I felt that night. It took weeks for my body to heal. I know there is something inside of me, I can feel it moving around, like it's trying to claw its way out."

Karyn dropped her hands to the side and looked out the window to her right at the blue sky and fading sun that was beginning its timely descent.

In a downtrodden tone, Karyn said, "I came to America three years ago, hoping to find some way to…rid myself of this. But, it only seemed like it became worse once I got here. I never meant to pass it along to you, Isaac."

Isaac balled up his fists while his dark face took on a more sinister, disgruntled expression. "You don't forget that kind of pain that I went through that night."

Karyn twisted her head around and said, "Don't talk to me about pain, Isaac. I've had to live with this for fourteen years. Do you know how many times I've thought about killing myself? Or wishing someone would do it for me?"

"There has to be a cure, dammit!" Isaac angrily said out loud. "There has to be someone out there that can help the both of us! Why didn't you tell me about this before we laid down?"

Karyn eyeballed Isaac with a confused contort on her face before slowly asking, "Would you have believed me? You don't just go around telling people that sort of thing, Isaac, lest I too end up in a mental institution. Besides, I'm not the one who chose to cheat on my girlfriend. That was you."

Out of a sense of both anxiety and frustration, Isaac covered his face with his gloved hands and wiped tears away from his eyes. With every passing moment he could see both Lynnette and Isaiah slip away from him.

"You don't know what it's like, man." He openly wept. "I'm supposed to be getting married soon. I got a kid. I'm trying to keep myself together, but it's getting harder every day. Sometimes…I don't even know what day it is. Everything just keeps running all together. When I got home the other day, I looked in the mirror and there was blood and feathers all over my mouth and teeth. I keep having these damn blackouts. I can't remember shit!"

"Wait a minute." Karyn hastily interrupted. "When was the last time you had a blackout, Isaac?" She nervously inquired.

Shaking his head from side to side, Isaac replied, "I don't know, I think I had one yesterday in church. One minute my father was preaching, then…there's this wide gap in my brain. It happened a few days before that too, I think."

Karyn's entire face grew a shade lighter right there. It was expressionless, as if she had seen her own existence shatter into a million pieces in mere seconds.

"Isaac," she stammered, "the blackouts mean that the cycle is beginning all over again."

"Cycle, what the fuck is a cycle? What are you talkin' about?" Isaac helplessly threw his hands into the air.

Karyn's hands trembled on the table. "It wants to feed again, Isaac. It's trying to come back again."

"No…no," Isaac loudly resisted with huge tears falling from his eyes. "Do you mean that I'm gonna…change again?"

With tears forming in her own eyes, Karyn leaned forward, took Isaac's shaking hands into hers and carefully stated, "The demon has lain dormant inside of you for the past few months. It has been resting, and it will continue to do so until it is ready to feed again. Sometimes it will hibernate for weeks, months or even years. I went a full four years without changing before. I figured that maybe it went away, that is until the blackouts. It's like the demon takes over for a little bit. Sometimes anger, spilled blood or even pain will arouse it. Isaac…when it is ready to feed, it will emerge, whether you are ready or not."

Slowly, Karyn began to slide out of her seat, all the while

keeping a cautious eye on Isaac. "Stay away from people, Isaac. Don't go back home." She sobbed as she stood up and started for the door.

Isaac, too, rose and grabbed Karyn by the arm." You need to tell me how to stop this!" He yelled into her face.

Everyone in the diner stopped what they were doing to watch in amazement the unfolding events before them all.

"Let go of me!" Karyn barked while snatching her arm away.

Isaac watched the woman storm out of the diner before following in behind her in the hopes of grabbing her once again.

Being careful not to slip and fall in the snow, Isaac chased after Karyn, only to miss her by inches before she was able to jump into her car.

"Stop the car, bitch!" Isaac insanely yelled as he pounded on the driver side window. "Please help me!"

But rather than stop, Karyn only put the car in drive and tore out of the parking lot and onto the road. Frantically, Isaac whipped out the keys from his pocket, ran to his father's car and tried to start the engine. He repeatedly twisted the key, but all the vehicle wanted to do was sputter and whine. It had been behaving irrationally all day long. The old, worn down car wasn't equipped to handle a long haul to *Cuyahoga Falls.*

Isaac pulled the hood's release lever, got out of the vehicle and inspected the supposed dilemma. Desperately, he pulled a few hoses here and there while examining the warm engine.

"Looks like you got yourself some car trouble." A heavy, velvety voice said from behind.

Isaac spun around to see a stocky, middle-aged white man dressed in a fancy coffee colored long winter coat, a smoke grey fedora and a pair of tight blue jeans and brown cowboy boots. The man stood in the middle of the lot holding a Styrofoam cup full of steaming coffee.

"Uh, yeah, I think it's the carburetor." Isaac grunted as he lifted his body out from underneath the hood.

"Well, I can tell you right now that this is no place to be stranded after dark, my friend, especially when all the truckers get here. I have a shop right down the road from here. I could get your car looked at if you want." The man kindly smiled while sipping away at his coffee.

Isaac was too enthralled with catching Karyn, who by then was at least a mile away, to think twice about taking a ride from a total stranger. At that juncture, he would have accepted help from *Satan* if he had offered.

"Sure." He carelessly shrugged. "How far down the road is your shop?" Isaac questioned while slamming the hood shut.

"About six miles," the man said. "C'mon, it's getting dark out." The man limped back to his blue, 1974 *BMW 3.0 CS* that was parked clear on the other side of the lot.

Isaac ran after the generous gentleman and got in on the passenger's side. The smell of cigarettes, coffee and fading perfume stunk up the entire vehicle. Isaac looked around, from front to back out of curiosity at how well kept the vehicle appeared.

"Was that your girlfriend you were chasing after?" The man asked before putting his cup down into the holder in front of him and cutting on the ignition.

Isaac blew heat back into his hands before saying, "Uh, no. Just someone I happened to know."

"Are you cold?" The man inquired as he pulled onto the open road.

"Not really, man, I'm just really upset at that woman."

"That's a woman for you." The man laughed. "They're always good at making a man upset. So, I saw the tag on your plates. You're from *Arkin County*. What are you doing all the way out here?"

"I just came to see her, that's all." Isaac nervously chuckled while keeping his eyes on the passing farmland outside the window.

"Yeah, I've been to *Cypress* a few times myself over the past few months. It used to be a real nice city years ago."

Isaac could hear the gregarious man chatter on, but his thoughts were lights years away. Even if he could get the car fixed, Karyn was long gone. It was dumb luck that he found her at the diner to begin with.

"Did you hear me?" The man glanced over.

"Huh?" Isaac stuttered as he turned towards the man. "My fault, I didn't hear you."

"I said I like your eyes. You don't see too many black guys with eyes like yours."

To hear a man comment on how alluring his eyes were was unsettling to him, but it was all just meaningless words.

"Yep, it was sure a pretty snowstorm we got last night."

Isaac said nothing. His eyes started to water up as they passed by an all-white church that sat alone in a valley.

Every so often he would glance over at the man and see only his lips moving. Isaac seemed unfazed by all the incessant babbling. All he could ponder was the look on Karyn's flushed face as she explained cycles and hibernating demons.

It was all foreign to him. But the one thing that brought the most fear out was being told not to go back home. Lynnette's trusting image flashed before his eyes.

Isaac shut his eyes and exhaled before opening them to see a white man and four little girls climb out of a brown station wagon and walk towards a red and white brick house.

His eyes rolled upwards to the orange sky that was growing darker with every passing minute. Isaac tried in earnest to recall one of his father's strong sermons, anything that had something in it concerning God's forgiveness and unconditional love for people, no matter what sins they committed.

"Hey, man, does this shop of yours have a phone? Because I—

At that very split second, Isaac felt an incredible sting of blazing heat surge throughout his entire body. Almost immediately his head hit the window beside him.

He was slipping in and out of unconsciousness. Isaac couldn't lift a single finger or even open his mouth to mutter a word. He could feel his body jerk from side to side as drool lazily dripped out and down from his mouth.

"Do you like music, sweetie?" Isaac heard a deep voice ask.

He could hear a song, but only for a few scant seconds before his warm ears could no longer pick up anything more.

CHAPTER 15

BY THE TIME THE *BMW* reached its destination the sun had already ducked itself behind the dark clouds for the evening. A brutally cold, stiff wind blew past the valley in which the driver's brown and white ranch-style home was located.

The driver pulled the eight-track from out of the deck before tossing it in the backseat. He then got out, slammed his door behind him and made his way around to the other side. His warm, fidgety hands could hardly grab a hold of the door's handle.

The second he was able to take a hold of the knob he flung open the door with such a force that it caused Isaac's lifeless body to fall out of the car and onto the snowy ground. The driver closed the door and picked the young man up into his burly arms as though he were an infant.

From there, he carried him from the curved driveway and on to the house, a total twenty-two feet. Somehow, with Isaac in his arms, the man managed to reach into his right pants pocket and pull out his house key.

The man opened the door, but before even shutting it behind him, he carried Isaac over to a black leather couch and carefully laid him down, allowing his head to softly hit the pillow at the foot of the sofa.

Then, like the rush of the wind, the driver ran back over,

shut the front door and clicked on the lamp light next to the television before feverishly tearing off his clothes and tossing them to the floor in reckless abandon.

His soft, multicolored carpet felt squishy and smooth in between his feet as he shuffled across the floor to a glass table where a *Panasonic* stereo rested.

From underneath there was a small drawer. Before reaching inside, the driver raced across the floor and retrieved his pants. He rooted around the pockets until he found his Taser gun. He then went back to the drawer, placed the gun inside and pulled out a record which he promptly placed on the stereo's turn style. Right beside the stereo was placed a tape recorder. With one finger the driver hit the record button.

Just like that, *Chicago's, 'If you leave me now',* began to play on the stereo, filling the entire living room with *Peter Cetera's* light, harmonious voice.

The man then reached over and began to pull off Isaac's clothing. From his coat, shirt and tie, all the way down to his *Fruit of the Loom* underwear and socks.

Once he was through, he raised up and shut all the blinds in the front window before stretching behind the couch and pulling up a half empty canister of *Vaseline*. He twisted open the metal container and with his two right fingers scooped out a glob and proceeded to lubricate Isaac's rectum with the gel.

After he was done, the driver just happened to look up at all the pictures that were placed on the mantle above the fireplace of a white man that resembled a younger version of himself. His pain stricken eyes didn't want to even catch a mere glimpse of the man's face.

He ducked his head down and kissed Isaac on the cheek before spreading his butt cheeks and entering.

The event lasted no more than two and a half minutes. The sweaty, out of breath man slowly pulled out and stood up, jerking from side to side while semen oozed from his penis and onto the carpet. The song that was playing on the stereo ended right on time.

With sweat lacing his forehead and hairy chest, the gasping man looked back at Isaac's body that was dangling off of the sofa. There were drops of blood that emanated from the young man's rear.

The man, in all his unbridled nakedness, stepped over and turned off the stereo. He then began to pace the floor back and forth in the quiet living room, trying his hardest not to look at the young person that he had brought home with him. It was a cross-like burden that seemed to weigh him down. Suddenly, he wanted nothing more to do with the individual that was lying helplessly on his brand new couch. To him, the young man was nothing more than a piece of trash that needed to be discarded and forgotten.

Without warning, Isaac's teetering body fell off the couch and onto the carpet. With semen still streaming from his penis the man walked over, picked Isaac up and carried him from the living room to the kitchen.

Within the spacious kitchen was a door. With one hand, the man unlocked the wooden door before opening it wide and throwing Isaac's body down the stairs. The second he heard him hit the bottom, the man slammed the door shut.

From the basement door he regrettably marched over to a nearby cabinet and took out a sharp knife. Placed on the counter beside a cookie jar was a blue and white electric knife sharpener. With the flip of a switch, the machine came to life. With steady precision, the man placed the knife's edge against the loud contraption and watched with his bare eyes as sparks flew from left to right.

It had never occurred before in times past, his house was newly built, there was never any problem of sorts with such a thing, but all of the sudden, the lights in the kitchen began to flicker off and on. The driver, startled only a slight bit, paused for a few moments before resuming his meticulous sharpening detail.

The basement, much like the kitchen, was brightly lit, with four ceiling fans spread out along the expansive room. Lanced upon the ceiling were sixteen hooks, all of which were supporting sixteen blood soaked, brown cloth sacks, each one with its own bulge.

The cement floor was layered from one end to the other with blood. It looked as though someone had spilled red paint and didn't bother to clean up after themselves. The pungent odor of dead, decomposing bodies was akin to an overflowing sewer on a hot summer's day.

Maggots swarmed and feasted on the bloody floor while Isaac's body laid still, curled up in a ball. Right above him hung a lonesome young woman who was dangling inside her own special brown, cloth sack.

With a tiny hole that she herself had carved open, she looked down upon Isaac's body in utter dismay, realizing that with yet another victim added to the lineup, her odds of escaping had all but shrank.

She held her naked self as tight as she could while resuming her daily regimen of desperate prayer time, hoping beyond all hope that someone would come and save her from the barrage of collected death that she was reluctantly gathered amongst.

The more she prayed, that was all the longer time seemed to stretch out for her. Every so often she would take quick glances down at the motionless body on the floor just to make sure he wasn't moving.

"Dog kcuf," Isaac grunted aloud with his eyes still closed.

The young lady's ears perked up like an attentive dog at

what she hoped she had heard. She poked one eye out of the hole and noticed that Isaac's hands were moving.

"C'mon…c'mon and get up." She gasped with just about every ounce of air inside her lungs.

She watched in fervent exultation as the man's hands slapped the bloody floor all while repeating the words he was shouting.

"Shh," she strongly whispered, "don't talk too loud or else he'll hear you."

Isaac didn't utter another word, he only rolled over onto his back and opened his eyes. The woman in the sack saw two eyes, but there was something different. The man's eyes rolled backwards to where all she could see was nothing but white.

His body then turned back over until it was on its hands and knees. The man breathed in and out as though he were fighting for air. To the shock of the captive woman above, Isaac began to growl an unearthly noise.

The woman's entire body clinched itself as she watched the man's arms expand in size. His legs and feet cracked and extended in length while his fingers scraped across the floor until they began to bleed.

Soon, sharp claws shot out from Isaac's fingernails while thick, black fur protracted from just about every aperture of his body until there was nothing left but a larger sized, hairy version of the man.

The woman hung in her sack while her petrified eyes caught way too much of the unspeakable. At first, she threw it all up to delirium. She had been kidnapped, raped and nearly murdered, both her mind and eyes could have been playing all sorts of cruel jokes on her at that point.

The young man that at one time she hoped would be her escape, was seemingly gone, what lurked about on the basement floor was nothing but a mutated former human being.

The woman could still see Isaac's white eyes and what

resembled a face, a face that astonishingly began to stretch outwards into what appeared to be a snout and sharp fangs. The man could be heard crying out in unbearable pain until his human voice had all but morphed into that of an animal's roar.

She couldn't contain herself a moment more. Not only was she shaking like a leaf, but she was also urinating at the sight of seeing pointy ears extend up from the beast's head before its once white eyes drew back to amber.

With her one eye the woman watched as the creature sniffed at the floor. It snarled and licked up spots of blood until it came upon the warm, wet space below her. On its powerful arms and hind legs it lurched its way over and smelled before looking up with its shining eyes at the sack.

She wanted to shut off her brain, or at least go into a fit of hysterical blindness. Just as it seemed as if it were about to attack, the buzzing noise from the floor above captured the beast's attention.

The woman watched as the thing appeared somewhat confounded. Its head turned from her to the stairs and back again before growling in anger and galloping for the steps.

Her eyes had captured the ungodly; it was time for her ears to take over. She heard the creature tear through the basement door before letting out a devastating roar. Her captor didn't seem to even have enough time to let out a simple squeal before being mauled by the thing.

Two things, and only two things she heard, the animal roar and growl, and the crashing of a human body being tossed from one end of the kitchen to the other. It sounded as if someone were taking a jackhammer and using it on the floor with as much reckless noise that was taking place.

Just for the briefest of moment's, the young, captive lady actually felt a glint of sorrow for her uncaring captor.

Then, after seemingly endless minutes, the crashing racket stopped. The woman could hear what sounded like sharp teeth tearing and chomping before another rumble entered the home. To her it sounded as if an entire door had been knocked down again.

There was a bitter hush. The knife sharpener was still operating, but inside the woman's head was jarring stillness. She could no longer hear the beast. She couldn't hear roaring or teeth tearing flesh. There was nothing but hushed silence inside the home, along with a whistling wind that she prayed would serenade her to sleep that evening.

CHAPTER 16

NIGHTFALL WAS A HARD and acrimonious plight in the quiet valley as the beast crunched its way across the snow and towards a crippled forest.

Its enormous paws and hind legs stretched forward at a pace that would be quite unusual for a creature of its enormity. It trekked along as though it was aware that food was near, even though its stomach was nearly full by that point in the evening.

Its hot breath steamed out in front of it as the demon entered the dark forest roaring and growling an ever-present warning to anything that may be in its sprinting way. The withered trees were more of a nuisance that only stood in its path. One by one, the demon's hairy arms bumped and crashed against the oaks that dared stand in front of it.

The thing's shiny eyes pierced the sheer blackness of night; its sight was flawless. The temperature was well below the teens that evening, and yet, the demon's thick coat of fur provided the ever so perfect insulation that it required for lurking.

As soon as the creature cleared the forest thick, its eyes caught sight of a brightly lit house just a few yards up ahead. Like a charging steed into medieval battle, the demon trampled further towards the large home, snarling and snorting across a snowy, open field that young boys would often play football in.

"You've been on my ass ever since me and the girls got

home this evening! And it's only eight o'fucking clock!" An angry, balding, middle-aged white man raged as he slammed the refrigerator door shut and advanced towards his shuddering wife.

His wife, who was adorned in a pink bathrobe, hairnet and slippers, stood in the middle of the kitchen floor, staring a distraught eye at her fuming husband while holding her cold arms together.

"I told you to bring the girls home at four o' clock, Gary! You know full well that they have to eat before seven!"

"Well excuse me all to hell for wanting to spend a little quality time with my own children!" Gary screamed while waving his arms in the air. "You're the one that keeps on bitching about how I don't spend enough time with them, and when I finally do, you jump all over my ass! What the hell do you want from me, Sarah?"

Sarah stepped away from Gary and began to pace the floor as though she were trying to think up something important to say at that instant; like she had something to get off of her chest, but didn't exactly know how to let it go.

Gary only backed away and rolled his eyes in blistering frustration. The backdoor was only a few feet to his left, and there was nothing more he wanted than to storm away.

"Gary," Sarah pathetically whimpered, "I think...I just think that you and I should get a divorce."

With a drained appearance on his face, the man stared deep into his crying wife's eyes. It was as if his very breath had inexplicably been snatched away. His skin grew a shade whiter.

With tears flowing, Sarah said, "You can't be surprised, Gary. It's been a long time coming. I can't talk to you anymore. If you're not in Cleveland then you're in New York! If it's not New York, then it's Chicago! You're hardly even home anymore! And you want to stand there and take credit for taking the girls out for ice cream?" She hollered while stomping her right foot on the linoleum.

"I work, Sarah." Gary said. "I'm not like your brother who just sits around all day long and does absolutely nothing! Or you're instigating mother who just lets herself in our house every morning like she owns the damn place! I have a fucking career! And for that, I get this?"

"Oh, God, Gary," Sarah shouted at the top of her lungs, "This is not about you!"

Gary stood back, and with a smug expression on his face he asked, "A divorce, huh? Did *Gloria Steinem* tell you to do that?"

Sarah just rolled her eyes in defeat and exhaled as though the fight had taken everything completely out of her.

"Well...if that's the way you want it, then I guess I'll see your sorry ass in court." Gary sternly replied before re-opening the refrigerator door and resuming his search for food.

With her left hand covering her mouth, Sarah carried herself back into the dimly lit living room and dropped herself down onto the couch.

Hearing his wife cry in the other room suddenly caused Gary's rage to gradually dissipate. Like angry storm clouds, he could see the destruction of their union from miles away, but he honestly never imagined that he would hear the word 'divorce' said straight to his face.

He rooted around in the refrigerator, pretending to be in need of sustenance. Gary didn't want Sarah to think that he too was falling apart.

In an aimless blunder, Gary recklessly sifted past an open box of baking powder and a carton of milk in order to reach a block of cheese before hearing a loud crash, which was followed by a heavy thud from the basement.

Gary shut the refrigerator door and leisurely stepped over to where the basement door was located.

The ferocious ruckus could have been yet another raccoon

SHAWN A. JENKINS

or possum, even though neither creature had ever made such thunderous, violent racket before.

Gary reached behind him and grabbed a red broom that was placed next to the sink; he then opened the basement door only to see nothing but darkness below. The noises had suddenly ceased.

The longer the quiet down below reigned, the more Gary began to realize that whatever was at one time down there could have possibly run off the moment it heard the door open.

Just as Gary was about to shut the door, out of the corner of his eye he caught what looked to be two bright beams of wavering light appear in the blackness of the basement. Gary stood back as the beams began to slowly advance towards him. His own heart nearly jumped out of his chest at that second. He was accustomed to seeing animals shine their night eyes in the dark, but the thing that was apparently skulking about on his basement stairs had a strikingly different kind of sound to it, like that of an angry, snarling lion.

Both man and beast stood opposite the other, staring each other down. Even the light from the kitchen wasn't able to shine bright enough to where Gary could catch a more precise glimpse of the supposed animal that was prowling about.

As Gary began back up the steps, he felt his right arm being snatched forward. Before he could even let out a single scream, the beast tore into his face, ripping away at his eyes and mouth with its sadistically sharp fangs.

All that could be heard was the bumping and thrashing of Gary's legs as they kicked from left to right, knocking over a canister of nails that was perched in a nearby corner.

Sarah, still seated on the couch in the living room, rolled her eyes in disgust at all the rumpus that she assumed Gary was making. She immediately shot up from off the couch, carried her tired self into the kitchen and sighed, "What are you doing now? I thought you were getting something to eat."

When she received no response, Sarah looked at the open basement door and figured that Gary was downstairs; it was customary for him to retreat downwards whenever a fight broke out between the two.

"Can you at least try and keep it down?" She irritably yelled. "I'm going upstairs to be with the girls!"

But still, there was no reply, only the racket of what resembled something being torn apart, and snorting coming from the stairwell.

"Gary, why don't you have the light on?" She shook while noticing the red broom lying on the floor.

As she leaned forward to pick it up, her trembling left hand managed to cut on the light switch. Glorious light filled the top half of the basement, enough light for the woman to see an enormous, hairy animal ravenously eating away at her husband's stomach.

Without blinking, Sarah dropped the broom, turned and ran away, only to be chased down into the living room, hollering for help.

The beast pounced onto her back and proceeded to tear into her soft flesh. Pieces of red hair were torn out of her head to where the woman was nearly bald. The demon then used its powerful jaws to crunch into her skull.

Meanwhile, upstairs in the parents' bedroom, four little girls, two red heads and two blondes, all sat on the queen sized bed, watching *Wonder Woman* on the *RCA* television in front of them and wondering why their mother had squealed for help the way she did.

Three of the scared children looked over at the eldest sister that was seated at the foot of the bed. Her little hands and legs shook with unyielding fear.

They had heard their parents fight before, but never had there been such an aggressive commotion as there was that evening. Never was there a plea for help.

"Is daddy hitting mommy again, Jamie?" The second youngest girl asked while wiping tears away from her eyes.

"Don't worry...I'll go and see." The young lady stammered before reluctantly rising to her trembling feet and marching her way over to the door.

As she twisted the knob, her only thoughts were that her father would not take out his aggression on her and her sisters.

When she finally opened the door and looked out into the brightly lit hallway, all Jamie could see was the blue laundry basket that was full of clothes sitting next to the bathroom door.

Too petrified to go downstairs, the girl carefully closed the door and climbed back onto the bed alongside her sisters.

Right behind the child, a loud chorus of thumps could be heard rumbling up the stairs. It sounded as though a series of people were chasing after one another.

"Daddy's gonna get mommy!" Another one of the girls screamed out.

Jamie covered her sister's wailing mouth with her hand while holding her own knocking knees together and thinking only of her three sisters that were gathered amongst her.

When the rumbling clatter ended, a new sound began to resonate. There was something on the other end of the bedroom door, sniffing up and down like a dog. The girls held themselves in silent, dreaded anticipation. Not one child moved an inch as *Lynda Carter* spun around in a circle to reveal her alter ego on the TV in front of them.

One...two...three seconds passed by. Like a bulldozer, a fur covered arm crashed through the door. The arm was followed by a loud, unearthly roar.

The girls all yelled out in blood curdling unison as the hulking beast rampaged its way into the bedroom.

Outside, and from a clear distance, the bedroom lamp could be seen wildly thrashing all about, until finally, it went completely dark inside.

CHAPTER 17

AN EMPTY, SMALL, QUIET church inhabited an equally isolated pasture. Eight pews in all; four on both sides. Down in front, a short pulpit, behind the pulpit, a ten foot tall porcelain statue of Christ Jesus, nailed to a cross that was lanced onto a wall above, looking down with a woeful demeanor.

Like a sudden explosion, the beast crashed straight through one of the windows and into the church, landing on the newly cleaned red carpet. It shook off shards of glass from its thick fur while its mouth was completely soaked with blood.

Its face appeared as evil as the sins that it had been committing all evening long. It crept about the building as though it were in search of something. Its heavy breathing echoed throughout the church.

The demon's immense paws tracked snow, mud and blood all over the floor, leaving both a mess and deep crevices behind it. As it prowled, large globs of feces dropped from its anus; some in small clumps, and others in elephant sized layers.

The ungodly creature, on all fours, plodded around the sanctuary until it found itself in front of the altar. Its glaring eyes happened to look up to see the crucified savior. At first, the beast only shook its hairy head from side to side like an agitated bull, until it managed to catch the statue's eyes slowly creep open and look back down upon it.

At first, both individuals gave each other only hard stares, as if they were waiting for the other to make a move. Then, the beast, possibly out of a confused rage, opened its mouth wide and let out a vicious roar before slumping down to its knees in agony.

It lied on the carpet, writing in pain. A minute or two passed before the Nazarene, with his crown of bloody thorns perched upon his head, picked the demon up by its shoulders and dragged it away, leaving only a black streak behind on the carpet.

Ever so gradually, the beast's snout was beginning to shrink.

There was an uncanny, almost appalling silence in the deep farmland that evening. The natural nighttime sounds, from the hooting owl, to the occasional rambling barking dog, were nowhere to be heard.

A February winters twilight never felt so alone and frigid; it was as if the entire world had left *Cuyahoga Falls* behind.

Silence never sounded so ugly.

CHAPTER 18

6:37 A.M.

THE SUBZERO, OVERCAST SKY bared down upon the seven brown and white police cruisers that crept into the driveway of 1941 Prosler Road that following morning.

Both Detective Linus Bruin and his partner, Detective Alan Fitzpatrick climbed out of their vehicle with their individual pistols already in hand. Fourteen other police officers tagged along behind the two, all with their respective weapons drawn.

Bruin's white sideburns coiled in the harsh wind as he brashly stalked towards the house. He pulled down his black wool hat tighter on his head as his pale white face grew a shade lighter from stomach dropping anticipation. The man was never prepared to engage a suspect, and at 53, physical combat was practically a forgone fantasy.

He poked his head up to see through the frosted front window of the stylish home. He wasn't sure just what he would end up finding, but he was certain that nothing was going to catch him off guard; the man had invested entirely too much time and effort into the case to allow it to collapse before his eyes.

SHAWN A. JENKINS

The detective stepped up onto the porch, knocked on the door and loudly hollered, "Police! Open Up!"

After five seconds, he looked back at the waiting officers before returning his attention to the door where he proceeded to muster all of the strength in his right leg to kick it in.

After three striking attempts, the door went flying wide open. The instant he stepped inside, the piercing buzzing sound of a loud device could be heard clear from the front door.

"Hello?" Bruin called oud, pointing his gun straight ahead while skulking about for any signs of humanity.

One by one, Fitzpatrick and the other officers all cautiously made their way inside. Two ventured down a hallway, while the others stuck behind Bruin.

As Linus neared the kitchen, he was all the more convinced that there could have been someone waiting for him on the other end. The buzzing commotion was completely unfamiliar to him.

Right then, a blustery wind rushed into the living room from the kitchen. At first he reckoned that his suspect had escaped through a backdoor, which was exactly why his heavy feet paced even faster towards the kitchen's threshold.

The very second he crossed through the kitchen's doorway, his brown eyes were immediately bombarded by the grotesque visual of blood layered walls, and what resembled a mass of both torn bones and ripped flesh lying in a heap on the floor.

Every officer that viewed the mutilation stood back in both awe and repulsion at the horrendous scene laid out before them.

Bruin, a man who had always hoped that a gunshot victim would be the worst thing that he would ever have to experience in his storied career as an officer, suddenly became ill to his stomach. He didn't want to step into the kitchen, but there were others behind him that were a lot more daring. Without giving it a second glance, the officers stampeded their way inside the freezing kitchen.

"Well," Fitzpatrick cringed, "I'll be dammed."

"No one in the other rooms, Detective," a black officer announced as he ventured into the kitchen. "What the hell?" He suddenly gulped.

Bruin and his fellow officers all tip-toed around the disfigured corpse, but with all of the blood and body parts that littered the floor, it was nearly impossible not to step in something gruesome.

"Is this him?" Bruin examined, kneeling down and poking at the body's mangled face with the tip of his gun.

"Leroy Cummins The Third." Fitzpatrick replied while clicking off the switch to the knife sharpener on the counter. "Age fifty-five."

In total astonishment, Bruin looked up to see the gaping hole in the wall to his right. "And just what in the blue hell could have done that?" He pointed.

"Quite possibly the same thing that did this," Fitzpatrick motioned to the body while crouching beside Bruin.

The two men glanced over at each other with confounded glares on their cold faces as the hostile wind slammed into the kitchen and on top of them.

"Look at this." One officer pointed at the destroyed basement door. "We're going down." He brazenly proclaimed, taking seven other officers along with him.

Bruin and Fitzpatrick handed each other unsettling stares as though they had been one-upped by the other officers.

Just then, a young, heavy set, brown-haired white man with thick glasses and a brown winter coat came rambling into the kitchen. Unlike his fellow officers, he didn't appear to be all too shaken by the macabre sight that lay before him.

He carelessly stepped over the carcass, nearly knocking over both Bruin and Fitzpatrick in the process, before approaching the open wall. "What is this?" He questioned as he stooped down to the snowy ground.

"It's called snow, Brice." Fitzpatrick snidely remarked.

"I don't mean that. I mean, what kind of animal left these tracks?"

Bruin and Fitzpatrick stood to their feet and made their way over to where Brice was already crouched. They looked closely at the oversized paw prints that were creviced in the snow in amazement.

"Could it be a bear?" Bruin curiously inquired while jabbing at one of the tracks with his finger.

"I've never seen a bear leave these kinds of tracks before." Brice confidently replied while looking over to his immediate left to take notice of a few strands of black fur that was strewn all over the ground. "No, what we have here it far too big to be a bear, I'm afraid."

"What is that, mane?" Fitzpatrick ogled.

"Lions have mane, Detective." Brice smugly answered without taking his eyes off of the specimen. "This is more of a North American species, if you ask me."

"Well, whatever it is, it looks like it came up from out of the basement and got to Cummins." Bruin deliberated. "The tracks look to head west of here."

"Let's get a body bag for this one!" Fitzpatrick pointed to the corpse before stepping back into the house, whipping out a piece of chalk from his hip pocket and tracing a line around the cadaver.

"We've got sixteen bags down here!" An officer called out from the basement. "No survivors!" He then shamefully added.

"The sick fucker probably fed them to whatever he had hiding down there." Fitzpatrick sulked before stepping away from his outlining duty.

Bruin knew that he should have gone downstairs

immediately. Deep within, he realized that after so many months, finding any survivors was all but a pipe dream, and yet, to hear a fellow officer announce it to the world was like having his own chest crack in half. To him, it was all wasted hope and effort. He had no words or energy left in him to disburse.

"I only wish I could have personally fed Cummins to the damn thing myself." Fitzpatrick bitterly groaned before walking back into the living room.

Bruin was all too ready to leave the house altogether, the entire investigation and cleanup would take nearly all day. He stood to the side and meticulously observed two male coroners come into the kitchen to retrieve the body. Ever so carefully they reached down and attempted to pick up what was left of the dead man only to have his body split in two right in their hands.

"Fuck me!" One of the young men angrily yelled before kneeling down to pick up Cummins' bottom portion.

Completely deflated, Bruin dragged himself past the murder scene on his way back into the living room to find Fitzpatrick holding a tape recorder. He then watched as his partner pushed the rewind button and allowed the recording to play.

Everyone that was gathered in the living room stood and listened with disgusted faces as Cummins huffed and wheezed to a *Chicago* song playing in the background. It wasn't too difficult for everyone to figure out what the man was doing in the recording.

"Damn shit." Fitzpatrick growled as he placed the machine back down onto the glass table without stopping the recording.

"Hey, Jones," Bruin motioned to the floor, "there's a thing of *Vaseline* beside the couch there."

"Where's the fellow that he snatched yesterday?" One of the other officers asked.

"Maybe he's downstairs." Bruin miserably replied before starting for the bedrooms.

"I guess it makes sense in a way," Fitzpatrick mentioned while gawking about the sophisticated living room, "he's been using his own vehicles to snatch people."

"We've got a live one down here!" A voice gleefully shouted out from the basement.

Like little boys on summer vacation, both Bruin and Fitzpatrick raced through the living room, into the kitchen and down the basement stairs to see fifteen naked, dead bodies lying all over a bloodied floor, and one living, naked person curled up in a secure ball, holding her thin hands together as tight as she could while her blue eyes bulged out of her head in a horrific manner.

"Someone get Donaldson down here, now!" Bruin feverishly screamed as he got down to his knees and attempted to tenderly hold the woman in his arms. "It's okay, honey. It's all over now." He gently reassured the girl while taking off his coat and wrapping it around her shockingly warm body."

Right around the corner at the top of the stairs was a plump, blonde white female officer. The woman came rushing down the steps only to stop midway at the sight of the sadistic death that took hold of her eyes.

"Shirley, come here, we need you to take her upstairs!" Bruin yelled.

But Donaldson appeared too afraid to make another move forward. She slowly began to back away until she stumbled against one of the steps behind her.

"Get your ass down here now, Donaldson!" Fitzpatrick furiously gestured with his left hand.

The petrified woman skittishly stepped down the stairs and approached the young lady on the floor. From there she coddled the woman in her arms like a child.

"Talk to her, Donaldson, she's a baby girl!" Bruin urgently ranted.

"Hold on...sweetheart, we're gonna get you out of here real soon." Donaldson stammered while caressing the woman's long, brunette hair.

With his hands shaking, Bruin stood back up and surveyed every corpse that was lying on the floor. Each body, including the young woman's, had deep puncture wounds to the stomach area. Their pale, distraught faces told the story of their final moments of life. Handsome, young black men and pretty, young white women were all scattered from one end of the basement to the other.

Even the overwhelming stench of the room couldn't tear the officers and detectives away from the bludgeoning sight of all the death that stared ever so lifelessly right back at them. Every moment passed by in surreal slow motion.

"There's Calvin over there." Fitzpatrick pointed straight ahead.

Bruin turned around and watched as the medics helped the young lady from off of the floor and onto a gurney.

Bruin was handed his coat back by one of the medics before turning and saying to an officer beside him, "Smiley, contact the Cohen family. Inform them that we've found their daughter...alive."

Brice scurried his hefty girth down the stairs and began to examine the bodies one by one. After he had overturned each corpse onto its stomach, he coldly stated out loud, "Forced insertion wounds to the rectal areas. Looks like our man raped his victims before killing them all. That would explain the *Vaseline*."

"So where the hell is this fellow that Cummins took yesterday?" Fitzpatrick griped.

Ignoring his partner, Bruin noticed even more black fur that was located next to the steps. "Yep, it came out of here alright." He remarked as he gazed deep at the fur. "Pat, are you sure this isn't bear fur?"

Brice stood up, retrieved the fur from out of Bruin's hand and sighed, "Linus, forensics fucked it all up last November when their supposed bear attacked those Jamaican guys. Everyone down at the lab was in such a hurry to get home for the holiday that they would have said an elephant did it. This fur resembles that of a wolf rather than a bear. You saw the bite marks all over Cummins; it even left a tooth behind, for God's sake."

"So you're saying that a wolf did that to Cummins?" Fitzpatrick stepped up beside both men. "C'mon, Brice, you saw that faggot bastard, he was torn in half."

"Unless it was a pack of wolves, that's not too uncommon for these parts." Bruin said.

"There's only one set of paw prints tracked in the snow, Linus." Brice added.

"Well, let's only hope that this Mercer guy escaped while he could." Bruin exhaled.

"If he did end up escaping, he did so a naked man." Fitzpatrick said. "His clothes are still upstairs on the couch. I'm gonna call back to—

Right then, the bizarre roars of an angry animal shot out from upstairs. Every officer and detective that was in the basement pulled out their weapons before racing back up the steps.

Once they made their way into the living room, to their stunned surprise, the sounds that they were hearing were coming from the tape recorder that Fitzpatrick left playing earlier.

Each and every officer stood in the middle of the living room and listened to the roars and growls of the beast that was tearing a human being to shreds.

"Is that a bear?" Fitzpatrick's face turned up.

"I've never heard a bear sound like that before." One of the other officers chimed in.

They all continued to eavesdrop until the crashing of wood came into earshot, which was followed by utter silence. Bruin picked up the recorder and hit the off button.

"That's not all." Another officer pointed to the front window. "Look out there."

Every man inside peeked out the window to see news vans and reporters all descend upon the residence like a swarm of hungry bees.

"Well, you're the big TV star here." Fitzpatrick sarcastically grinned at Bruin. "Go get 'em, tiger."

The very last thing Bruin wanted at that stage was to speak with nosey reporters, or anyone else for that matter, but it was his case, it had been for the past six months, there was no turning back.

With cement feet, the detective stepped outside onto the icy porch with his hands slipped tightly into his coat pockets.

"Detective Bruin, is this the residence of the B.O.D. kidnapper?" A male reporter asked with a mini tape recorder pointed at Bruin's blushing face.

"Yes it is." Bruin bashfully exhaled. "We received an anonymous tip. The tipster described a black male in his early twenties accepting a ride from a man that fit our description. Upon our arrival here this morning, Leroy Cummins the Third was found dead inside his home."

"Wait a minute, Detective, are we talking about the same Leroy Cummins that owns *Cummins' Chevrolet* here in town?" A female reporter questioned in a flabbergasted tone.

"That is correct." Bruin shook his head. "We discovered sixteen bodies located in Mr. Cummins' basement this morning."

"Were there any survivors, Detective?"

"Just one, so far," Bruin stated. "One Gloria Cohen was found alive, but in a shell-shocked condition."

"What about this person that Cummins abducted yesterday?"

"So far, we haven't been able to locate Mr. Mercer. We're only hoping that he managed to escape and is on his way back home as we speak."

"Detective, you mentioned that Cummins was found dead. What exactly was the cause of death?"

Bruin held his tongue for a few seconds before uttering, "We are not releasing that information at this time."

"Detective, there are rumors that an animal, possibly a killer bear, murdered Cummins. Is this true?"

"Like I said, we are not at liberty to discuss Cummins' cause of death at this point, but, we are working in conjunction with *Cuyahoga Falls'* authorities and informing residents to stay clear of wooded areas for the time being, until we are able to investigate further. That is all for now."

Bruin turned and stepped back into the frigid confines of the house, leaving the ravenous reporters screaming for more.

"Just how the fuck did the bear story get out that quick?" Bruin snarled at Fitzpatrick who was holding a Taser gun in his right hand.

"You know how some people are." He shrugged. "Someone else probably saw the tracks, too. Look at this." Fitzpatrick said while holding up the weapon. "How much you wanna bet he used this to incapacitate his victims?"

"Where did you find that?"

"Right behind the sofa here," he said.

Ignoring the Taser that his partner seemed so proud to embrace, Bruin stepped towards the hallway that led to the bedrooms before an officer approached him and said, "We found more tapes inside his room, Detective."

"Thanks, Dudley." Bruin despondently replied, glancing past the officer and straight ahead at Cummins' bedroom.

As he made his way inside, Bruin began to stroll about the room that smelled of *Old Spice* cologne and unclean laundry. The unmade, queen sized bed was layered in nothing but dirty men's and women's underwear. There were spots of blood sprinkled all over the tan carpet, along with dirty tampons and cut out pictures of famous black males, noticeably *The Jackson Five* and *Jimmie 'JJ' Walker,* to *Billy Dee Williams.* Pasted on the cream colored walls were photos of well-known white woman from *Diane Lane* and *Jodie Foster,* to *Linda Blair.*"

With a pen that he pulled out from his back pocket, Bruin picked up a pair of blue panties from off the bed before asking, "Hey, Al, what was the name of the guy from the diner again?"

Fitzpatrick stopped snapping pictures with his *Kodak* camera before saying, "Mercer, I believe."

"No, his first name," Bruin said.

Fitzpatrick paused again and remarked, "The car was registered to a Charles Mercer. Fifty-eight years old, from *Cypress.*"

Bruin dropped the panties back onto the bed and frowned, "Fifty-eight? I thought the waitress at the diner said he was a young guy."

"You're right, Detective." A young, black officer announced as he abruptly entered into the bedroom. "I found his I.D. in his pants pocket. His name is Isaac Mercer. He's twenty."

"Thanks, Smith." Bruin responded, securing the wallet from the officer's hand. "If he's from *Cypress,* what in the world was he doing all the way out here in the sticks of all places?"

"The waitress did say that he was arguing with a woman there before she got up and took off. Maybe they were lovers or something of that nature." Fitzpatrick clarified while slipping on a pair of blue rubber gloves. "Christ, I feel filthy just being in this room." He turned up his nose.

"I'm guessing that Isaac is the son of Charles, and Charles

is probably wondering just where in the world both his son and his car are right about now."

Fitzpatrick knelt down to the floor and said, "I think we need to head back to *Cypress* and quick, before this guy's family goes insane worrying about him."

"Not only that, but I'd also like to follow those tracks in the back as well. From the sound of it, I don't think this was the last place our furry friend visited last night." Bruin said as he turned and wandered out of the bedroom and back into the living room.

He stood next to the sofa looking on in silent aversion. Everything he had expected, minus the slaughtered kidnapper, had come to vibrant and horrifying life.

Once the busy path of pacing officers and medics was clear, Bruin stepped lightly back into the slippery kitchen. There was still more evidence to collect down in the basement, but he was in no such rush to get down there anytime soon. Just staring off at the hole in the wall was jarring enough.

"Detective, we've got a report of a murder just a few miles west of this location." An older officer announced as he stepped inside through the gaping hole.

"Just west of here, huh," Bruin cynically shrugged. "We get rid of one animal, we end up with another. Any more surprises?"

His conscience couldn't decide on what was more terrifying, a kidnapper that rapes and kills his victims, or a supposed animal that splits the kidnapper in two and leaves a seven foot wide hole in the sturdy wall as a calling card.

His beating heart wanted ever so much to grieve over the victims and their long suffering families. Bruin's hands at that instant began to tremble, even though his entire body was on fire.

Mournfully, Linus turned away from both the officer and the hole before making his way downstairs.

CHAPTER 19

"WHAT TIME IS IT?" Linus moaned while driving all too slowly down the desolate highway on a day that was nearing noontime.

Fitzpatrick looked out at the passing farmland scenery and asked, "Does it really matter?"

Linus must have sighed at least three to four times since leaving the house. The man's entire body felt as if it were carrying a load of bricks tied to his heels. No matter what, he just couldn't get the fog out of his brain.

"It's hard to believe that this thing hiked almost three miles away just to eat more people."

Stirring awake from his dull stupor, Linus glanced over and grunted, "Huh?"

"I said, I can't believe the thing hiked three miles just to eat more people." Fitzpatrick replied a bit louder.

"Yeah," Linus sighed again."

"You gotta be kidding me." Alan griped.

"Whaddya mean?"

"What's with all the damn sighing? You sound like my wife whenever she wants sex from me?"

Linus shrugged and said, "We just wrapped up a five and a half month kidnapping investigation, and you're asking what's with all the sighing?"

"For Christ's sake," Alan grumbled, "it's not the first kidnapping we've ever covered."

Linus didn't bother to look over at his partner, instead, he gazed upwards into the grey, brooding sky. "What would make a person do all of that, Al?"

"Do what?"

"Kidnap, rape and kill. He even raped the guys, for God's sake." Linus shook his head in shame. "I'm sitting here trying to figure out what sort of twisted event in this man's life could have brought him to such a point."

"Who knows?" Alan groaned. "He obviously had some kind of sick fetish that needed to be fulfilled. You mentioned it yourself back at the TV station."

"And the smell," Linus lamented. "How can any normal human being tolerate having all those dead bodies in that house and not become sick themselves?"

"After a while, even the most perverted person becomes accustomed to his or hers perversion. The man was obviously tormented."

Bruin only scanned the grazing land that passed by at 33 mph. "I wonder if Gloria saw—

"That's enough!" A frustrated Fitzpatrick hollered.

A momentary quiet took place inside the car before Linus again sighed and said, "I suppose you're gonna tell me that I'm feeling sorry for myself, right?"

"No, it's not that." Fitzpatrick huffed. "You're shitting bricks because after all these months someone or something else got that fucker before you could. We all wanted to plug a bullet in the guy, but we missed out."

Linus rolled his eyes in the other direction, hoping that he could possibly ignore his partner's rant, but it seemed that the more he tried to focus on other matters, Gloria's pale, terrified image would cross his path in stunning full color.

"Whaddya think?" Fitzpatrick looked over.

"Think about what?"

"About what Brice said about the fur. Do you believe that there could be a pack of wolves running around out here?"

"Who's to say?" Linus gripped the steering wheel tighter. "I can't see wolves tearing through a wall like a wrecking ball. Maybe it's something that escaped from the zoo."

"The zoo," Fitzpatrick chuckled. "If I ever see the thing that could eat the way that fucker did last night, then I hope we never find it."

Linus actually wanted the creature to materialize inside his mind, but he had to sift through the dead bodies first before he could even place the image of an overgrown killer beast prowling the countryside into his psyche.

"A wolf," Fitzpatrick sniggered. "I swear that Brice gets dumber by the day."

Linus smirked before asking, "You don't think too much of Pat, do you?"

"It's not that I don't like the kid, it's just that...well, he's a kid." Alan tossed up his hands. "An Ivy league, smarty pants, know-it-all kid. He's just twenty years younger than you and I. The guy is creepy, if you ask me."

"Are you trying to say that we're old men?"

"Nope, I like to play it like my wife; I turn twenty-four with every passing birthday."

Linus smiled at the remark while glancing down at the speedometer to notice for the very first time that he was driving extra slow.

"Damn kids are taking our jobs." Fitzpatrick begrudged in a doleful tone.

"Is that all you're concerned about?"

"No, I also hope I get home in time this evening to watch *Battle of the Network Stars*."

Linus wanted to burst out laughing, but he restrained himself as a semi-truck roared past them on the other side of the road. The first sign of life ever since leaving Cummins' house.

"I was thinking about calling Linda." Linus muttered.

It took a few moments before Fitzpatrick said anything. "It's a shame that you have to actually think about calling home."

"Yeah...it is." Linus bitterly sulked with a far off expression hanging on his face.

"I hate to say this, but I think you have a better chance of speaking rationally with someone like O'Dea than you do with Linda."

"I can handle O'Dea, in small doses, mind you."

Once more, a drowning silence took place inside the cruiser. For a few moments Linus actually believed that he had slipped into another trance.

"Did you catch the body on that one reporter?"

"Which one," Linus glanced strangely over at his partner.

"The black lady," Fitzpatrick smirked.

"Oh yeah, she was a looker."

"I can see you with a black chic."

Linus grinned...and drove along.

As Linus parked the cruiser behind a coroners van, both he and Alan noticed a barrage of officers and reporters all milling about the yard of a red and white brick house.

Without uttering a single word, they climbed out of the vehicle and dragged themselves towards another squad car just a few feet away where a bald, middle-aged black officer was standing with a C.B. radio in his hand.

"Good afternoon, guys." The officer greeted as he placed the radio back into the holster inside the car. "Long time no see." He shook both Linus and Alan's hands.

"How are you, Phelps?" Fitzpatrick asked.

"Not too well, I'm afraid." Phelps pouted before turning to the house to his right. "We got six dead bodies. A mother, father and their four daughters. The mother was found in the living room. Her entire skull was cracked wide open. The father was found in the basement with his guts lying all over the steps."

"It even got the daughters, too?" Linus regrettably inquired.

"Upstairs…all four girls. Two, four, seven and ten," Phelps chocked. "Something just…just tore its way through the bedroom door and got them all."

"Who found them?" Linus asked while zipping up his coat.

"The wife's mother," Phelps said. "She lives right across the street. She and the mother have coffee every morning. Can you imagine finding this, of all things?"

All three men looked over to a distant pine bush and watched as the loudly weeping grandmother was consoled by a number of female neighbors.

"You two should see the bedroom." Phelps murmured. "You can hardly take two steps without…it's like something from out of one of these dickhead horror movies."

"We would like to take a quick peek inside, just to see what we're dealing with." Linus said while glancing nervously over at the foreboding house.

"I heard you found your guy."

"It was more like we found what was left of him." Fitzpatrick snickered. "But, as it so happens, something else found him first."

"And whatever found him made its way here." Phelps rubbed his face in weariness. "It broke in through a basement window."

Linus stepped forward, placed his right hand on Phelps'

shoulder and sympathetically whispered into the man's face, "We're sorry about Calvin, Lou."

Phelps dropped his head in a noble lamentation before glancing back and saying, "Sometimes, losing a nephew feels like losing your own son. This is all his mother needs right now. Does anyone know what did all of this? A bear or something?"

"That's what we're still trying to sort out." Linus responded. "Our man kept a recording of all the rapes he committed. Last night, right after he got through with his last victim, something came up from out of his basement and tore him limb from limb, literally. He left his recorder on the entire time. We can't seem to make heads or tails of just what exactly it is."

"Brice, from forensics, doesn't believe it's a bear." Fitzpatrick added. "He says that the paw tracks are too large."

"Come inside and take a look at this." Phelps said as he stepped away from his cruiser and led Bruin and Fitzpatrick to the house ahead.

From left to right, all three men dodged officers and four covered stretchers that were being wheeled out of the house. Ironically, both Bruin and Fitzpatrick had the same thing in mind when it came to who was up under the black blankets.

As all three men entered into the house, the strong odor of exposed human organs slapped them across the face hard enough to where Linus had to cover his nose with his fingers all over again.

"Here they are." Phelps somberly announced while holding up the picture of the entire family in a frame. "The Sanders. The husband, Gary, was an architect. The wife, Sarah, was a homemaker."

"What were the girls' names?" Linus inquired while glancing down at the floor to see strands of red hair sporadically sprinkled all over the carpet.

"Jamie, Giselle, Jodie and Terry," Phelps remarked.

Linus paced forward and examined the frame closer. "That's nice." He regrettably frowned. "They were a handsome family."

"What I have to show you guys is unfortunately upstairs."

"Let's go check it out." Fitzpatrick said in an almost eager manner.

Linus stared at the man as if he had lost all control of his mental faculties. He himself was still trying to grasp the fact that an entire family had been ostensibly wiped out in one night; heading upstairs to witness even more ugliness wasn't in his agenda.

Phelps and Fitzpatrick carried on up the stairs, with Linus bringing up a very reluctant rear. As the men rounded a corner, a sudden whiff of cold air sprang out into the hallway. A streak of blood was smeared along the wall right above a blue laundry basket.

"Here it is." Phelps broadcasted, stepping into the blood spattered room.

"What the hell?" Linus astonishingly inhaled at the hole in the wall that led outside.

"Yep, apparently after it was through, it jumped out not only the window, but it took half the damn wall as well." Phelps explained. "Take a look at this." Phelps pointed to the bed.

Linus and Alan peered down at the destroyed, bleeding bed. Almost immediately, beyond all the blood, the one thing that Linus took notice of was all the black fur that was littered from one end of the bed to the other.

Piece by piece, Linus picked up strands. "Can we take some of this with us?"

"Be my guest." Phelps said. "There's not much else anyone can take anymore. The damn thing was strong enough to throw one of the girls out of the room and clear into the hallway. That was the two year old."

Fitzpatrick, holding his nose, gradually backed out of the bedroom while mumbling, "This was a bad idea, guys."

"You were the one that wanted to come up here so bad, Evel Knievel." Linus replied with an uneasy smirk.

"That's the one problem with living way out in the sticks, no one can hear you whenever trouble arises." Phelps observed while marching over and picking up the shattered glass lamp from off the floor before placing it onto the nightstand. "We're there any survivors in that guy's house?"

"The woman he kidnapped some days ago." Linus answered. "You should have seen her face, Lou. She'll have to live with what that man did to her for the rest of her life. All that poor girl could do was stare off into space."

Phelps quaintly chuckled, "You get rid of one animal, and here comes another."

"I have a feeling that we'll be hearing a lot more of that phrase in the days to come." Fitzpatrick chimed in from the safety of the hallway.

Both Linus and Lou exited the bedroom. For Linus, he felt even heavier than he did before entering. All he could do was turn back and catch one final, brief glimpse of the bed from out of the corner of his eye.

"Officer Phelps!" A young, white officer yelled, running up the stairs. "We've got a report of a break in at a church, just a few miles west of this location!"

Phelps sniggered to himself, looking as if he had no idea as to what to do with such information. "Uh, as you can see, officer, we sorta got bigger fish to fry right here."

"Wait a minute, Lou." Linus breathlessly interjected. "What was the extent of the damage?" He then asked the young officer.

"That's easy, Detective, according to the guys already there, it looks like a bulldozer just crashed through a window. There's a big mess inside the place."

Linus looked over at Alan and shook his head up and down as to say that they were already on their way. Without speaking another word, both detectives handed Phelps a final nod before heading back downstairs.

"Ten bucks says our friend got a conscience and went straight to confession last night." Alan jibed.

CHAPTER 20

BRUIN AND FITZPATRICK GOT out of their cruiser. Standing at the entrance of the tiny church was Brice, who was shivering like an overstuffed popsicle with his hands lodged securely inside his pockets.

As the detectives made their way towards the man, Linus couldn't help but to glance over at the white man and woman who were staring down at a mutilated cow on the ground.

There was something inside of Linus that wanted so badly to veer off over to where the couple was standing behind an old rugged, wooden fence. But with as much restraint as he could amass, the man maintained his course towards the long-suffering Brice and the tiny church he was standing in front of.

All three men entered the church through the double doors. Once they were inside, they caught sight of two, white officers who were conversing with an elderly white minister who was bundled up in a black winter coat.

Brice happened to look down at the carpet to find the same mammoth paw prints that he examined earlier, while Linus and Alan surveyed the freezing church.

"I sure hope to God no one was in here last night." Linus' teeth chattered while kneeling down to pick up even more strands of fur from off the floor.

"Guys, take a look at this." Brice said, pointing to the floor.

Linus and Alan made their way over to Brice's direction to observe what looked to be a smelly heap of waste.

"Is that what I think it is?" Linus turned up his nose.

"Yep," Brice replied in a snippy sort of voice while taking out a pair of small tongs from his coat pocket.

Linus and Alan looked on at the young man as though he were doing something wrong. They stood and watched as Brice poked and prodded at the dung like a science experiment until he was able to grab a hold of something.

"Do I even want to know what that is?" Alan cringed, too afraid to step any closer.

"You got it." Brice despondently replied as his tongs scooped up a partially eaten human thumb from out of the thickness of the feces.

Trying not to appear jarred by the scene, Linus too stood back and asked, "What is that over there?"

With his human body part still lodged in between the tongs' tight grip, Brice scooted forward and examined what appeared to be a glob of clear mucus lying on the floor, just a few feet away from the altar.

"Is it blood?" Fitzpatrick mumbled.

"It's blood, and then…some saliva." Brice answered.

"How do we know it's the saliva of the animal?" Alan questioned. "It did kill seven people last night. It could just be residue."

"True, but this is the only saliva sample that I've managed to collect all morning long so far. It looks as though the thing vomited. Most animals regurgitate their food, and then eat the remains."

"Excuse me, gentleman." The short, bearded minster approached the three men from behind. "Are you men police officers?"

"Yes, sir," Linus replied. "This is Detective Fitzpatrick, Brice, and I'm Bruin."

"Good to meet you. My name is Pastor Gabriel Longfellow." The genial man greeted, wiping the cold fog away from his eyeglasses.

"Mr. Longfellow, how old is this church?" Fitzpatrick asked.

"Oh my," Longfellow pondered in his head, "this place has been around since 1883. It's the oldest in the city. Why do you ask?"

"No particular reason, I'm just fascinated with old things."

"Tell me, does anyone know just what it was that left those kinds of tracks, or what killed the Franklin's cow out there?"

"We're still working on that, sir." Linus seriously responded.

"Hey, guys, look at this for a second." Brice stirred, crawling about on the floor in the direction of the paw prints. "The tracks seem to end...right here." He motioned.

Linus, Alan and the pastor all gawked down at the muddy carpet in disbelief.

"Hold on," Linus panted, "look here. It appears as if the thing crashed through the window over there, took a stroll down the aisle, then...look at that."

Everyone looked to their immediate left to see a long, dark smudge streaked across the floor in an almost orderly fashion.

"There aren't any tracks leading out of this place either." Alan noted. "Judging by the direction of the streak, it looks as though it were dragged away."

"Who could've dragged something that enormous?" The pastor asked.

"We have no clue, sir." Linus replied while kneeling down and rubbing against the smudge. "It ends right here. Now, unless our friend can fly, there is absolutely no way in the world it could have gotten out of here without leaving any tracks in its wake."

"This church has only one floor, Detective." One of the officers commented. "We searched every corner. We're the only people in here."

Linus looked over at the pastor and asked, "Sir, was there anyone else in here last night?"

"No, sir, Mr. Bruin," Longfellow scratched at his beard. "Last night we had our prayer meeting at six. I locked up around seven, and that was that."

Studying the carpet with a sharp eye, Linus began to pace back and forth until he found himself face to face with the crucified Christ that was lanced on the cross down behind the altar. The detective then turned around and wearily exhaled, "Somebody, please kick me in the head."

"It makes no sense trying to rack our brains over this, Linus." Fitzpatrick said while standing next to his exhausted partner. "The trail ends here. And we still got one fella that's missing."

"Can you tell me, detectives, did the kidnapper leave any survivors?" Longfellow desperately asked.

"Yes, sir, we have two." Bruin sighed.

"Thank the good Lord." The pastor graciously smiled.

"Thank the Lord?" Linus smirked in a coy manner. "Where was the Lord when all of those kidnapped people were murdered? No offense, padre, but four little girls were eaten alive last night. It makes no sense whatsoever."

"Sir, the Lord works in mysterious ways. I cannot explain it, but his love does endure forever. I can only hope and pray that the two survivors can pull their lives back together again in Jesus' name."

In silent rebuttal, Linus turned to Alan and whispered, "We need to get Mercer's address."

"Let's get the hell outta here." Alan grumbled before

turning back to Longfellow and smiling, "Thanks for all your help, sir."

"I'm here whenever you need me." The pastor waved.

"You comin' with us, Brice?" Linus looked down at the young man.

Standing back to his feet, Brice, with a plastic pouch in hand, said, "I think I'll hitch a ride back with some of the other officers. There's still a wealth of info I need to collect just right here."

Linus glanced over at Alan before turning and walking out of the church. "Perhaps you're right about that guy, Al." Linus whispered into the man's ear.

"A wealth of what, poop," Alan asked with a snicker. "What the hell is wrong with that generation anyways?"

As they made their way outside, still standing behind the fence was the couple who were still ogling down at the deceased cow in the snow.

Linus' once rapid pace back to the cruiser gradually slowed the longer he stared on and on at the couple before he eventually paused and made a direct approach towards their direction. The man just couldn't help himself.

"It killed our last cow." The middle-aged, ragged looking woman said without even being asked.

Linus stopped short of the fence before looking down at the animal that had its entire stomach torn wide open.

"I was just wondering, do you two happen to live around these parts?" Linus asked.

The woman turned her attention back to the dead animal while the man lifted his head to stare at Linus. His entire face was full of unshaven, silver fur that ruffled in the brazen wind. His brown eyes shot bullets at Linus like the question he asked was sinful.

"We live around here." His scratchy voice answered. "Are you reporters?"

Unfazed by the man's piercing demeanor, Linus pulled out his badge and replied, "No, sir, we're Detectives Bruin and Fitzpatrick."

The man stared on at Linus for a bit longer before saying, "My wife and I live around here."

"Can you tell us if you saw or heard anything last night?"

The man, with his hard stare still stuck on Linus, replied, "I was born and raised in these parts. I've lived here all my life."

"Did you manage to see or hear anything?" Linus' tone urged.

The man turned his face away from Linus and pointed it behind him. "You see that field out there? Last night, I saw something that I've never seen before in my life."

"Let's get out of here." Alan whispered into Linus' ear. "This guy looks like he's about three sheets to the wind."

"Last night, I saw it." The man's tone turned suddenly methodical.

"You saw what?" Linus' attention perked up.

"Last night, in that field, I saw it running around."

"Was it a bear?" Linus asked.

Shaking his head, the man said, "No, bears don't look like the thing I saw last night. This thing had hind legs. A snout and eyes."

"So it was a wolf." Fitzpatrick shrugged.

"I never said that. I was taking out the trash when I saw it racing through the field. It didn't look or sound like anything I've ever seen before. But it did look at me."

"It looked at you?" Linus frowned.

"It had these eyes. These glowing eyes that just glanced at me for a few seconds before it took off again."

"Wait a second, if you saw this thing, did you ever contact the police?" Linus questioned in an agitated voice.

The man just kept his face pointed towards the snowy

field. "Perhaps I should have, but I just remember its shining eyes."

"You gotta be kidding me." Alan moaned. "We didn't come all the way out here for this *Rod Serling, 'Night Gallery'* bullshit. Let's get back to *Cypress.*"

Without another word, the mysterious couple meandered away from the detectives and plodded their way back across the field.

Right then, the wind found it within itself to become even more stiff and rampant, but that didn't seem to deter Linus who began his own jaunt over the fence, past the cow carcass and out into the field.

"Are you crazy?" Alan hollered. "It's 19 degrees out here!"

Linus carried on and on until he managed to stop halfway between the church and the middle of the field. He stood and eyed the spacious landscape from front to back and side to side before looking down to spot a set of tracks layered in the snow.

Linus stuck his booted foot in the track and noticed that it was about five sizes bigger than his own.

There was more fur lying in the tracks, but the man had no desire to gather any more evidence for the day. Instead, he remained in the middle of the sprawling field all to himself, just where he wanted to be.

CHAPTER 21

WITH THE PHONE TUCKED securely underneath his right armpit, Mr. Mercer anxiously paced from the living room and back to the hallway, totally forgetting that the phone's cord wasn't as long as he would have wished it could have been while fussing with the police over the line.

Adorned in his all blue janitor's jumpsuit, Mercer looked at the clock that was nailed to the wall in the living room and realized that heading into work would be futile at that point in the day.

"I don't understand why no one can give me any information about my own son!" The man irately yelled. "He's out there somewhere, for God's sake!"

He dragged the phone back into the living room where he just happened to look out the front window to see a police cruiser parked right in front of the house. Without saying a simple "goodbye", Mr. Mercer hung up the phone, and with quivering knees, stepped across the floor and to the door, opening it before the detectives could even get out of their car.

He stood at the doorway watching and waiting with bated breath for the two men to make their way to him. Over and over again he kept on replaying the worst scene in his head.

As cold as it was outside, his palms couldn't stop sweating. His knees were ready to collapse right where he stood; the stiff, unrelenting wind splashed into his sweaty face like a bucket of ice cold water.

Just then, the law officers opened their doors, climbed out and began their march towards the home. Mercer gritted his teeth to the point where they started to hurt the closer they approached.

"Good afternoon, sir. I'm Detective Linus—

"Is my boy dead?" Mercer impulsively jumped in.

Taken aback by the very question, both Bruin and Fitzpatrick blushed. Bruin then glanced over at his partner and then back again at Mercer who was shuddering, not from the cold air, but from heartbreaking fear.

"Uh, sir, we aren't quite sure yet." Bruin slowly uttered. "Can we come in and talk for a moment, please?"

Steadily, Mr. Mercer moved aside to allow the men into his warm home. The moment he shut the door behind him, Mercer crossed his arms and asked, "Okay, where's my son at?"

"You are Charles Mercer, right?" Fitzpatrick questioned.

"That's me." He intolerantly sighed. "Now, where's my son?"

"Mr. Mercer, this is Detective Bruin, and I'm Detective Fitzpatrick. I don't know if you are aware of this or not, but we found the B.O.D. kidnapper this morning."

"I heard all about that, yes." Mercer said.

"Well, sir, your son Isaac was last seen taking a ride with the aforementioned person yesterday evening."

Right then, Mercer's sullen eyes opened to twice their original size. He dropped his arms to his side and slowly stuttered, "What...was he doing with that man?"

"A witness at the diner where Isaac was last seen said that your car seemed to be having trouble. That was when your son accepted a ride from Cummins." Fitzpatrick clarified. "Mr. Mercer, right now we don't have a clue as to where Isaac is."

"Wha...whaddya mean you don't have a clue?" Mercer

breathlessly stammered. "He went with that kidnapper, didn't he?"

"Yes, sir, but when we arrived at the residence this morning, Isaac was nowhere to be found."

"Well, maybe he escaped and went back to this diner to get the car." Mercer eagerly said.

"Sir, the car was still at the diner this morning." Fitzpatrick continued on. "Some of our people are having it brought back here, and—

"I don't give a damn about that car!" Mercer angrily hollered. "I want my boy!"

"Sir, please calm down." Fitzpatrick urged.

"Calm down?" Mercer threw up his hands. "My son is out there! He could be dead or waiting for someone to come and rescue him! And all you can talk about is my car?"

Both Bruin and Fitzpatrick turned their heads in a manner that would have suggested that they had nothing left to say at that point.

With his hands outstretched, Mr. Mercer cried, "Isaac has a son...he's two years old. He's got a fiancée. What on earth was he doing all the way out in *Cuyahoga Falls* to begin with?"

"Our witness mentioned that—

"Our witness informed us that Isaac was asking for directions at the diner." Linus brazenly cut right in between his partner.

"Well, Isaac never did have a good sense of direction." Mr. Mercer dropped his hands. "But that still doesn't explain why he would take a ride from a complete stranger."

"Would there be any other place Isaac would possibly go? Other places he would hide out? Because for all we know, he could be on his way back to *Cypress* as we speak." Linus insisted.

"If he's not at Lynn's house, then I don't have a clue."

"And who is this Lynn?" Linus questioned, taking out a pen and pad from his back pocket.

"Lynnette Glover is his fiancée. She lives at *909 West Seventh Blvd*. I tried calling her a while ago, but her line was busy." Mercer exhaled before reaching over to the mantle and pulling out a photo of Isaac. "Here's his picture, if it'll help any."

"Okay, thank you, sir." Linus replied, taking the photo and slipping it into his pocket. "I assure you, Mr. Mercer, we are doing everything in our power to find your son. It's been a long, trying day for us all. Hopefully Isaac will be in a safe frame of mind when we do find him."

All of the sudden, like a door violently slamming shut, Mr. Mercer looked up at the detectives with a sadistic frown on his face. It was menacing enough to where both Bruin and Fitzpatrick actually had to take a slight step backwards in unison.

"My son isn't crazy, Detective." Mercer uttered in a foreboding murmur. "Do you hear me? Isaac is just fine. You'll do best to remember that."

"Yes, sir," Linus muttered right back while sliding his pen and pad back into his pocket. "Your car should be arriving sometime before six this evening."

At that very second, with an evil eye pointed directly at both detectives, Mercer stood still, right in the middle of the floor, while attentively watching the officers turn and walk out the door from which they entered.

From left to right, the heavy burdened man looked on as though the walls in his own home were caving in on him. He then sat down on the sofa, clasped his hands and closed his eyes.

A quiet, lone tear dropped down from out of his left eye and onto his folded, hardened hands.

"What the hell was that all about?" Fitzpatrick blurted out while climbing into the passenger side of the cruiser.

"I don't know for sure." Linus reflected as he got in and slid the key into the ignition. "The guy looked like he was going to gun us down."

"So tell me," Fitzpatrick smirked, "what gives with the little lie back there?"

Linus put the car in drive and pulled out onto the road before replying, "Call me a cynic, but something tells me that Isaac may have been up to a little risqué business, if you know what I mean. Did you see that man's face? He was about as clueless to his son's whereabouts as we are. Isaac has a fiancée and a young son, and yet, he drove all the way out to *Cuyahoga Falls,* of all places, just to meet up with and argue with some mystery woman? That man inside that house is going through enough right now."

"I say that if's he's not at his fiancée's house, then we go back to *Scats* and get some info on this so called mystery woman he was with." Fitzpatrick said. "Who knows, maybe she has an idea where he is?"

"This oughta be fun." Linus sighed. "What time you got?"

"Uh...ten after five," Fitzpatrick looked hard at his wristwatch.

"I wonder if this day will ever end." Linus lamented.

CHAPTER 22

THE 5TH DIMENSION'S, 'UP, *Up and Away'*, rang out triumphantly throughout the glorious, blue sky as Isaac sat calmly in the Indian style upon a huge rock.

Surrounding the rock were ten children of varying races, all seated Indian style as well. The little girls were wearing pink dresses while the boys were adorned in black and white tuxedos.

Isaac was wearing a black and white tuxedo himself, the same one that Lynn noticed in the window at *Clancy's*. Upon his face, in the warm mountaintop, Isaac wore a peaceful smile, one that perhaps he wore long before he and Lynnette ever had a falling out. A serene smile that he took with him everywhere before ever meeting Karyn.

All ten children that sat below Isaac were all holding hands while rocking back and forth to the melodious tune that just would not stop playing. For Isaac, it was a song that he hadn't heard since his youth, and yet adored with all his heart.

The young man sat with his hands folded as his normal looking eyes took in all the spacious and wondrous surroundings that were the mountains; mountains that he had never once visited in his entire life.

The man sat and pondered on and on until he heard the

soft pattering's of what resembled feet creep up behind him on the rock he was sitting on.

Isaac subtly turned around to see a ragged looking German Shepherd trot up beside him. The animal stood for a moment before turning to Isaac and saying in a male's human voice, "I see you made it this far."

Unfazed by the uncanny creature, Isaac, with his head still pointed at the beauteous mountains ahead of him simply replied, "I guess so."

"I can't say that I'm surprised, you were always a trooper. Your mother even knew that."

Smiling ever greater, Isaac said, "Yeah...I remember her saying that, too."

The dog looked down at the children below before turning back to Isaac. "How long do you think it'll be before you fucking die?"

Still smiling, Isaac dropped his head and exhaled, "Oh, I don't know. I figure I have at least another week or so. How long do you think I have?"

The dog began to pant before saying, "It is unknown, my friend."

Isaac wrapped his left arm around the dog's body and patted it on the side while humming the song that he loved ever so much.

The two enjoyed each other's company for as long as the intruder that was creeping up behind them both would allow. It was the naked phantom, and unbeknownst to both Isaac and his canine companion, its ghastly presence was lurking closer than expected.

"Don't look at him, Isaac." The dog warned.

But all the animal's warning seem to do was incite curiosity inside the young man. Without thinking, Isaac gradually turned to see the phantom's face, a face that he had never managed to see in times past.

The man had red eyes and fangs that were drooling blood all over the rock that it had ascended.

Isaac looked over to see the dog gone. He then glanced back to see the phantom's hands.

With the same hands, the phantom grabbed Isaac by the throat and proceeded to strangle the life out of him.

Isaac tried with all his might to pull away from the slathering demon, but no matter how hard he tried, the phantom was entirely too strong to withstand. Suddenly, and without warning, both the music and children all vanished. With every passing second, Isaac was finding it more difficult to grasp even a single breath.

"I don't know where Isaac is!" Isaac unexpectedly heard Lynnette's hysterical voice scream out loud.

In fact, the sound of her voice was so clear and audible that it sounded as if she were right behind him, or at least very near.

Isaac shut his eyes and re-opened them to see nothing but total darkness all around him. Gasping and spitting for air, the man looked up to see the phantom pull away and sink into the wall behind it until it vanished away completely.

Isaac couldn't tell if he was asleep or even alive at that point, all he wanted was to breathe again. Hearing Lynnette and Isaiah scream and cry caused Isaac to fight even harder to regain his breath. Unexpectedly, he decided to hurl himself off of the soft foundation that he found himself lying on. Once his body connected with something hard, Lynn's screaming ceased, and a series of footsteps slowly began to creep towards his direction.

Isaac wallowed about on the ground like a wounded animal, unable to even let out a simple grunt, let alone a word. He coughed and panted while listening to his helpless son cry out for his mother to return.

Isaac heard what sounded like something twisting. He held his fleeting breath and waited until the sound ended.

Like an explosion, stinging light from an opened door blasted into his eyes. Isaac covered his face for a second or two before removing his hand to see Lynn standing at a doorway with a baseball bat in hand.

"Who the fuck is in here," she shouted out.

Without hesitation, Isaac opened his mouth and muttered, "It's me, Lynn. It's me."

Lynnette cut on a light. Isaac covered his face all over again and only removed two fingers to see that he was inside the warm confines of Lynn's bedroom. He himself was completely naked.

"Isaac!" Lynn hollered wildly as she dropped her bat to the floor and ran to Isaac's aid.

Feeling as though his arms weighed fifty pounds each, Isaac lifted his right hand to touch not only Lynn's hair that was wrapped in pink curlers, but also his own sore jaw.

Weeping uncontrollably, Lynn screamed, "Isaac, did you just get here?"

Too stunned and disoriented to reply, Isaac rubbed his mouth and nose and listened as his stomach rumbled and churned. "I...don't know." He pitifully wept, sounding as if his mouth was full of cotton.

Coddling the man in her shaking arms, Lynn wiped her face and asked, "Isaac, where were you last night? The news said that you were kidnapped by that guy!"

"I don't...remember." He mumbled, holding his throbbing jaw. "I don't remember anything."

"How did you get here?" She tossed up her hands. "I was just in here ten minutes ago! How did you escape?"

Without answering another question, Isaac slowly got up from off the floor and staggered his way out of the bedroom and towards the bathroom. Lynnette followed and watched as he bounced spaghetti-legged from one end of the hallway to the other like a pinball, until he found himself face to face with the toilet. Isaac lifted the lid, knelt down and vomited.

"Do we still got any of that *Ben-Gay?*" Isaac sobbed, wiping excess waste away from his mouth and chin.

Lynnette opened the medicine cabinet next to her and took out a half empty container of *Ben-Gay* before handing it to Isaac.

Isaac immediately snatched the cream away from her hand and squeezed out the remainder. He lathered his entire sore face with what was left inside.

"This is it?" Isaac raged before tossing the empty container to the floor.

Shaking, Lynnette wept, "You used the rest of it back in November after...after the last time."

"Then fuckin' get me some more!" Isaac yelled into her face.

Terrified, Lynnette stumbled backwards into the sink, holding her hands up in defense. Just seeing the fear in her eyes, Isaac quickly reclaimed what was left of his senses and lurched towards her.

"I'm sorry...I'm just in so much pain right now." He shivered while crying. "I don't know what happened. It's like every bone in my body is...broken. I need help!"

As though she had a choice in the matter, Lynnette took Isaac into her bosom and cradled his frail body. "I don't know how to help you, Isaac. You have to tell me what happened so I can help you." She nervously muttered into his ear.

"I can't remember a damn thing." Isaac held on tight to Lynnette's arms. "One moment I was driving, and then... everything went black. I need more *Ben-Gay*, and some *Anacin*, too."

"Well c'mon and lie down for awhile." Lynnette said as she aided Isaac out of the bathroom and back to the bedroom where she gently laid him down onto the bed.

The very moment Isaac's head hit the pillow, four knocks at the front door erupted throughout the small house.

"Who's that?" Isaac looked up.

"I don't know." Lynnette answered. "Just lie down and I'll go see."

Isaac lay helplessly and watched as Lynnette left the room to go and attend to the door. He listened as what sounded like two men entered and conversed back and forth.

In Isaac's ears, the discussion from Lynn's point of view sounded tense and jittery. He could tell that she was searching for words to say to the men, words that she had no business trying to conjure on her own.

With about as much energy as he could assemble, Isaac climbed out of the bed before taking the bed sheet and wrapping it around his naked body. From there, he hobbled his way out of the bedroom and into the living room to find Bruin and Fitzpatrick and Lynnette, with Isaiah in her arms, all standing by the door.

"Here I am, officers." Isaac miserably mumbled as he leaned his sore body up against the wall.

With their jaws practically hanging to the floor, both Linus and Alan stared at Isaac as though they were viewing a miracle right before their stunned eyes.

"Isaac...Isaac Mercer?" Linus' tongue fumbled.

"That's me, sir." Isaac replied with his head shamefully hung low.

"Uh...Mr. Mercer, first off, are you alright?"

"Yeah, I just feel real tired." Isaac exhaled.

"We received a report early this morning that you were seen at *Scats* diner in *Cuyahoga Falls.*"

Isaac looked up to see Lynnette's eyes connect with his in a manner that suggested she was as lost as the detectives.

"Yes, um, the waitress there said that you seemed to be having car trouble and that you hitched a ride with one, Leroy

Cummins." Linus explained. "Mr. Mercer, Leroy Cummins was the B.O.D. kidnapper. He was found murdered this morning inside his home."

At once, Lynnette crumbled to the floor in tears, nearly dropping the baby along the way. Fitzpatrick attempted to help her back up, but Lynnette only shoved his hand away while remaining on the floor.

"We went over to your father's house. He told us to come here and see if you had shown up." Fitzpatrick clarified.

"What about my dad's car?"

"Our people are having it towed back to *Cypress* as we speak." Linus stated. "Mr. Mercer, we'd love to know just how you were able to escape Cummins' house. And how were you able to get back home?"

Wanting to break down and cry himself, Isaac said, "I don't remember. When I woke up a few minutes ago, I was in the bed. Everything else is a blur."

Isaac observed as the detectives handed each other skeptical glances. The young man held on to the wall that he was seemingly attached to with all his might.

Isaac then noticed Detective Bruin gawking at him from top to bottom as if he were studying a clue.

"Mr. Mercer, how tall are you?"

Rolling his eyes, Isaac responded, "Man, I don't know, six one or two I guess. Why?"

"Just procedure, sir," Linus plainly replied.

"Are you sure you're okay?" Fitzpatrick pressed on. "Do you require medical assistance of any kind?"

"No...I'm fine." Isaac sighed. "I just need to rest."

The detectives gave each other one more quick stare before heading out the door. "If it's not too much to ask, Mr. Mercer, we would like for you to come down to the station and provide us with a full statement. Whenever you're up to it, that is." Linus said. "Good evening."

Once the door was pulled shut, Lynnette gathered herself and gingerly got up from off the floor. From there, she laid Isaiah down onto the couch before boldly approaching Isaac.

"Lynn, I really need some more *Ben-Gay* for my mouth and—

"Stop, Isaac!" She powerfully commanded, placing her right hand in the air and nearly pressing it against his face. "Something isn't adding up. Both the news and those cops said that kidnapper was found in *Cuyahoga Falls*. Isaac, *Cuyahoga Falls* is an hour from here. What, you couldn't find a job here in *Cypress*? What were you doing all the way out there?"

Inside his brain, Isaac searched and plotted, but he couldn't find the words he needed to explain all that was taking place fast enough. Most of what had occurred the day before, much like in past instances was a dark haze. He was aware that the small fragments of what he could recall would only get him into even more trouble. He stood there, slumped against the cold wall, waiting for Lynnette to abandon her attack and walk away.

With a shaking body and red eyes, Lynnette hollered, "I'm waiting, Isaac!"

"I ...gotta go throw up again." Isaac slurred before dragging his heavy body back into the bathroom and heaving into the toilet.

From the bathroom, Isaac could hear Lynnette slamming cabinet doors and dishes from the kitchen as though she were rearranging the room.

Once he was through vomiting, Isaac flushed the toilet and stumbled his way over to the medicine cabinet mirror.

He had seen his face in the deformed manner in which it was at that moment once before. He knew that it had happened all over again, just like Karyn said that it would, except, it hurt a lot more at that instant than it did back in November. It was hard for him to make a simple fist, let alone lift his arms that felt as if they were on fire. It felt as if his bones wanted to explode into dust at any moment.

In his ears, the blood curdling shrieks and screams of children played over and over again loud enough to where he thought they were inside the bathroom along with him.

Isaac shut his eyes and listened to his rumbling stomach gurgle like a boiling cauldron. He truly didn't remember what had taken place after accepting the ride from the so called kind stranger, but unlike the occurrence three months earlier, the physical pain that he was swimming in had taken a backseat.

Inside of him was growing an unrelenting sense of sorrow the likes he had never experienced before in his life. It overwhelmed him to the point where tears just suddenly began to fall from his bloodshot eyes. He was no longer weeping for himself.

Isaac slowly opened his eyes and turned around only to see the entire bathroom floor flooded from one corner to the other in nothing but blood.

Like a cat, the man jumped backwards into the mirror, nearly cracking it in half. His startled face grew a tone lighter. He had hoped that what he was seeing was a mere illusion, something that his inner self craved.

"Here's the *Anacin*." Lynnette sharply announced as she entered the bathroom with a half full bottle of aspirin in hand.

Isaac watched her face that didn't appear startled. He looked back down at the floor to see the blood all but gone. At once, he breathed a sigh of relief, a relief that lasted only seconds.

Gazing strangely at him, Lynnette asked, "What are you doing?"

Isaac uncoiled himself and said, "Nothing…I just thought I saw something on the floor."

Lynnette slammed the bottle down onto the sink before moving closer to Isaac. There was a vigilant appearance festering on her face. Isaac could tell that she was still scared, but curious all at once.

"Isaac," she gritted her teeth, "what were you doing in *Cuyahoga Falls?*"

With his private parts dangling beneath him, Isaac stepped forward and answered, "Lynn… I had to go out there and see something with my own eyes."

"What?" She tossed up her arms.

"It's hard to explain, but—

"Don't talk to me like I'm some damn child that can't understand anything, Isaac!" She screamed out loud. "I wanna know now!"

Isaac deeply exhaled before saying, "I got lost. I just got lost, and then the car broke down."

"You got lost between *Cypress* and *Cuyahoga Falls?*" Lynnette suspiciously shrugged.

"Some of the roads were still covered over." Isaac quivered. "I missed one exit and ended up at another. Before I knew it, I was at some diner. I had no idea I was even in another city."

Isaac watched as Lynnette glazed over his face with a mysterious frown before she turned her head to the sink and asked, "Okay, so how did you get away from that guy? Isaac, he could have killed you. How did you get home? Before I found you in there, I was in the bedroom just ten minutes earlier, and I never once heard you come in. What, did you just magically appear out of thin air?"

Being bombarded with one blistering question after another only caused Isaac's heart to race even faster than before. He hated to lie to Lynnette, but lies were the only thing that he could dole out without hurting her even further.

"Lynn, you gotta understand, these past few days have been real crazy for me." He stuttered.

"Crazy for you," Lynnette yelled into his face. "Isaac, I've been here crying my eyes out all night and day wondering where you were! I had to miss my writing class this morning because of you! Isaac, if I miss another class then I'll get expelled! On top of all that, your son has a cold, and you just show up out of the fucking blue, butt ass naked, and can't remember anything! Look at your face, your legs! I hardly even recognize you! Are you gonna go through that same shit that you put everyone through back in November, Isaac?"

Out of fear, Isaac cringed in the corner behind him, too afraid to even look the young woman in the eye.

"I don't know what you want from me, Isaac." She sobbed. "I'm almost out of tears, and I can't take this anymore. I can't even stand to look at you anymore. That's how much all of this hurts."

Isaac stood and reluctantly listened to each and every word. It was all he could do. Lynnette's words of pain were all he had left to hang on to.

"I know you're hiding something from me. Do you have a disease? Is that why your face looks the way it does? Is that why you're in so much pain? Did you catch something from someone? Are you on some of Larry and Marvell's drugs? I need you to talk to me, Isaac!"

Feeling the dire need to escape, Isaac pulled himself away from his safe corner before barging his way past Lynnette and out of the bathroom altogether.

"Where are you going?" she questioned, following Isaac to the bedroom.

"I'm going out to the shed for the night." Isaac nonchalantly replied while searching for clothes inside the cabinets.

"The shed," she turned up her face. "What the fuck for?"

As though he were in a rush, Isaac anxiously slipped on an undershirt, a blue sweater and a pair of blue jeans before saying, "I gotta be to myself for the night. I'll come back inside in the morning." He then put on a pair of socks and tennis shoes.

"What good is sleeping in the shed gonna do? It's five degrees out there!"

"I know," Isaac huffed, standing up from off the bed, "but I need to be out there, just for the night. I can't be in here... not tonight."

Isaac looked on as Lynnette feebly dropped herself down onto the bed and allowed her bottom lip to hang downwards. Suddenly, much like himself, she had lost her original appearance.

"Don't come out there tonight, Lynn. I mean it." Isaac firmly warned before kissing her on the forehead and walking out of the bedroom.

He ventured into the living room to gather his coat. As he was slipping his coat on, he happened to look back at Isaiah who was steadily snoring away on the couch. There was absolutely nothing in the world at that moment that could keep him inside the house a second more.

He unlocked the front door, and like a rushing wind, he raced out and around to the dark backyard where the tiny toolshed was located, just ten yards away from the house.

He opened the shed's door and stepped in only to trip upon an empty gasoline canister and a lawnmower. He closed the door and sat himself down on the hard, ice cold cement floor.

Even with the door shut, the brutal wind still managed to seep its way through just about every crack and crevice that it could find.

Isaac reached into his right pocket and snatched out a cigarette and his lighter. Concealing the flame from the wind, he lit the tip and quickly inhaled the intoxicating smoke that he so richly savored. The nicotine provided an almost orgasmic, if not temporary, comfort from both the cold and his aching body.

The young man sat in the small space that he had carved out for himself shivering and watching through a tiny crack in the door the kitchen light that Lynnette had left on. He hoped that she wouldn't turn it off.

His bright eyes shined away in the absolute blackness that he found himself in. Isaac knew what was inside of him, even though he would never be able to successfully explain it to anyone else.

For the time being, the shed was the safest place on earth for him to be...away from people.

CHAPTER 23

FLEETWOOD MAC'S, 'YOU MAKING *loving fun',* played on low volume in the deck as Linus pulled his brand new, dirty orange *Chevrolet Chevette* into the parking lot of his four floor apartment complex.

The keys were taken out of the ignition. The eight track was placed on the passenger's seat and a load of papers and folders were gathered into his aching arms. Like a battle weary soldier, the detective slumped out of his car and carried on to the front door, holding tightly to the contents that were securely tucked underneath his right arm as to not allow the wind to take them away.

He hated to fiddle with his keys in such cold conditions, but it was the only way to enter the building since the night guard had left for the evening. Linus feverishly cycled through his ring of keys until he spotted the gold key that he was searching for.

Before he could even slide the key into the lock, the door abruptly swung open, revealing behind it an elderly white woman and her black Labrador retriever.

"Edna?" Linus lost his breath. "Edna, it's ten past one in the morning, honey. What are you still doing up?"

Coming down from being so alarmed, Edna replied, "Oh

well, I was just waiting for Stanley to come home, that's all. I figured you were him."

Gladly stepping in from out of the cold, Linus looked upon the sweet, frail thing before saying, "Edna, Stanley is twenty-four years old. He's not a little boy anymore."

"I know," Edna bashfully smiled, "but you never know how folks can be these days." Edna then stood back and examined Linus as if she were studying a work of art. "I saw you on TV yesterday morning. I heard you found that kidnapper fella. Good for you." She grinned while proudly pinching Linus' left cheek.

Linus only blushed before reaching down to pet Edna's dog. "Something got to him before I could. But at least he's gone."

"That's right, good riddance to bad rubbish, I always say." Edna said, giving Linus a spunky punch in the arm. "Go get 'em!"

As Linus raised back up, unbeknownst to him, strands of fur fell from out of his pocket and onto the linoleum floor. Both he and Edna continued to converse as the dog sniffed the fur.

Suddenly, like a loud bang, the dog began to bark and snarl at the strange fur that it was sniffing. Linus and Edna gawked down at the animal, wondering just what had it so spooked all of the sudden. From one end of the hallway to the other, not a single soul could be seen or heard, and yet, the dog, which was usually the gentlest beast in the complex, became incredibly angered at a few shards of fur.

"Oh my, Edna bemoaned, trying to keep the dog from breaking its chain, "I wonder what's gotten into Earl all of the sudden!"

"I think you'd better get both you and him back to your apartment before he wakes the entire building!" Linus had to say out loud, taking three steps back just to avoid the agitated animal.

"I think so, too." Edna relented. "Goodnight, Linus."

Linus watched as the woman and her vicious dog carried on to the elevator and out of sight. He then looked down at the floor and noticed the fur lying about. Linus reached down to pick it up and study the filaments carefully.

He never bothered to stay behind that evening at the station to find out the results from the analysis that Brice took, and quite frankly, he was in no mood to investigate any further. He, much like the dog, sniffed at the fur before slipping it back into his coat pocket and carrying on down the quiet hallway to his apartment.

Linus unlocked the door, turned on the light switch that was on the wall and stepped inside. Warm, quiet and alone at long last.

To his right sat a bureau with pictures of his wife and two young daughters. Without taking another look at the files and folders that he had brought home with him, Linus dropped them all onto the dresser, along with the other fur samples, before taking off his coat.

The man felt like two hundred and twenty-one pounds of stale meat. Every joint in his body screamed out in agony for their master to take a long, hard stretch. But before even doing so, Linus went straight for the bathroom where he lifted the toilet seat, unzipped his pants and let out an exhaustingly endless stream of urine into the commode.

Once he was through, he flushed, cut on the light and washed his hands. In the midst of washing, he looked up into the mirror. The exhausted man that was staring back at him caused Linus to shudder in subtle disbelief. Wrinkles that were not present the morning before arose in striking, living color. He actually had to remind himself just how old he was just to make sure that he was looking at the right person.

Linus cut off the light and carried on into the kitchen. He opened the refrigerator door, loosened his tie and rooted around for anything to eat. The instant he came across a *Swanson's* TV dinner located beside a can of *Genesee* beer he right away grabbed both items.

He turned on the stove behind him before looking down at the cardboard box that contained beef and vegetable inside.

Just then, every muscle in his body decided to tense up. He wasn't even hungry. Sluggishly, he turned off the stove before carrying both himself and his can of beer into the small living room.

Late nights were customary for the man; it was all part of the job. In the past five months alone Linus couldn't recall one time getting home from work before ten p.m. Being that he had to report back to the station in about five and a half hours again only caused his stomach to bubble with dreaded anticipation.

He wasn't sleepy; rest was the last thing on his mind. Every image of the long day before kept his eyes jolted wide open. The sinking feeling that he got every time he dared recollect upon the body bags in the basement only made him want to freebase coffee for the rest of the evening. There should have been the long awaited calm after then storm moment. The unwinding relief, but the enthusiasm was nowhere to be found.

Linus dropped himself down in his recliner, picked up the remote control that was sitting on the coffee table beside him and cut on the set ahead. One station after another was flipped through. From *Benny Hill's* outrageous and lewd womanizing, to *Ralph Kramden's* ever constant threats of violence to his long suffering wife.

The Texas Chainsaw Massacre just happened to be playing on the late show. The scene where the killer cracked a young man over the head with a hammer and watched as his legs shook and twisted was enough to make Linus turn off the television in complete disgust. It was all he could digest.

He wanted to toss the remote clear to the other side of the room, but instead of being angry, he chose a completely different approach, one that he figured would settle his frayed nerves. Linus reached up under his chair and pulled out the March issue of *Playboy* with *Susan Kiger* on the front cover dressed in a red and black wet suit.

Her nearly exposed chest and long, wet, blonde hair only made Linus rip open the book with the gusto of a child opening a birthday present.

The very moment he viewed the first set of breasts inside the magazine he quickly unzipped his pants, took out his part and started to slowly massage it up and down. The harder he pulled at his own member, the stiffer it grew, until it was a rock hard tip in the air.

The longer he gazed into the young woman's brown eyes, the more his left hand that he was holding the book in began to tremble. Her precious eyes and face staring back at him in a sultry, sensual stare caused his stomach to turn. Her legs spread wide open for the world to see made Linus drop the book, turn and vomit all over the carpet beneath him.

When he was through convulsing, the man rose back up and wiped his mouth with his own shirt sleeve. He closed his eyes and gently stuffed his gradually shrinking penis back into his pants.

The warm silence inside his apartment began to cave in on Linus, making him feel as if he were losing his breath. The staggering image of a young woman stuffed in a bag like dirty laundry punched at him like a boxer in the twelfth round.

Linus sat back in his seat, placed his frazzled hands on his two knees and stared up at the ceiling above as though there were something there to see.

Behind him on the dresser sat the pieces of fur, gently moving from side to side as if a stiff breeze were blowing in the apartment. A wisp of thin, fine smoke began to billow from the fur. At first, it was a placid, smoldering sensation, like incense, that is until the smoke grew thicker and the sound of sparks whistled into the air.

Linus spun around not only to hear the popping racket but to also smell the raw odor of what resembled burning flesh. At the drop of a hat, the man jumped up from out of his seat and ran over to put the lone flame out.

He knocked the burning fur off the dresser and began to stomp out the flame, but no matter what, the fire would only grow even more intense. Before it could become more of a hazard, Linus scooped up the blazing hair, raced directly to the kitchen and drowned it under the cold water in the sink.

"Shit!" He irately yelled, washing his hands under the scolding cold water faucet.

Once the smoke had cleared, he cut off the valve and watched as the remains of the burnt fur whisked away down into the drain. Nothing was left but smoldering ash, which too was slowly dissolving.

At that point in the night, there wasn't much more that could possibly take place. In one day, Detective Linus Bruin had witnessed evil on a supreme level, and to think that it had followed him all the way home only made the very thought of sleeping all the more contemptible.

With his hands buried in his pockets, Linus dragged back into the solemn confines of the living room and sat back down in his chair. He wanted to ponder on just why the fur had burst into flames in the first place, or just how in the world Mercer had managed to escape his captor without incident, but it was all mere afterthought as one-thirty rapidly approached on the clock that sat on the coffee table.

The lonely, combat burdened law officer hung his heavy head to the floor and listened to the beating of his heart that seemed to drum a bit slower with every passing minute.

CHAPTER 24

CAPTAIN KANGAROO WAS CONVERSING back and forth with both *Mr. Green Jeans* and *Mr. Moose* on the television while Isaac spoke in a low, overcast tone to his father over the phone.

Dressed in the same clothes from the night before, Isaac watched Isaiah crawl and romp about on the floor with his *Fisher Price* toy phone while he sipped away on his fourth cup of coffee for the morning.

Isaac's mind was from the TV and drifting even further away from his son. Every so often he would stare down at his scarred fingernails that felt as if someone had pierced each of them with sharp needles.

"Isaac, are you still there?" Mr. Mercer worriedly asked.

Shaking himself awake, Isaac replied, "I'm fine, dad. I just got a bad headache. Did the fuzz bring your car back yesterday?"

"Yeah, they brought it back last night. I think the carburetor needs replaced." Just then, a long pause prevailed. The pause was soon followed by a moan from Isaac's father. *"Son…is everything alright with you? You sure don't sound fine."*

Just judging by his father's stretched out gap in speech Isaac could sense that he was stressed over his grueling ordeal. All the young man could do was sit and shut his eyes in angst.

"Yeah, dad, I just need some time to…to work things out."

"Where's Lynn at?"

"She went out to get some more medicine for Isaiah. She said she'll be back before nine."

"Isaac, just relax and let the good Lord take care of everything. You've got a friend in him."

Out of helpless frustration, Isaac threw himself backwards into the couch where he was sitting and began to silently weep.

"Dad...I got something to tell you later on." He flinched, trying with all his might not to sound like he was crying.

"I get off from work at five, come down to the church and we can talk then. I'd stop by, but the car won't start."

"Okay, I'll be there." Isaac hesitantly said, sitting back and wiping the wetness away from his face.

"I gotta go to work now. Be careful, son."

"I will, dad," Isaac sniffed before hanging up the phone.

Isaac noticed a frightened shakiness in his father's tenor that he hadn't heard before; it startled Isaac enough to where he even lost track of where Isaiah was and what he was doing.

"Dah," the child squealed out as he handed his father his toy phone to play with.

A forced smile came across Isaac's battered face before taking the plastic receiver, holding it to his ear and saying, "Hello?"

The mock conversations were customary; Isaiah would just sit and clap his tiny hands as though a parade were trolling right through the living room. The boy was happy to see someone enjoying his toys as much as he did.

Back and forth father and son played until the newsbreak on the television re-ran reports of the murder of the kidnapper, the dead bodies in his basement and the mutilation of the entire Sanders family.

There were the usual speculations from the usual talking heads on just what kind of animal could have possibly killed all seven people in one night, and just what authorities were planning on doing to capture the thing.

With Isaiah frolicking in his arms Isaac's eyes were locked firmly on the TV as the screen scrolled through every little Sanders girl. Their angelic faces were alive with euphoric vitality as their smiling parents held all four of their children in their arms.

A steady stream of drool dripped down and out of Isaac's bottom lip the longer he concentrated on the screen. He was completely void of any emotion at that instant, as though someone had shut off a light and left the room.

"Here!" Isaiah blurted out, handing his father his red *View-Master* to play with next.

Isaac's hands and knees all shook in perfect unison as Leroy Cummins' sharply dressed photo appeared on the television. He remembered the generous man offering him a ride two days earlier, but what seemed to cause Isaac's head to ache even more was the shock of knowing that he ended his life.

"C'mon, man," Isaac struggled as he lifted his aching body from off the couch, "your mom wants you to take a bath before she gets back."

Once he managed to limp his way into the warm bathroom Isaac promptly removed every item of clothing from off the child's body, cut on the warm water and then placed his boy inside the tub. With only a bar of soap Isaac scrubbed Isaiah from head to toe.

Unlike most children, it was never a strenuous chore to bath Isaiah. The child actually enjoyed being wet; just splashing about in the water was all playtime for him.

He knew that he should have been paying close attention to the baby at every second, but Isaac's brain just couldn't remain focused. He stared straight ahead at the grimy tile while listening to the little girl's scream in his head in a high pitched tone.

Much like the proverbial 'fingernails across the chalkboard', Isaac couldn't help but to drown in the hellacious notion that everything that happened two nights earlier was nowhere to be found in his mind. Even the remembrances of the grueling strain of his physical transformation had ostensibly been erased, which was hard to fathom considering the pain that he had been in since waking the night before in Lynnette's bed.

He recalled screaming of all sorts, from that of adults to children, and yet, had it not been for the TV, not one person's face could materialize inside the man's head.

All of the sudden, sprinkles of soapy water splashed into Isaac's dead face, alerting him to find his son fiddling with his own private part.

"Quit playing with that thing, boy, it'll turn into a habit." Isaac scolded, shoving the child's right hand away from his submerged midsection.

As soap suds drizzled into the baby's face, Isaiah sneezed. What came out of his nose was an amalgam of mucus and blood; he had been sneezing that way for days.

Instead of cleaning away the mess, Isaac paused. Behind him was a clean rag, but rather than turn and grab the cloth, he remained on his knees and inhaled. Isaiah looked up at his dad with an odd glare on his tiny face.

Isaac closed his eyes at that moment and allowed his flaring nostrils to take in the aroma of fresh blood that was drooling from his son's upper lip.

Right then, from seemingly out of nowhere, Isaac heard yelling come from the living room. Startled, he quickly opened his eyes and looked up to see the baby licking his own mucus. Immediately, he turned and snatched the rag from behind and wiped the child's nose completely clean. He then snatched the boy out of the tub before rushing both himself and his wet and naked son into the living room to find something very unusual...the room was gone.

Isaac stood and watched with downright stunned eyes at crashing waves, a bright sun beaming down and a young, black girl running away from a shirtless black man down a sandy beach.

He never questioned where or why the scene was inside Lynnette's living room, all Isaac could do was stand in complete silence and watch as the two individuals gave chase until the girl came upon a small, wooden shack that was located directly in the middle of the beach.

Screaming for all that she was worth, the girl ran through the door, only to have the ravenous black man trap her inside. To Isaac, the girl appeared somewhat familiar, but the man was as recognizable as his own face in the mirror. It just happened to be the same man that had been invading his life ever since his first transformation way back in November.

The girl's clothes were already torn and tattered to where all she had left was her ragged skirt. With a pair of white eyes and blood stained fangs, the man slowly stalked the petrified girl until he was able to grab her by the arms and restrain her.

The man then opened wide his jaws and tore right into the girl's neck. All the young lady could do was holler until her pleas went dead silent. Her skinny body seemingly went limp. Isaac could see her eyes, her lifeless eyes, stare up at him as if she knew he were right there along with her as the beastly man snarled and tore away at her flesh like a wild and famished animal.

And just like that, as mysteriously as it appeared from out of nowhere, was as inexplicably as the scene vanished right before Isaac's frazzled eyes.

Gathering what little breath he had left inside his lungs, Isaac inhaled, "That's how it happened." He held Isaiah up in his arms. "That's how she became that...thing. That man did it." He endlessly droned on. "You see, she has to know how to stop it. If I could only find her, then it would all be over, son. It would all be over...we could be happy all over again."

"Isaac...what are you doing?" Lynnette's voice spoke out behind Isaac.

With a confounded expression on his face, Isaac's head twisted ever so slightly till his eyes connected with hers. The bones in his neck could be heard cracking and straining.

Lynnette stood at the front door, holding a brown paper bag in her hand and wincing at not only the vile sounds that she heard coming from Isaac's body, but also at the creepy glare in her man's eyes.

Without saying another word, she dropped the bag to the floor, stepped over and immediately snatched Isaiah from Isaac's grip.

Isaac remained still for a minute more before he eventually limped past her on his way over to the coat rack where he grabbed his coat and steadily walked out of the house.

CHAPTER 25

WITHOUT LOOKING BACK, LINUS shut the door to the empty, grey bricked interrogation room before sitting himself down behind the small desk that was placed directly in the middle of the cement floor. Besides the bathrooms, it was the only place in the entire police station where an officer could grab a piece of momentary privacy.

On the desk sat a tan telephone that was layered from top to bottom with multicolored transfer buttons. The man loosened his blue spotted tie for more neck room.

Linus sat and stared blankly at the phone on the table in the interrogation room as though it were a bomb ready to go off at any second.

His stiff right hand wanted more than anything to pick up the receiver, but the circuitry in his brain wasn't exactly prepared to register such a strenuous task yet.

He looked up at the blurry window ahead of him in the door to see large silhouettes pass by in the hallway. Back and forth his eyes zoomed, from the door to the phone, until at last his hand managed to disobey the ongoing orders that his brain had been receiving. Slowly, he punched the number nine and seven more numbers after that one. As if he could sense a slap coming right at his face, Linus clinched his body in anticipation for an answer.

"Hello?" A young, female's voice eagerly spoke.

"Hey there, kiddo, how are you?" Linus cleared his dry throat, just grateful to hear the girl's playful voice.

"I'm find, dad." The girl giddily replied. *"How are you doing?"*

"Not bad, I just called to see how everything was going with you ladies."

"It's going pretty good, I guess." She sighed.

"You guess?"

"Well…I guess I'd better get it out in the open before mom tells you. I got a D in algebra."

Linus gladly exhaled before asking, "What are you doing getting a D, Tabitha? You're a smart girl. And just what are you doing home from school today anyways?"

"I know, dad, it's just…algebra is so damn hard, and our teacher is such a witch. The teachers are having their conferences, by the way."

"Does your mother know that you're using that king of language, young lady?"

"Sorry. So darn hard," Tabitha groaned.

Smiling, Linus said, "You just have to keep working at it. You may not realize it now, but that witch of a teacher could be the best thing to ever happen to you."

"I suppose so. So, uh…we all heard about what happened up there in Cuyahoga. How you caught that kidnapper and all."

"I didn't catch anyone; something else beat us to the punch."

"Yeah, well at least it's all over now."

"For now, or until the next perv comes crawling out of the sewer." Linus sighed before taking a long breath. "How's your sister doing?"

Tabitha hesitated at first before replying, *"She's okay. She still won't eat much. Mom says she eats like grandma used to when she was still alive."*

"Like a bird?" Linus' smile shrank.

"Something like that."

"Listen, uh, is your mom around by any chance?"

"Yeah, she's in the kitchen. Do you want me to go and get her?"

"Would you please, honey?"

Linus held his breath and tightened his fists. In the background he could hear Tabitha's mother speaking. He could tell just by her distant tenor that he was the last person she wanted to talk to.

"Hello?" The woman answered in a melancholy nature as though she were being inconvenienced.

"Hi there," Linus perked up. "How are you?"

"I'm fine, Linus. How are you?" She defensively replied.

"Not bad, not bad. I just called to see how everything was."

"Everything is going just fine." The woman sarcastically said.

"Tabi tells me that Liz is still...still not eating."

The woman sighed, *"Well, after what she went through, eating is probably the last thing on her mind. I'm glad that you were able to catch your kidnapper, though. Were you able to find whatever it was that killed him?"*

"No, not yet," Linus rolled his eyes. "But I didn't call to talk about that."

"What did you call about then, Linus?"

"Actually, I was wondering if it...if I could come down this weekend and see you guys."

There was an inflated pause over the phone at that instant. Linus held his breath and shut his eyes.

"Linus...I don't think that would be a very good idea; at least not yet."

Sitting back in his seat, Linus asked, "And why not, Alice? I haven't seen the girls since Thanksgiving, for Christ's sake."

"Linus, you just got off of a case that you've been working on since last September."

"What does that have to do with anything?"

"You know full well how you get too involved in your cases. You

bring them home with you. I don't think it would be wise to bring this particular one all the way down to Xenia."

Linus dropped his head to the table and rubbed his blushing face in anguish. "I only wish you could have seen the girl we found in that madman's basement, Alice. The look on that child's face," Linus gulped. "She looked just like—

"Stoppit, Linus! Just stoppit!" Alice furiously screamed into the phone. *"Do you see what I mean? I don't want to know what happened down in some murderer's basement, and I surely don't want our daughters to know! Elizabeth is a vegetable, and you want to come all the way here with that hanging over your head?"*

"I need to see them!" Linus suddenly roared into the phone.

There sat another stretch of silence before Alice calmly uttered in a condescending tone, "And you wonder why we left."

Linus pulled the phone away from his ear and began to massage his pulsating temples as though they were ready to explode.

"Linus, just give yourself some time. Give us all some time; perhaps around spring, when all of this has finally died down. When Liz is better, then…then maybe you can come."

Without replying, Linus slammed the receiver down before shoving the phone away. He held his aching head in his hands while sitting at the desk and brooding over his daughters' faces, as well as the smug manner in which his wife carried on during their conversation. He wanted to tear right through the phone. Not once did the thought of saying goodbye even enter his brain.

Right then, the phone rang. The red button on the bottom repeatedly flashed. Linus reluctantly picked up the line and soberly answered, "This is Bruin."

"Hey, buddy, the old man wants to see us." Fitzpatrick adamantly announced.

"Okay," Linus sighed, "I'm on my way."

The detective hung up the phone, straitened his tie and marched towards the door. The second he stepped out into the busy hallway, he found himself instantaneously bombarded by the vibrant sights and sounds of ringing telephones, arguing hookers and every day, garden variety thugs being carried in from off the cold streets for whatever crimes that had committed.

He secured his gun belt around his shoulder and began down a long, grubby hallway that led to an equally dingy stairwell.

"Hey!" Fitzpatrick called out while rounding the corner with a manila folder in hand.

Slightly alarmed, Linus looked back with a morose glaze on his face and asked, "How did you know I was in interrogation?"

"It's not hard to put two and two together." Alan said before both he and Linus started up the stairs. "How is everyone?"

"Same as usual," Linus shrugged.

"You sure," Alan glanced at the man.

"Yeah," Linus kept his eyes to the passing wall.

As they reached the third floor, both men just happened to stop right in the middle of the hallway beside a water fountain.

"Same as usual," Alan asked with a hard stare into Linus' eyes.

Linus dropped his head as to not allow his partner to see his misty eyes; he then looked back up and asked, "You and Peggy got any plans this weekend"

Alan glared at Linus with a glum appearance on his chunky face, looking as if the words that he wanted to say were still trapped inside his head.

With a straight face, Alan bellyached, "I missed *The Battle of the Network Stars* last night, dammit."

Linus chuckled before sarcastically asking, "Oh darn, you

mean to tell me that you missed *Rerun* leaping his big self over a hurdle?"

"Make fun if you want, but it's the only thing on TV that Peggy and I actually enjoy together, if you can believe that."

"Hey, you guys, the captain is waiting." Officer Donaldson feverishly motioned from her desk.

Linus and Alan carried on to the captain's office. The second Linus opened the door, the powerful aroma of cigarette smoke almost immediately struck him across the face.

"C'mon in, you two," the gruff, country speaking captain ordered as he put out his cigarette in the glass ashtray that sat on the edge of his cluttered desk.

He was an older white man in his early sixties. His nearly bald head was littered with liver spots while his thin build suggested that life on the force had taken its toll on his body. His rugged facial feathers were straight out of a *Marlboro* magazine ad, complete with a thick mustache and ice cold blue eyes.

"Well, if it isn't *Starsky and Hutch*, in the flesh." The captain coughed while gesturing for the detectives to take a seat in the two chairs in front of his desk.

"Damn TV show." Alan griped, taking his seat."

"Thought you'd quit that, especially since you're carrying a cold." Linus said as he sat down next to Alan.

"The cigarette has nothing to do with this cold I have." The captain hacked again. "When you have a wife that teaches second graders, she's bound to bring home some of their germs sooner or later. Congratulations, by the way."

"Everyone keeps congratulating me, but I wasn't the one who ended it all." Linus modestly turned away.

"Perhaps not, but quite frankly, it's all over now. But, speaking of the one who ended it all, I was just listening to this tape right before you two stepped in." The captain said before pressing the play button on Cummins' tape recorder.

Everyone gathered listened to the beast's roars and snarls all over again. Linus sulked in his seat like a five year old, still not believing that it was only a day removed from first hearing it.

"Poor schmuck," the captain offhandedly mumbled while pushing the off button. "He barely got a word out before getting the ax."

"Yeah, poor baby," Alan arrogantly sucked his teeth.

"Now, so far I've been getting a lot of feedback about this thing being a wolf, or something of that nature. But what everyone around this place seems to forget is that I was born and raised out in the hills of Montana, and in all my years I've never heard a wolf sound anything like that. And believe me, I know exactly what a wolf sounds like. Hearing a wolf out there is as common as hearing a car horn here in the city. This damn thing sounds like it's from the mouth of hell itself." The captain explained.

"Well, sir," Alan shrugged, "we have reason to believe that we may be dealing with something else, perhaps a bear, maybe."

"Knock, knock." Brice gaily chimed as he opened the captain's door ever so slightly.

"Come on in, Patrick." The captain said.

"Sorry to barge in like this." The young man humbly panted as if he had been running while holding two green folders underneath his right armpit. "I was told that you three would be here, so I just thought I'd go ahead and bring my data as well."

"Whaddya got?" The captain asked while leaning back in his creaky wooden chair.

Nervously rummaging through one of the folders, the young forensic examiner said, "Well, three things. First off, I ran the animal's recording through the voice analyzer. Believe it or not, this is not a wolf, or even a bear for that matter. The

machine keeps telling me that the sound is unrecognizable."
Brice gasped.

"Calm down, son." The captain motioned. "Just slow
down and breathe for a second."

"Wait a minute." Linus stepped in. "You mean to stand
there and say that our so called state-of-the art equipment
couldn't tell you what this thing is?"

"Hold on, Linus, there's more." Brice continued to grab air.

"There always is." Alan sighed.

"I also ran an analysis on the fur follicles we found. It's all
wolf hair, every single strand. But on top of that, and you're
not gonna believe this. The saliva I found in the church…it's
human saliva."

The entire room at that moment grew eerily quiet. The
captain, Linus and Alan all looked up at Brice with sour
expressions on their warm faces; not a single hint of emotion
could be seen. They possessed the appearance of someone who
could sense that the world as they knew it would end the very
next day. Brice stood by the door, waiting to see or hear what
was going to take place next.

"Close the door, son." The captain calmly ordered.

With a completely pale face, Brice did as commanded
before standing straight and still in front of his superior.

The captain then eyeballed the nervous young man while
slipping his frail fingers into the other before asking in a
composed and dignified demeanor, "Son…just what do you
suppose we do with that bit of information? Do you think it's
wise that we just allow you, or anyone else for that matter, to
leak that out to the public? This is a police station, not *The
National Enquirer.*"

All Linus could do was sit and watch Brice, who was
still stuck in statue mode, stare at the captain as if he were a
medieval warlord of sorts.

"Now, here's what I want you to do. I want you to strike

everything you just mentioned about that saliva off the plate, right now. Do you understand me?"

"Captain," Brice uneasily smiled as though a searing hot spotlight were glaring down upon him, "you're not just gonna ignore this, are you?"

The captain looked dead into the man's eyes and simply asked, "What do you think?"

Linus, Alan and Brice all looked back at the captain with the most innocent and confused poses on their faces as though they were locked in a moment of absolute clarity.

"Let's just say that you got the animal's saliva mixed up with some of the victims."

Seemingly too wound up to be contained, Brice opened his mouth and said, "But, captain, that's impossible. You see—

"Shh." The captain nodded. "We're gonna say just that. Okay?"

"Yes, sir," Brice hesitantly recoiled. "We'll say that."

"As a matter of fact, let's all say that. Let's pretend this is *Sesame Street* and we'll say it together. There was no saliva sample to speak of. Alan?" He pointed with his head.

As if he had a choice in the matter, Fitzpatrick simply uttered, "There was no saliva sample."

"Linus," the captain dead-eyed the man.

"No saliva sample, sir."

"Brice?"

"No sample, Captain." The young man blushed while grudgingly stuffing his all-important data back into its folder.

"Good. Now, what about this wolf hair?"

"Well, it's one hundred percent wolf fur alright. No doubt about it."

"But your analyzer, or whatever it is, said that it wasn't a wolf. How do you explain that?"

"Captain, I didn't make the thing, I just operate it." Brice haplessly shrugged.

"Not unless we're talking about the quote, unquote, *Jaws* of all wolves. Something that's super big and running free and loose out there somewhere." Linus elucidated.

"Yeah, you didn't see the size of those holes that it left behind, Captain." Alan added. "It seemed pretty damn big to us. God help anyone if something like that is out there on the loose."

"Captain, I measured this thing's strides in the snow. It has a…foot size of at least sixteen. Just on all fours, it measured up to six and a half feet long. Assuming this thing is capable of standing, like a bipedal, I'd say it was possibly close to seven feet tall." Brice said.

The captain once again leaned back in his seat and glanced over at the gloomy sky outside his frosted window.

"*Summit County* police aren't equipped to handle such a thing." The captain sulked while spinning back around. "And quite frankly, neither are we. We've got entirely too much to handle here in the big city to be chasing after some overgrown…whatever. But I was thinking, right before you fellas came in here. All of this sounds damn familiar. Do you guys remember that incident back in November, with those Haitians or Jamaican's, or whatever the hell they were?"

"Yeah," Linus spoke up, "Brice mentioned that yesterday. Something just broke into that house and tore those guys apart. Who covered that one?"

"Wilson." The captain answered. "Both he and his wife finally took that vacation to *Hawaii*. I guess they watched that *Brady Bunch* episode with *Vincent Price* one too many times."

Linus, Alan and Brice all sniggered while shaking their heads.

"I do remember Wilson saying something about some hair being left behind." Brice pondered. "I sure wish I were there to pick some up."

"So that means either we have two of these things running

around, or the same animal is hitting different cities." Alan examined.

"Here's how it's gonna go." The captain said, placing his hands on his desk and leaning forward with a serious presence behind his mustache. "Cummins is dead. That now leaves us with something that is possibly even more dangerous. So, it killed three drug dealers and a sicko car salesman. Big fucking deal. As far as I'm concerned, we're all better off. But two nights ago, it managed to break into a house and kill four little girls and their parents. Inside their own damn home," the captain strongly clarified. "We here at the *Cypress* P.D. don't hunt animals. We're police officers, not animal control. But, if this one thing can take out four large men on its own, then we've got one helluva problem on our hands, gentlemen. Personally, I don't wanna wait another three months for it to strike again."

"Well, what do we do, hire an old time search posse?" Alan snickered to himself.

"That's exactly what we do, Fitz, for now at least." The captain remarked. "I want you to put a task force together by the end of the day. No more than four men. Hook up with *Cuyahoga Falls* and the highway patrol. We all seemed to work pretty well with each other these past few months; I don't see why the love affair should end now. Let's see if we can put some of those country boys to work; I'm sure they'll enjoy the change of pace."

"Yes, sir," Alan said, promptly wiping the cheesy grin from off his face and exiting the office.

"Brice, I want you to retrieve Wilson's file and see if you can dig up something more on this thing. As I was telling Bruin and Fitz before you dropped by, I've never heard a wolf sound like this thing before."

"I'm on it, Captain." Brice, with a dower expression on his face, replied as he too bolted out the door.

The moment the door slammed shut, Linus sat back and relaxed into the wooden chair that he was attached to.

For a few brief moments there melted a quaint silence between he and the captain that actually felt comfortable.

"So, it took you six months, but you finally did it." The captain smirked at Linus.

A forced grin graced Linus' face at that second. He was visibly weary of all the attention that was being tossed at him from every direction.

"Finally," he apprehensively muttered. "I'm just glad that it's over."

The captain sat and stared unceasingly at Linus in humble adoration before saying, "I know how bad you wanted to kill him, Linus."

Linus slumped his limp body into his seat as though his bones were melting into jelly. The anger that had been foaming up inside of him for the past few months was all but wasted energy, by then, there wasn't an outlet of any kind to expunge it all.

"How's Elizabeth doing?"

Linus pressed his lips together before saying, "The same."

"Are you going to go see her?"

Linus ducked his head and said, "Alice doesn't think it would be a good idea just yet."

"For crying out loud, your twelve year old daughter was raped, and she thinks that it wouldn't be a good idea for her own father to come and see her?" The captain grumbled.

"I know, Roy." Linus breathed as he lifted his head back up. "I still can't get that Cohen girl out of my damn head. I still haven't finished all my paperwork. I feel like I'm trapped inside a *Karen Carpenter* song, for God's sake."

"Take the rest of the day off then, you've earned that much."

"And do what, go back home and be alone? Do you know

what daytime TV can do to a person?" Linus grimaced. "I need to stay active."

The captain shoved aside a collection of papers before pulling out a paper clipped bundle from underneath the stack. "I didn't bring this up when the others were in here but, what about this Mercer fella? What's his story?"

"Not quite sure yet," Linus sat up. "When Alan and I went over to his fiancé's house yesterday evening, the guy was wrapped in a blanket like a mummy. Judging by his face, it looked as if Cummins had worked him over pretty badly."

"Just how in the hell did he end up escaping not only Cummins, but the animal also?"

"He can't seem to remember."

"Bullshit." The captain obstinately pointed. "He remembers something. You don't go through all of that and come out with a blank memory. You're not gonna sit there and tell me that he just up and walked all the way home. *Cuyahoga Falls* is forty-five minutes away. Did you ever find out who he was talking to at that diner?"

"Judging by the shifty way he was behaving in front of his fiancée, I'd say our man was meeting up with someone. I didn't want to bring up the subject; I figured that he'd been through enough as it was. But, there was one thing, among many, that seemed out of place."

"What's that?"

"Either my eyes are going bad, or he looked taller than he was described to us by the waitress. That woman said that Mercer stood about six foot or so. I looked this guy up and down. Either he was standing on something, or else he just suddenly got one helluva growth spurt overnight."

"When does he plan on showing up for a statement?"

"He never gave an approximate time. I'll give 'em till this evening."

"And I wanna be here when he does show up. He can't play

the *Manchurian Candidate* role forever." The captain adamantly responded while studying Isaac's record that was lying on his desk in front of him. "Born January 12th, 1957. Father's name, Charles. Mother, Lucy Mae...deceased."

"His father was an interesting trip to say the least."

"How's that," the captain asked, still reading over his paper.

"Before Alan and I left his house yesterday, he practically ordered us not to forget the fact that his son wasn't crazy."

"Hello?" The captain suddenly buzzed to life.

"What's up?" Linus shot up from out of his chair.

"I don't flipping believe it. This joker was the sole survivor of that mutilation back in November."

Linus' eyes perked up also. "Is that right?"

"You bet."

"Judging by the shifty way he was behaving yesterday, I'd bet bottom dollar he was dealing along with the other fellas. Perhaps he was meeting up with a contact over in *Cuyahoga*."

"Says here he's got a clean record," the captain mentioned. "Never been arrested or any of the sort."

"So what the hell was he doing at that house that night? And better yet, how did he manage not to be swallowed up by our animal friend? Talk about the luck of the Irish."

"We've got to bring this joker in, Linus, before the sun sets on this city." The captain smirked. "Either he's the luckiest son of a bitch alive, or we may have another suspect that we've overlooked all this time."

"I'm on it." Linus intently replied as he leaned forward, far enough to where he could smell the captain's smoke riddle breath. "I was thinking about going over to *Saint Titus* later... to see the Cohen girl."

"Do you think that's wise?" The captain doubtfully queried with worry in his eyes.

With a plain face, Linus said, "No."

From there, the man turned and walked out of the captain's office. As soon as he closed the door behind him, he caught sight of Brice standing over an attractive female officer's desk in the rear of the busy room.

Linus criss-crossed desk after desk until he reached the man who appeared more upset than flirtatious towards the young woman who was steadily typing away.

"Pat, can I get your ear for a second?"

Brice, with his folders gripped tightly in his hands, stepped away from the officer's desk and followed Linus who was heading into the hallway.

"What now?" Brice asked in a frustrated manner.

"Listen, before you throw a bitch-fit at the whole station, just understand what you're coming at the captain with. You may think that you've stumbled upon the *Loch-Ness Monster*, but in the captain's eyes, it's all smoke and mirrors."

"Smoke and mirrors," Brice strongly contended. "Linus, the data is never wrong! It's all right here!"

"Put that away." Linus tried to calm the man down. "Not yet, okay? Not yet. You may think that everyone here is out to get rid of you, but it's just not that way. You still got a lot to learn."

Brice looked away as though he were about two seconds from jumping out the nearest window and away from the whole situation altogether.

"I need for you to answer me something."

"What's that?" Brice looked back.

"The fur samples," Linus carefully said. "Did you notice anything...peculiar about them when you performed your analysis?"

Brice glared at the detective with a weird contort on his pudgy face and asked, "Peculiar in what other way than what I discovered already?"

Linus bobbed his head from side to side as though he were

trying to convince the man that what he was searching for was right in front of his face already.

"I don't know...perhaps some fire?" Linus gulped.

"Fire," Brice squirmed. "Detective, what is this all about?"

"Look, all I need to know is...did anything happen when you analyzed the fur?"

"Nothing that shouldn't have happened, I suppose." Brice simply shrugged.

Linus cut his eyes away from the man's cynical face as fast as he could; too bashful to admit what he experienced just a few short hours earlier inside his apartment.

"Forget it, I need sleep, lots and lots of sleep." Linus exhaled, patting Brice on the back before heading down the stairs that led to the second floor and into the melee that was the police station.

CHAPTER 26

NEARLY TWO HOURS LATER Linus found himself face to face with Leroy Cummins' house once again. He sat inside his cruiser moping over the gut-wrenching fact that there were dead human beings gathered inside just a day earlier.

Upon finishing all of the paperwork that he had set aside the day before, Linus needed to escape the disorderly confines of the station. As luck would have it, he chose a murderer's homestead to find solace.

In his head, it was all like putting together a thousand piece puzzle in the dark; no matter how hard he tried to gather everything mentally, nothing seemed to connect, the emotions and memories kept slipping through his fingers like water.

Linus pulled the keys out of the ignition, got out of the car and sheepishly stepped forward to the front door. The sharp wind seared straight through his heavy coat, leaving his chest nearly frostbitten. In vivid color he recalled the sights and sounds of men carrying body bags out of the home one by one.

There the man stood at the front door of one of *Cuyahoga Falls'* wealthiest former residents. He remained face to face with the door as if it were supposed to open at the very sight of him before he suddenly remembered that just about every door to the home was locked, which meant that only an exterior tour would have to ease his inquisitive cravings for the time being.

He stepped down from off the doorstep and made his way around to the back of the house where the wind just happened to be even more spiteful than it was up front.

Upon reaching the spacious backyard the flapping of plastic could be heard loud and clear. The hole in the wall was covered with two large layers of plastic that were nearly coming apart at the seams, thanks to the severe wind that was pushing against it.

"Hey there, buddy!" A young, white highway patrolman hollered from the other side of a chain-link fence.

Linus spun around to see the man hop over the fence with his right hand clutching his sidearm that was still lodged in its holster.

"You can't be here, mister!"

Linus ever so carefully pulled out his badge from his pants pocket and held it up for the patrolman to see in plain sight.

"Detective Linus Bruin," he called out in a stutter. *"Cypress Police!"*

The officer stared closer at the detective before removing his trigger happy hand away from the butt of this gun.

"I'm sorry, sir." The officer humbly blushed, scratching his thin, blonde mustache. "I thought you were another reporter or another kid trying to get in there again."

Slipping his shield back into his pocket, Linus said, "Don't mention it. I didn't mean to intrude."

"You're not intruding." The officer waved. "It's just that last night, after all the others left from here, we got some reports of some kids running around, trying to get in. The little bastards even tried to tear down the plastic you guys put up."

"Is that right?"

"Yeah," the officer panted heavily. "Hey." He gazed on at Linus. "You're that guy that—

"I'm gonna stop you right there, Officer—

"Oh, Officer Stamp, sir," the young man smiled.

"Officer Stamp. I'm gonna tell you the same thing I've told just about everyone else that wants to give me kudos. I got here too late."

"Yeah, maybe, but at least the guy is gone."

Linus turned around to face the mildewed plastic. "Just how many times have you guys been out here since last night?"

"Um, I think about maybe seven times or so."

"Seven times," Linus gasped.

"Yeah, this place is real famous, or infamous. We kept getting calls from folks that live near here saying that they keep seeing kids peeking in there."

Linus turned, cracked a cynical smirk and asked, "Folks that live near here?"

"That's right."

"I suppose those same folks that saw those kids just happened to miss all those bodies that Cummins brought up in here these past few months, huh?"

Officer Stamp uncomfortably lowered his head and mumbled, "I guess so, Detective."

"I'm not beating up on you, son, it just...amazes me."

Officer Stamp glanced at the house before saying, "I still can't believe that it was Leroy Cummins of all people. My dad bought his last two cars from that guy. He seemed like a real nice fellow."

"That's what people are saying...but." Linus shrugged.

"Um, did you want to go in there? I mean, we can tear a hole in the plastic if there's something you need."

Linus paused, trying to remember why he even bothered to drive completely out of his way in the first place.

"Uh…that's okay." He took a nervous glance of the house. "I just saw everything that I needed to see."

"Yep, I guess coming back to the scene of a crime always haunts a person." Stamp remarked while taking a peek over Linus' shoulder. "I'm still having a hard time figuring out just what in the world could have that big of a foot."

Linus turned around to see the paw prints, along with traces of blood still lined in the snow on the ground. Every other second the spark of a large animal's face would appear before his eyes. He had been trying in vain since the day before to imagine what it could possibly look like.

Teetering back and forth with his hands in his coat pockets, Stamp said, "God help us all if that thing attacks again."

"If you saw what it did to Cummins, then I guarantee that not even God himself can help anyone." Linus stated.

"I still can't believe what it did to the Sanders down the road there."

"Were you familiar with the family?"

"Sure was." Stamp replied with a pessimistic grin on his face. "The mother and girls were really nice, but the dad, Gary, that guy was a character."

"How do you mean?"

"Well, he would always beat on his wife, Sarah. Every so often, she would call the police on the asshole, but Gary had a few connections down at the station, if you catch my drift."

Linus twisted his lips and said, "I'm afraid I do, officer."

"Well, all I know is that those girls didn't deserve any of what they got the other night. You think you're safe, and then…then something like this happens."

Linus exhaled before looking back at the house and then turning back to Stamp. "Tell me something, besides snooping kids, have you or your comrades noticed anything out of the ordinary here since last night?"

Stamp stood in place at that very moment. He took

his hands out of his pockets and folded his arms. He then peered deeply into Linus' eyes as though the question had offended him.

"I don't know." Stamp seemed nervous to utter. "I'm not supposed to say anything about it. I'm sorta sworn to secrecy on the whole subject. But since you're the one that cracked the case, I guess it's okay."

Linus braced himself, and that's all he did. He didn't budge or even blink. All he could do was stand and wait for the man to speak; and the sooner Stamp explained the situation, the sooner Linus himself could breathe again.

"Last night, two of our guys were patrolling out here, just like they do every night, nothing out of the ordinary. Well, when they got down to the Sanders' house, they see the downstairs lights coming off and on. So, they go into the house, and in the living room they said they saw a naked, colored guy sitting in a corner, talking to himself. When they asked the guy what he was doing there, the guy gets up, runs down to the basement, and…just vanishes. They couldn't find him anywhere. Mind you, we don't see too many blacks around these parts, but this guy was completely butt naked." Stamp exclaimed.

All Linus could do at that point was continue to stand. To say that he was frozen in place would have been cliché. He was drowning within himself, trying desperately to come up for air.

Clearing his throat, Linus asked, "You say they never found him?"

"That's right."

"Maybe he escaped through the opening where the animal came in."

"That's what they figured, too, but they remembered that the officers before them had boarded that opening shut before leaving yesterday afternoon. The guy just vanished into thin air, detective."

Linus stood back and watched Stamp's mustache bristle in the blowing wind before asking, "Would it be okay if I went there, just to check things out?"

Grinning, Stamp answered, "You can go anywhere you need to, detective."

"I'm glad you said that." Linus grinned back while heading for his squad car.

"Would you mind a little company?" Stamp followed. "It's not that I don't trust you or anything, it's just that I don't want you to be spooked all by yourself."

Smiling from ear to ear, Linus said out loud, "Company? Hell, I'd rather you bring the entire *Cleveland Browns'* squad with us!"

Both men got into their respective vehicles and took off down the road. For Linus, what seemed to keep his foot so light on the gas pedal was the harrowing fact that he actually believed Stamp's tale; every last bit of it.

Just a few minutes later, both lawmen arrived at the Sanders' residence. Unlike Cummins' home, the Sanders' house appeared even more sinister in Linus' eyes. He threw it all up to the fact that young lives were taken inside the place.

Both men dragged their snow burdened feet towards the home as if they were too afraid to walk any faster. Every so often Linus would turn around to see if anyone else was near or around the property.

Right before reaching the front door, Linus could see the backyard where a pink swing set was located. All of the sudden the man couldn't seem to move anymore.

"Let's get inside before the mother-in- law sees us." Stamp urged, pushing against the front door to get it open. "She lives right across the street."

Linus had to snatch his brooding eyes away from the empty

swings just to look at the young man in front of him barge his way inside.

The moment the door opened, the stench of fresh blood stung his nose. Linus shut the door behind him and covered his mouth.

"There's nothing worse than that 'day after a death smell,'" Linus said in a muffled voice.

"Really," Stamp asked. "Someone said that the animal took a dump somewhere in here before it took off."

"I wouldn't be surprised." Linus replied while listening to the furnace suddenly kick on. "Do you know if the officers came across any of the animal's fur in here?"

"Uh, I can't say for sure." Stamp answered, trekking towards the stairwell. "Neither of them stuck around for long after what went down. Do you need to go upstairs?"

Linus gawked strangely at the man as though his question were the most outlandish thing he had heard in his life.

"Uh, no thanks," he gulped. "That's the last place on earth I want to go. I'd rather see the basement."

Stamp led Linus through the living room where the brown carpet was stained with blood, and into the kitchen where a large crack in the linoleum could be seen.

Linus knelt down and inspected. "I wonder if Lou saw this." He murmured to himself.

"Jesus H Christ." Stamp exclaimed, gazing on in amazement at the deep indenture. "Was the thing that damn big?"

"For it to leave such a print, I'm guessing so, officer." Linus said without taking his eyes off of the dent in the floor.

He then looked up at the brightened kitchen and the refrigerator that was littered with *Holly Hobby* magnets and school papers with the letter A written in red on the top left hand corner of each.

"There's the basement." Stamp announced, pointing

directly at the door. "I bet you could find some more fur down there, considering that's where it came through."

Linus stood back up and neared towards the door while trying not to appear skittish in front of the young officer. He then cut on the light and immediately caught sight of more blood trails that were lined up and down the steps.

"I honestly wouldn't blame you if you didn't want to go down." Stamp stammered.

Linus glanced back for a moment to not only see the officer, but also an old, grey-haired white woman standing behind the man with a broom in hand and a hateful look on her face.

"What in the hell are you two doing here?" She angrily screamed while waving her broom at the men in a defensive fashion.

Out of shock, Linus slid down two of the steps while Stamp spun around and hollered, "Ma'am, we're police officers! We're just doing some investigating!"

Holding on for dear life to the slick wall, Linus looked back down into the pitch blackness of the basement, hoping not to descend any further into its gaping mouth.

"Ma'am, we are terribly sorry about this!" Linus panted, struggling to regain his footing. "I'm here on official business. This officer was escorting me."

"I don't care what kind of business you're doing; I don't want anyone else around my daughter's house!" The woman irately yelled.

"Ma'am, put the broom down or else I'll have to take you in!" Stamp warned with shaking hands.

"I don't care anymore! You can go on and take me anywhere you want to! I don't have anything more to live for!"

Approaching the woman with extreme caution, Linus explained, "Ma'am, my name is Detective Linus Bruin. I'm from the *Cypress* Police Department. I've seen all I need to see. We'll be on our way now."

"Good, and don't come back here, ever again!" The old woman ranted while following both men out. "Don't you people have any respect for the dead? First, some nigger comes hiding out around here, and now this!"

"We apologize, ma'am." Linus sheepishly remarked while both he and Stamp made their way outside to their vehicles.

From a distance, Linus and Stamp watched as the woman slammed the front door shut, stood and waited for them to leave.

"I could've arrested her for that." Stamp scornfully stated. "We're police officers; we have every right to be here."

"It's all the better that you didn't. She has every right to protect that house." Linus modestly responded. "To tell you the truth, I had no business coming out here anyways. This was supposed to be my day off."

Stamp stood and stared on and on at the house before asking in a far off whisper, "Who'd want to live here anymore after what happened? Kind of reminds you of that incident that happened three years ago in *New York* with that family and the kid that went crazy with the shotgun."

"You mean with the *DeFeo's?*"

"Yeah, that's it."

Linus looked over at Stamp with a glint of fatherly admiration in his eye. "Officer Stamp, how long have you been a lawman?"

Stamp looked back at Linus and proudly replied, "About three years now, sir."

Linus put his hand on Stamp's shoulder and said, "My friend, as a law officer, you're going to have remarkable days. Days that are going to be remarkably boring, remarkably great and remarkably ungodly. What happened inside that house two nights ago was remarkably ungodly. But as long as we get to go home at the end of the day and see our families, then everything just falls into place."

Linus and Stamp stood in front of their respective cruisers and stared on at the dreadful, empty home ahead of them, without another word being spoken.

CHAPTER 27

"I NEED TO SPEAK with Doctor Sanyupta, please! Doctor Benjamin Sanyupta!" Jeremiah intently shouted over the phone to the operator.

With a clutter of papers in both hands and his eyes firmly locked on the clock above the door, Jeremiah anxiously awaited the doctor's speedy response.

"Uh, yes, good morning," he jittered, dropping his papers flat on the floor beneath his feet. "Or should I say, good evening, Doctor? Sorry to disturb you. I was just calling to fill you in on a couple of patients that require some much needed attention."

"*I see. What can I assist you with, Doctor?*" Sanyupta replied, sounding as if he had just awoke from sleeping.

"Well, first I wanted to discuss Isaac Mercer. You won't believe this, but, Isaac was kidnapped two days ago."

First, there was a long gasp, then Sanyupta appallingly uttered, "*Oh my.*"

"Don't worry, I believe he is fine. According to reports, somehow he managed to elude his captor. Apparently he was abducted by the B.O.D. kidnapper."

"*I'm sorry, the who?*"

"The Broad Open Daylight kidnapper," Levin sighed while rolling his eyes. "I apologize for the acronym usage."

"Ahh, I understand. Tell me, how was Isaac able to gain his freedom from this individual?"

"It's still unknown at this time. But, the kidnapper was found murdered inside the same home where he took and murdered his own victims."

"Murdered? By whom," Sanyupta inhaled.

"More like a what," Jeremiah said. "The police say than an animal, a very large animal, killed this man, along with six others up along the *Cuyahoga Valley.*"

"And Isaac was able to escape unharmed?"

"That's correct. I would love to know just how he was able to do so."

"Wait a minute, just what was Isaac doing up in Cuyahoga Falls?"

"I'm not quite sure, sir."

"Are you seeing him again this month?"

"As a matter of fact, he has an appointment on the 28th. But I wanted to bring that incident to your attention, as well as a curiosity. I saw Isaac last week, and I was not aware that he was bilingual."

"Ahh," Sanyupta chuckled, *"I see you have come across that phenomenon as well. I am afraid that Isaac does not speak another language, rather, he is speaking backwards."*

Jeremiah's mouth grew dry at that second, trying to find the words to explain his sudden confusion.

"Backwards, you say?"

"Precisely," Sanyutpta sounded confident. *"I too was taken aback at first. He and I were having a conversation one day back in December, and out of nowhere, he begins to speak what I assumed at first to be a completely different vernacular. I replayed the tape recorder over again during our discussion when it suddenly occurred to me to play it backwards."*

"And just what exactly was he saying? If you don't mind me asking."

"Mostly obscene words of the four letter variety," Sanyupta sighed. *"Some random sayings about blood. I believe his final words that particular day were something to the effect of structures collapsing and a fateful train ride. Once again, random gibberish. Just the rants of a person who has endured a traumatic experience. Even his very tone seemingly changed. One would possibly believe that he was, dare I say, possessed, if you subscribe to such a preposterous notion that is."*

"I see." Jeremiah slowly spoke as he scribbled down words on a sheet of paper that was lying on his desk in front of him. "Well, as I mentioned, I will be seeing Isaac again later this month."

Jeremiah kept on speaking with Sanyupta. His lips were moving, but his mind was far from the conversation. Even when the subject switched from Isaac and to another issue, the man's thoughts remained solely upon Isaac. Somehow, even with the knowledge that Isaac was free from his captor, Jeremiah could still see the young man in some sort of distress; an agony that he himself would fear in a nightmare.

Rubbing his aching neck, Isaac stood in the back corner of the elevator and watched with hungry, scurvy eyes as the overweight, young white woman in front of him squirmed from side to side as though her elevator companion were readying himself for an all-out assault upon her.

Isaac scratched his unshaven face up and down as if his own skin were on fire. In his eyes there was really nothing attractive about the woman. He wasn't interested in looks, just smells.

He inhaled her strong perfume with just about every last ounce of lung power he could muster until his nostrils began to twinge.

The woman nervously glanced back at the young man while gripping her purse that was wrapped around her shoulder.

When his nose could no longer breathe in any more fumes, his body unclenched itself. Isaac leaned up against the wall and stuffed his cold hands into his coat pockets.

Just then, the elevator stopped. The very instant the door slid open, like a passing wing, the woman sailed out and into the hallway as though she were being chased down. Isaac remained up against the wall while a crass grin blessed his swollen face.

Realizing that he had arrived at his floor, the young man nonchalantly limped out into the quiet warmness of the soft-colored hallway. 'Moonlight in Vermont' was playing in the speakers above his head as he walked on.

Cream colored, block-like arrows pointing people in the right direction lined the walls that young Mercer passed by as his head hung low to the carpeted floor beneath his sore feet.

Without even looking up to see if he had arrived at the correct locale, Isaac pushed open the door and noticed right away Doctor Levin talking on the phone.

"Isaac?" Jeremiah choked, hanging up the phone.

"How you doin', man," Isaac cracked a lazy smile while dropping himself onto the leather couch as if he owned the place.

Levin, with a face of complete disorientation, sat himself down beside Isaac, took off his glasses, and with outstretched hands asked, "Isaac...are you okay?"

Without looking in Levin's direction, Isaac said, "Yeah, man. I've just been through some stuff lately."

"Some stuff is a helluva of an understatement, my friend." Jeremiah exclaimed while examining Isaac's face. "Isaac...I honestly don't know what to say. I...I can't believe you're here. How did you even get here?"

"I took the bus all the way out here, man. I just needed someone to talk to." Isaac lethargically replied, sounding as though he were ready to fall right asleep. "I've been freebasing coffee ever since this morning. I don't wanna go to sleep ever again."

"Well," Levin briefly sighed while glancing at the clock above his head, "I have an appointment with a patient in about twenty minutes or so, but I guess you and I can talk until then. I just have to ask, how were you able to escape that kidnapper? It's all over the news."

Isaac let out a hearty, hapless belly laugh before saying, "Man, everyone has been asking me that same question since yesterday. Truth is, I can hardly remember anything that happened the other day."

"Well, what was the last thing you remember? The news keeps saying that you were seen over in *Cuyahoga Falls*. What were you doing out there?"

Isaac immediately shot up from off the couch and began to pace the floor in front of the doctor. There was so much rambling chaos cluttering his brain that pulling out one thought seemed to drain his already depleted energy.

"I had to see someone up there. Someone very important," Isaac carried on. "I had to see the woman that made me."

"Made you?" Jeremiah shrugged with strange eyes.

"Yeah…made me into this," Isaac pointed to himself. "Just this morning, I saw how she was made, and I needed to find her so she could tell me how to reverse everything."

"I take it you're referring to your so called Lycanthropy?"

Isaac stopped his incessant pacing to give the doctor a strange scowl, as if the word were completely foreign to his nature.

"Isaac, you've got to understand, there's no such thing as that. It's nothing more than guilt." Levin urged.

Isaac faced the window and planted his hands back into his coat pockets. He then closed his eyes, inhaled the fresh new carpet smell of the office and said, "I think I'm ready to tell you what happened back at that house."

"You mean back at Leroy Cummins' house?"

"No…back in November."

"Oh…I see." Jeremiah softly reacted.

All Isaac could hear was Jeremiah's body settling into the leather couch. The very moment the man stopped moving, Isaac opened his eyes.

"Me and Lynn were arguing Thanksgiving afternoon. So I got pissed and went over to Karyn's place."

"Who's Karyn?"

"Some broad I met back at the garage where I was working. She and I had been messing around since October." Isaac steadily explained. "So anyways, I went over to her place, we did it, and then she suggests that we go over to some guys' pad to play poker."

"Isaac, you don't have to tell me all of this." Jeremiah sat up on the couch."

Isaac then turned around and stared at Levin while saying, "No, I need this, for me. You see, me and Karyn get over there, and these Jamaican cats are there smokin' and drinkin'. There's drugs and guns everywhere. For the first hour or so, everything is going alright. Then one of the Jamaican guys starts yelling at Karyn. He thinks that she's cheating him out of some money. Next thing you know, they all jump up and start beating her like she was a dude. I hate to admit it, but I got scared. I ran into the closet and hid. There these cats are just kicking and beating this woman half to death, and I'm in the closet like a little bitch."

"Isaac, were you ever able to find Karyn in *Cuyahoga?*"

"Yes, but that's not important now." Isaac's eyes began to water. "You see, when they got through with her, they start coming after me. And that's when I heard this sound. At first, I'm thinking they got a dog up in there, but it doesn't sound like a regular dog. Those men turned around. I could see everything that was going on through the keyhole."

"Tell me more about the sound."

"The sound gets louder and louder. I can see Karyn shaking and saying all these crazy things." Isaac himself began to tremble. "I saw her."

"You saw her do what?" Jeremiah shuddered.

"I...I saw her change." Isaac's voice faltered.

"Isaac, what exactly did Karyn change into?" Jeremiah appeared confounded. "I'm trying my hardest to understand you, but you have to quit being so vague with me."

"I saw her change into something." Isaac balled up his fists. "All those guys could do was stand there and watch. We all watched that woman turn. She turned until she wasn't a woman anymore. People aren't supposed to do that, man! People aren't supposed to change into other things!" Isaac yelled. "That thing got up and tore those guys apart! She ate them all! One by one! Hell, they even tried to shoot her, but the bullets didn't work!"

Looking both confused and frustrated all at once, Jeremiah began to stand up while saying, "Isaac, you have to understand, it was—

"I ain't done yet." Isaac interrupted while slowly turning around. "You see, the more I watched her kill those men, that's all the more scared I became. There was blood everywhere; all over the floor, the walls and the furniture. I could feel something inside of me. I could feel it moving around like it was caged and wanted to get out. Do you know what it feels like to have your own bones crack and twist? My whole body felt like it was on fire. I could feel my face just...explode! That's when I blacked out."

With utmost urgency, Jeremiah rushed over and grabbed Isaac by the shoulders. He stared the desperate man into the eyes and screamed, "Listen to me, Isaac! You didn't kill anyone! The police ruled that it was an animal! Possibly an escapee from the zoo!"

"A zoo," Isaac yelled back, snatching himself away from the doctor. "Man, I know what I saw that night! I know what I turned into! You don't forget how that shit feels! Look at my face! Look at how tall I am all of the sudden! It took a few days for me to heal the first time around, and then even after you've healed, you still have to limp around like a fuckin' cripple!"

"Isaac, listen to yourself!" Jeremiah pleaded. "It's like you've made no progress whatsoever!"

"I keep on hearing these kids in my head! I can't sleep because I keep hearing people screaming! All day long, I've been hurling my guts out! I think I even shit out somebody's eyeball before I got here! So don't stand there and tell me that this is all in my mind! You don't know what this is!"

Levin humbly stepped back and rubbed his eyes. He then held out his hands to ease Isaac while calmly explaining, "Okay, you're right. I don't know what it is. But, Isaac, I can't allow you to think for one moment that you had anything to do with those murders the other night. It's utterly impossible. This isn't the twelfth century. There are rational explanations for all of this. I believe that perhaps you were sleepwalking. It is conceivable that you walked all the way back from *Cuyahoga Falls,* that would explain the pain your body is in. It's plausible that you were somehow incapacitated and beaten by Leroy Cummins, that right there is a possible explanation for your face."

Isaac wandered around the office in an aimless blunder, trying his hardest not to listen to what Levin was saying. Trying to drive out the words that in his mind were just plain gibberish.

"Believing that you're some mythical demon doesn't exactly constitute you as being a murderer. I may be sounding like my father, but I personally blame *Hollywood.* It just seems that in the past few years they're releasing more and more films that have caused irrational behavior in a lot of people."

Isaac paced before he eventually found himself leaning up against one of the bookshelves. Exhausted, he sobbed into his hands, "I never meant for my life to end up like this. I had so many dreams. I was gonna open up my own garage. Me and Lynn were gonna get married. We were gonna get out of *Cypress* once and for all. Now…now it's all gone because I fucked up. All I see is darkness in front of me. It's like you're awake, but you can't open your eyes…no matter how hard you try."

"It's not all over, Isaac." Levin steadily persisted. "You just have to come to terms with the fact that this overwhelming sense of regret inside of you is what's causing all these delusions."

Exasperated, Isaac turned his head away as to not look at the doctor in front of him. He was telling him things that he neither wanted nor needed to hear at that moment.

"Your affair with this Karyn person is the burden that you've been carrying all these months. The guilt manifests itself as something unrealistic. Do you remember last week when I told you about my other patients?"

Right then and there, Isaac's entire body, from head to toe, ignited with blazing fury. Without warning, the man lunged forward, seized Levin by the neck and squeezed as hard as he could while angrily hollering, "I ain't no fuckin' vampire!"

Isaac squeezed as tight as he could before Jeremiah's eyes began to bulge forward, and a stunned expression came upon his bluish face.

Then, just as abruptly as the assault began, was just as sudden as it ended. Isaac released the helpless man before bolting out the door.

CHAPTER 28

LIKE A LONE DRIFTER, Isaac stumbled across the old, filthy train yard that dated back to the eighteen hundreds. He wasn't lost, the man was well aware of his current location; it was the simple matter of biding his time to meet up with his last hope in the world.

As he trekked along the live rails, Isaac couldn't help but to recollect upon the times when his father would take him down to *Cypress Underground* to watch the trains go by when he was only a child.

He recalled with fond quietness how much he wanted to hop onto one of the giant steam engines and take off down the track that seemingly led to anywhere on earth.

It was his undying desire to rid himself of not only his demonic affliction, but also the burden of his illicit affair, but deep down, there was always that one 'something' inside of him that constantly reminded Isaac that it would be virtually impossible. Watching Karyn speed away in her green *Monte Carlo* two days earlier left him with the emptiest feeling. He knew that he would possibly never lay eyes on her again.

Isaac was nearing *Lake Logan*. The icy chill in the air was becoming increasingly harsher as snow flurries blew past his face at wild speeds. He carefully stepped over a track where a huge black *Conrail* engine was slowly towing itself down towards his direction until he met face to face with the mighty body of water ahead.

Isaac stood at the pier. Every so often he would catch a sudden glimpse of déjà vu the longer he remained still, as if it hadn't been so long since he had visited the same sight.

He watched with bleary eyes as the choppy, foam riddled waves jostled up and down. Isaac stepped aside to allow the seagulls to gather the remains of a partially eaten fish that was lying frozen on the pier next to him.

The very first and only time in his life Isaac ever contemplated the notion of suicide was when his father took him to *Ashlandview*. But at that moment, he was all alone. There were no orderlies or compassionate speaking doctors to monitor his every movement.

He recalled the look of complete shock in Lynnette's eyes as she stood and watched him hold Isaiah in his arms earlier in the day. What she thought he was doing would be just as hard to explain as what was dwelling inside of him.

He closed his eyes and allowed the fierce February wind to push his body back and forth. Isaac was only five steps away from the edge of the rickety pier. The closer he inched forward, the more he could feel the animal inside of him claw about. It was such a nauseating sensation, much like a rat scraping its way out of a burning building.

"Hey…hey, you," a heavy male voice hollered from behind. "Hey, get away from there! That area is closed!"

Isaac abruptly opened his dreary eyes and turned around to see a black figure running towards him from out of the snowy distance, waving his arms as if he were landing an airplane. The young man stepped back from the edge and began to walk away.

"Didn't you see that sign there, man?" A heavyset black man with a full beard panted as he caught up to Isaac.

Isaac stopped walking long enough to notice an orange sign

to his immediate right that read **BOARDWALK CLOSED FOR REPAIRS**.

Nonchalantly shaking his head, Isaac wearily uttered, "No...I didn't see that."

"Had you stayed out there any longer, the damn thing would've collapsed, with you on it!" The man said out loud.

Isaac never bothered to reply to the gentleman; he instead stuffed his frozen hands into his coat pockets and walked away, not looking back once.

CHAPTER 29

THE CYPRESS GUARDIAN
WEDNESDAY, FEBRUARY 23RD 1977

IN WHAT RESEMBLED A *grisly scene from the latest horror flick, the owner of Larry's Garage & Auto Parts, twenty year old Larry Tate, and his twenty-six year old cousin, Marvell Tate, were found bludgeoned to death inside their place of business last night.*

As of now, police do not have a suspect, but nearly seven thousand dollars' worth of cocaine was discovered within the establishment, which leads authorities to believe that perhaps a drug deal had possibly gone awry.

The manager of the Tri-State Savings & Loan Bank, located right next door to the garage, told police that the garage was rarely ever open, and an assortment of "shady" characters would be seen coming in and out of the business on a daily basis.

The murder weapon, which was found lying next to the owner, was a blood soaked Phillips head wrench. Both victims were repeatedly beaten over the head with the tool.

Forensics officers are speculating that the victims had been dead for at least over a week, judging by their extreme decomposition. Tri-State bank manager, David Khan, noticed something was wrong when he heard the owner's Doberman pincher barking non-stop over the past few days. That was when he decided to call police.

Larry Tate leaves behind four toddler boys. Marvell Tate was the father of two young daughters.

With his issue of the *Cypress Guardian* in hand, Mr. Mercer sat in his pew and tried to regain his fleeting breath while pondering on the dreadful news he had just read.

He gripped the paper in his hand as tight as he could as he kept his dreary eyes locked on the crucifix down behind the pulpit ahead of him. As vexed as he was at the headline, Mr. Mercer was more strained on how he was going to break the news to a son that was barely hanging on to life as it was.

The man stretched his arms forward until they rested on the back of the pew in front of him. There was a distressed manifestation lying heavy on his face. Every so often flashes of his late wife would appear before his eyes. Mr. Mercer required her patient, maternal wisdom when it came to such situations.

For the very first time in years, the man tried and tried to communicate with God, but no matter how hard he wanted to shut his eyes, he just couldn't seem to bring himself to do so.

He wanted to see Isaac, but not in the scathing condition he could be in when he spoke with him over the phone in the morning.

Right before Mercer could even take another gulp, desperate knocks at the front door interrupted the quiet that he was lurking in.

Immediately, Mr. Mercer dropped the newspaper onto the pew before getting up and racing towards the door. He flung open the door to find Isaac shivering and wild-eyed.

"Isaac, come on in, son." Right away, he pulled his boy into his arms and squeezed tight. The moment he released him, he looked into his son's eyes and asked, "Son…did you know that Larry and Marvell were murdered a few days ago?"

Completely sidestepping his father's harrowing news, Isaac barged his way into the church and gawked around the dimmed sanctuary as though he had never set foot in the place before in his life.

"Dad, I gotta talk to you." Isaac huffed and puffed.

"C'mon, we'll go in the back." Mr. Mercer shook his head before leading Isaac towards the rear of the church and to his office.

As Mr. Mercer walked on, he suddenly realized that he was void another presence beside him. The man stopped and turned to see Isaac standing and staring at the cross behind the pulpit as if the symbol had possessed him to the point of absolute, solid shock.

"Isaac...c'mon, son," he said, holding out his right hand.

Instantly, Isaac snapped back and resumed his trek behind his father until they both made it to the study.

"Go on and have a seat." Mr. Mercer said before leaning against the wall with his burly arms folded against his brown jacket.

Isaac sat himself down on the stool beside his father's desk while his hands remained securely tucked inside his coat pockets.

Mr. Mercer stared strangely upon his son's facial features before worriedly questioning, "Son, what did that man do to you?"

Isaac looked up at his father with an odd contort on his face and replied, "Dad, this isn't about that man. I got problems."

"Is it that bad, son? Did you go to the hospital?"

"No hospital can help me." Isaac depressingly stuttered as if he were still freezing cold. "I need you, dad."

"I'm right here, boy." Mr. Mercer reached out with his right arm. "Just tell me what you need and I'll see to it that you get it."

Isaac's head twisted and turned from one corner of the

tiny office to the other before he looked down at the floor and said in a muffled tone, "It…it happened again the other night."

"What happened again?" Mr. Mercer held his breath.

"The same thing that happened back in November," Isaac bashfully looked up.

Mr. Mercer, completely spent, rolled his eyes and sighed, "Isaac, I thought this was something serious."

"It is serious, dad!"

"We've been over this once before." Mr. Mercer began to pace the floor. "I don't know what happened to you the other night, but whatever you think happened, didn't. Look at you, you look like death itself. When was the last time you slept?"

"Dad, you weren't there!" Isaac desperately said.

"And since we're on the subject, just what were you doing all the way up in *Cuyahoga Falls* to begin with? I thought you were going to look for work back on Monday." Mr. Mercer adamantly remarked.

"I did look for work, and after I got done with that…I went to go see someone."

Mr. Mercer stopped pacing and squared his eyes down at Isaac in an accusatory fashion before asking, "Who was this someone, son?"

"It was this woman—

Mr. Mercer once again rolled his eyes in agony. "A woman," he questioned. "Boy, what woman do you know in *Cuyahoga Falls?*"

"Dad, she knows what I am! She knows how to cure me!" Isaac frantically answered.

"Damn!" Mr. Mercer indignantly growled while storming out of the office and back out into the sanctuary with his son close in on his heels.

"Dad, you don't understand!" Isaac breathlessly urged, chasing after his father. "Me and Lynn was having problems, and…I'm not trying to make excuses, but, it just happened!"

Mr. Mercer stopped walking right in the middle of the floor and asked, "What, just happened? Is that who you went to see in *Cuyahoga*, this woman? You went to go see some woman, and then you're ass goes and gets kidnapped? It's by the grace and mercy of God that you got away from that man!"

Tears began to drip from Isaac's eyes as he wailed out loud, "I didn't mean it! We had sex! Next thing I know, I wake up with these eyes! I started having blackouts! And then...then that thing on Thanksgiving! Dad, she was lonely! She needed someone to talk to!"

"Then you should have told her to go and buy a damn dog!" Mr. Mercer roared at the top of his lungs while flailing his arms in the air. "It's not your job to keep company with another woman! You keep your own woman company!"

Isaac dropped to his knees and wept incessantly into the carpet. All Mr. Mercer could do was stand above his son and shake with fury.

"Nigga, you could lose your family! What were you thinking? This is your life we're talking about here!"

"I didn't mean to do it!" Isaac screamed to the ceiling above.

"I know exactly what's wrong with you!" Mr. Mercer continued to yell while making his way over to his son and yanking him up from off the floor by the hood of his coat. "You've done gone and caught some nasty disease from this gal! That's what's got you acting like a heathen!"

Mr. Mercer couldn't seem to stop his rampage. He shook Isaac nearly out of his own jacket while pointing his finger directly into his face.

"I can't imagine what's wrong with you young people today! You all get out there and fool around with any and every one that you see! And when something like this happens, you come crying to your parents for help! Well, I know exactly how to help you! C'mon, you and me are going down to the free clinic before it closes so we can get you checked out!"

"I ain't got no disease!" Isaac shot back, snatching himself away from his father's powerful hold. "I need you to take this thing outta me! I need you to do one of those exorcise things for me! Do me like they did that white girl in the movie! The power of Christ compels you!" Isaac insanely spat as he ran over to the half full baptismal font next to the pulpit and scooped out a few ounces of water into his hands. "C'mon, dad...the power of Christ compels you! Say it! The power of Christ compels you!"

Mr. Mercer stood and watched in utter astonishment and woe as his one and only child recklessly splashed water into his own face. Right there, his heart shattered into pieces. He no longer recognized his own son.

"You're a pastor!" Isaac furiously hollered, racing over and grabbing his father by the hand. "Do the exorcism thing on me! I need it! Do you need the crucifix up there?"

With painful tears in his eyes, Mr. Mercer held out his quivering hands and said, "Son...it hurts my soul to see you this way. *Proverbs* 27: 8 says that *As a bird that wandereth from her nest, so is a man that wandereth from his place.*"

"I don't wanna hear all that bible shit! If God really did love me then he'd help me!"

"You have to allow him to help you!"

"Dog denmad em," (God damned me) Isaac slurred in a coarse tone. *"Dog eta hem,"* (God hate me)

Out of gut fear, Mr. Mercer stumbled backwards into one of the pews. He watched with stunned eyes as Isaac began to draw closer to him.

"Oh, God, son," the man choked, clutching his chest.

"I'm so fuckin' afraid. I didn't mean to do any of it." The young man continued to cry. "Tell mama I'm sorry. Tell her that I won't do it again, daddy!"

Mr. Mercer held his breath while glancing past Isaac and down towards the pulpit, hoping that God would come down and settle the situation first hand.

"She told me to stay away from people." Isaac began to froth from the mouth. "I gotta go, dad. I gotta go away." Isaac said as he started to storm past his father on his way out the front door, only to have the man grab a hold of him.

For the large Mr. Mercer, it was akin to wrestling a man of equal or greater size. Never before had it been such a task to try and overpower his son as it was at that moment. But somehow, Isaac managed to outmaneuver his father to where he was able to slip out of his grip and race straight for the door.

Mr. Mercer watched the opened door sway back and forth for only a few seconds before running back to the janitor's closet. Inside the closet were two brooms, a vacuum, a red bucket, a mop and a black telephone. He snatched up the phone and feverishly dialed Lynnette's house.

The line was busy.

CHAPTER 30

IT WAS WELL PAST six that evening, close to half past the hour. A surly and numb Detective Bruin, along with three other persons, exited the elevator and stepped onto the seventh floor of *Saint Titus* hospital.

His crimson red face was still frigid, along with his hands that were lodged inside his coat pockets as he casually strolled down the semi-busy hallway.

The hustle of emergencies had all but seemingly died down, at least for the time being. With the exception of a couple of chatting doctors in a nearby corner and four female nurses going on about what they were planning on doing once their shifts ended, it was a relatively peaceful evening.

With every other step Linus found himself slowing down, either to listen to the female voice over the loud speaker paging a doctor or just biding his time to reach Gloria Cohen's room.

The closer he drew, the more his feet wanted to turn and walk away. For the sake of nagging, curious ambition, Linus wanted to see the young kidnap victim face to face one final time. For him, it was peace of mind to find out if she was alright; he wanted more than anything to be assured that the ungodly expression on her face that she was wearing two mornings earlier had forever vanished.

As he approached the room, a sudden wave of searing heat

slithered down his spine. His right hand shook as it neared the door's handle. He knocked first.

"Come in!" A female's voice called out.

Gently, Linus pushed open the door and noticed a plump, blonde-haired white woman, who looked as though she were in her early to mid-thirties, seated in a chair next to the bed where Gloria was lying comatose.

Gloria's brunette hair laid flat across her shoulders while her eyes were totally fixated on the television that was mounted up on the wall in front of her. For a second or two, Linus lost control of his own body to where he couldn't even move a single muscle.

"If you're another reporter or yet another police officer, "I've told you people everything. There's nothing more to talk about." The woman impatiently sighed while rising up out of her seat.

Linus blushed and explained, "Well, I am an officer, but I'm not here for questioning. Detective Linus Bruin, *Cypress Police.*"

Instantly, the woman's eyes grew large right before she extended her right hand. "Oh...I'm so sorry, I thought you were someone else." She suddenly caught herself off guard.

"Don't be sorry, I understand." Linus smiled while shaking the woman's hand right back.

"My name is Deborah Cohen. I'm Gloria's older sister."

"Good to meet you, Deborah." Linus humbly beamed as his eyes shifted from Deborah to Gloria's motionless body on the bed. "I, uh...I just stopped by to see how the young lady was doing." Linus nearly forgot how to breath.

Looking down at her sister, Deborah feebly snickered, "Well, as you can see, she's taking it the only way she knows how right now."

"I can see that."

"Yep, she hasn't eaten anything or said a single word to

anyone since being brought here. She won't even speak to me. All she does is lay there and watch TV." Deborah clarified. "Every so often she'll start to cry, then she'll stop for a few hours, and it'll start right back up all over again."

Trying not to appear rude, Linus redirected his pitiful eyes away from Gloria and pointed them up at the television.

Linus sniggered before saying, "Nothing like a game of basketball to liven things up."

"That's the funny thing about it, she doesn't even like sports. I just got tired of changing channels, so I just left it there. I honestly don't think she even knows it's on. I figure whatever she went through in that man's house must've been pretty damn scary. I'd like to thank you, Detective, for saving her life."

"Don't thank me, something else got to the fella first."

"Yeah, it's all over the news. Do you think anyone can catch it?"

"We're prepping a task force as we speak. Hopefully we can find it before it strikes again."

"I still can't believe that it killed that family. Four little girls...all dead," Deborah gasped. "How do you cope with all of that, Mr. Bruin?"

Linus breathed in and modestly answered, "You try not to carry it home with you. Believe me, it only makes matters even worse."

"I'll admit that you're the first officer that's stopped by here just to pay a social visit. All of the other guys that show up just want to ask questions."

"Let's just say that...I just happen to know someone else in a similar situation."

"Someone close to you," Deborah questioned with deep concern.

"You could say that." Linus meekly responded as if he were too ashamed to answer.

"It's just hard to believe that there are people out there that are that sick. A car dealer of all things," Deborah cringed. "I remember watching those commercials with him and his son. His son was kind of cute, too."

Amused, Linus quaintly chuckled and switched his attention back to Gloria whose facial features hadn't changed in the slightest bit. Her entire body was as immobile as cement.

"Funny thing is, as many days as he missed at his own dealership, not even his co-workers noticed anything suspicious. You get rid of one monster and out pops another." Deborah flinched.

"That seems to be the running theme down at the station." Linus smirked.

Linus watched as Deborah began shaking her head in dismay before he glanced down at Gloria who had managed to move her bed covers enough to where a bible could be seen securely gripped in her right hand.

"Isn't that cute?" Deborah unusually smiled.

Linus looked over at Deborah and then down again at Gloria with a baffled glare on his face, as if to say he was lost on her question.

"My sister holding a bible, of all things," Deborah discreetly motioned to Gloria's hand.

It took a few seconds, but the detective eventually gathered the gist of just what Deborah was referring to.

"Usually, she would be a chatterbox; our parents had to tell her to shut up at least a million times when she was little. Now...now it's just haunting to see her so...quiet." Deborah frowned. "I honestly don't think she'll ever live this ordeal down."

Linus gazed upon Gloria's pathetic body; it was like studying an old woman who was waiting to die. He tried ever so gallantly to read her thoughts. He wanted to take her by the hand and hold her in his arms.

Feeling as if she could sense him staring at her, Linus turned his head away from Gloria and focused upon the television to see *Mr. Whipple* advertise *Charmin* toilet paper. Once the commercial vanished, the nightly newsbreak brusquely flashed across the screen. The young male anchor reported on the weather forecast which called for more snow flurries for the evening. The current score between *The New York Knicks* and *The Philadelphia Seventy-Sixers* game, and the day's news updates, which of course consisted of the ongoing investigation involving the murders from two nights earlier.

Gloria laid in her bed, stroking her bible's leather bound cover up and down as her energetic photo shined on the screen. Leroy Cummins' image appeared next, dressed to the nines in an all-black suit and smiling while standing beside a brand new white 1977 *Chevrolet Chevette.*

After Cummins' picture disappeared from sight, Isaac's happy, normal image came across the screen in a year old photo. Without any warning whatsoever, Gloria's eyes began to water up. Pitiful whimpers started to escape from behind her quivering lips.

"I can't tell you how tired I am already of them showing those little girls bodies being carried out of that house." Deborah griped before spinning around to see Gloria writhing about in bed crying. "Gloria, honey, what's the matter?" She frantically asked while trying to console her sister.

Linus stared down at the horrified young lady and then back up at the TV to see just what had spooked her from out of nowhere. As Isaac's face exited the screen, he glanced back at Gloria, and then again at the television. The man had to take at least five more twists and turns of the neck just to gather all of his thoughts at once.

"Can somebody help us in here?" Deborah said out loud, trying with all her might to restrain Gloria who was fighting to escape the safe confines of her bed.

Linus, on the other hand, just slowly began to back away before three nurses rushed into the room and aided Deborah in her mission to soothe Gloria.

The very instant the man found himself outside in the hallway he turned to his left and began down the floor until he came face to face with a phone booth.

The man stepped inside the booth and shut the glass door. Gloria could still be heard wailing clear out into the hallway. Linus reached into his pocket to secure a quarter before inserting it into the proper slot. His shifty contemplations were beginning to weigh him down to the point where his own hands couldn't even hold on to the phone.

Seven numbers were dialed. A four second ring sounded before a voice spoke up. *"This is Detective Fitzpatrick."*

"This is Linus. Pop quiz."

"Shoot."

"Call it a hunch, but why would a person be more afraid of a so called fellow victim, than the person who victimized her?"

There was a long pause which was followed by a long sigh. *"You got me, partner."*

"It's got me, too. I'm down here at *Saint Titus* visiting the Cohen girl. She was watching TV when the news came on. She sees a picture of Cummins, no response. Then, she sees a picture of the Mercer fellow, the kid goes insane. Whaddya make of that?"

"You don't think that Mercer could somehow be involved in all this, do you?"

"It's hard to tell." Linus exhaled. "I mean, the guy has yet to come downtown and give a statement. He meets up with some mystery woman at a diner, hops a ride with a kidnapper, and then somehow makes it home and doesn't remember anything."

"Nothing about this is adding up."

"I tell you this, though, whatever is going on, it's traumatic

234

enough to have a Jewish woman hold on to a Holy Bible like an Arab to a barrel of oil."

"Something tells me that we'd better get our boy down here, post haste." Fitzpatrick exclaimed, sounding as though he was smiling over the phone.

"Agreed, assuming he hasn't skipped town yet. I think I still have his fiancé's address. I'll head over and see if he's in."

"Oh, before you go, I forgot to tell you that I left my piece inside the car."

"Alan," Linus rolled his eyes while grinning, "why do you always forget to check in your weapons before your shift ends? The captain will skin you alive."

"That takes forever." Fitzpatrick groaned. *"Peggy would kill me first if I showed up late for dinner again."*

Linus hopelessly exhaled and said, "I'll check it in after I'm through with Mercer. But you owe me one."

"Alright, buddy, thanks, and good luck."

"Yep," Linus replied before hanging up the phone.

For a moment or two Linus sat inside the booth motionless, he then reached into his back pocket and pulled out a *Kodak* picture of his youngest daughter.

Her happy, carefree face caused Linus to crack an appealing, yet brief smile before it eventually turned into a hostile frown. At the very end of his frown he saw only his child being violated by some pervert, and him, behind his desk, working as usual.

With a twinge of rage inside, Linus got up, slid open the doors and began marching down the hallway towards the elevator. As he carried along, standing in front of the nurse's station was a blind white man and his Rottweiler dog that was attached to the man's hand.

Linus tried his best to ignore the animal; after all, it was only a simple seeing-eye dog. But no matter what, the detective just couldn't seem to go past the beast without handing it a salty stare. The dog returned the gesture, except its gaze was more sorrowful, almost appearing as if it was sad to see the man leave.

Linus wanted to stop, but he kept on right up until he came face to face with the elevator. Once he stepped inside, the man pressed the first floor button.

The doors began to close, while both man and dog continued to gawk at each other until there was nothing more to look upon.

CHAPTER 31

MUCH LIKE A FORESEEN tragedy that no one had the power to prevent, evening fell hard and cruel upon *Cypress*. The severe, five degree winter wind lashed through just about every living soul like the steel tip of a slave drivers whip.

With only a few lampposts that shined their dim, orange hue down onto the ground, Isaac stumbled his way through the alley, making only frequent stops to vomit into any trash can that he could rush to first. He was sleepy, hungry, thirsty and angry all at once, and judging by his wide open coat, the oppressive cold was apparently the last thing on his haywire brain.

Inside his body raged a hellacious war of good vs. evil; one man's divine struggle to fight off the demonic presence that dwelt within; an ongoing battle against the dark force that longed to inflict limitless devastation.

Back and forth his regrets wandered: Karyn had a sad story of being lonely in a new country, while Lynnette was always on his back for working at *Larry's Garage*. Karyn hung on to his every word, while Lynnette went on and on about how Isaiah needed new clothes. He screwed Karyn, but made love to Lynnette.

With each and every maddening ramble, Isaac found

himself wanting to just end it all right there in the alley, beside all the other garbage.

"You look like you're lost, friend." A medium-sized man with a shabby looking German shepherd by his side warmly stated from behind Isaac.

Surprised, Isaac spun around and tried to see into the man's face, but not only was it dark outside, but the dirty looking individual was wearing a filthy hood that was concealing his facial features. All Isaac could make out was the smoke that would exit the man's mouth whenever he spoke.

"Get the fuck outta here, man." Isaac slurred, trying not to fall against the trash cans that he was standing in front of.

"I apologize for troubling you, sir." The man's kindly, raspy voice continued on. "It just seemed like you were ailing."

"Man, I said get outta here!" Isaac barked back. "I ain't feelin' good!"

The ragtag man only remained in place. The chain in which he was holding his dog was rusted beyond recognition and looked as though it were ready to snap in half at any moment.

"Are you sure you want me to go, sir?"

Frustrated, Isaac began to advance towards the man, only to have the dog growl the instant the young man's feet moved.

Just then, two red eyes appeared from inside the man's dirty hood. Startled, Isaac staggered backwards into the garbage cans and held his hands up in a helpless defense from the man's sudden awful appearance.

The filthy one looked up into the pinkish sky as light flurries began to rain down. "Look at you, boy." He said in a more malevolent, hissing voice. "Sniveling like a mere rodent. You have a job to do."

Isaac's body was wracked in pain, but not to the point where he couldn't get up and run away. Immediately, he got to his feet and started for the opposite direction.

"Don't you dare move." The ragged hobo warned, pointing his trusty dog at the young man.

Out of fear Isaac ceased every movement in his body before turning and shuddering at the sight of the two evil eyes that stared him down like a feast.

"I...I gotta go." Isaac whimpered while violently shaking in place.

"I have waited for this moment for quite a while, and so far, you have not disappointed me. Now, I want that bitch and her child dead."

"Who," Isaac asked with a whine.

"Do not trifle with me, boy." The man impatiently remarked. "You know you want to kill her."

"No I don't, man." Isaac stammered.

"Don't you remember when you thought that Isaiah wasn't yours? You believed it to be Larry's at first. Then...then you changed your mind and accepted the bastard seed as your own."

"He is mine!" Isaac furiously stomped on the snowy pavement.

"You killed those girls; those sweet little bitches. Now, go on and kill that black trash and her child. You don't want her to get away with that, do you? Get away with having another man's baby? Go on, it's not like anyone could pin it on you. Just like the other night."

As if he were being dragged down, Isaac dropped to his knees in agony and moaned all over the ground. He beat his fists into the snow while gritting his teeth.

"Get away from me! Who are you anyways?"

"I am Unknown to you, but every man, woman, boy and girl comes to know me eventually."

"I didn't mean to do any of this!"

The insidious individual chuckled and said, "Your mother cried the day she went to the hospital. She cried for you, boy.

But you were busy running the streets. How does that make you feel?"

Isaac looked up into the sky and held out his hands to the heavens, pleading for mercy to fall upon him.

"Either you kill that bitch, or I will." The man lurched towards Isaac.

"I can't kill her! I fucking love her!"

The dirty man reached out with a clawed right hand, lifted Isaac's face to his and asked, "Did you love her when you were inside another woman?"

Enraged, Isaac snatched his face away from the man's claw before spitting at his face. The dog stared up at its master with the most bewildered look on its face.

"I am not your enemy, child." The man reassured Isaac before taking his claw and using it to scratch Isaac's right hand. "Kill her, or I will, boy."

Isaac grabbed his hand and held it to alleviate the pain. When he looked back up, he discovered that both man and dog were gone.

"I am Unknown to you, child." Isaac heard the man's ominous voice echo softly in the air around him.

Blood incessantly dripped down from his hand and onto the ground as Isaac got to his feet. He then looked around the alley to see nothing but a stray cat passing by. Right behind him was Lynnette's house. Unbeknownst to him, he had already arrived there just moments before the ghastly fiend appeared from out of nowhere.

He leaned up against two trash cans and took notice of the kitchen light which was shining brightly into the backyard; it let him know that Lynnette hadn't gone to bed yet for the evening.

As both wrong and ugly as it felt, Isaac couldn't shake the aching stir of how blood tasted. He realized that it wasn't him that longed for the substance, which was exactly why it turned his stomach each and every time the raw taste belched up into his throat.

Feeling a sense of impatient urgency, Isaac rapidly marched through the backyard and onto the steps that led to the house.

Before his hand could reach the doorknob, he stood and watched as the supposed broken lock on the backdoor unloosened itself.

Lynnette searched all over the bedroom. When she was done skulking about in there, she hysterically scampered into the living room where the television was playing the opening theme to *The Six Million Dollar Man*. But no matter how much and hard she kept looking, she couldn't locate the source of the little screaming girls that was apparently coming from within the small house she and her son were inside of.

The sounds surrounded Lynnette to the point where all she could do was stand in the middle of the living room floor and spin around like a dog chasing after its own tail. It was such madness that the young lady began to cry, believing that she was losing her mind.

Just as soon as she was about to head back into the bathroom along with Isaiah, Lynnette began hearing something rattle from within the kitchen.

She quickly pulled out the loaded revolver from her pants pocket and skittishly headed for the kitchen with the weapon pointed ahead of her. However, before she could even clear the kitchen's threshold, the backdoor swung open revealing Isaac on the other end.

"Isaac!" Lynnette abruptly screamed. "How did you get that door open?"

At first, Isaac had no words to express. He just shut the door behind him and bashfully frowned. "Uh...I just came by to see you and Isaiah."

"Isaac, how were you able to get that damn door open?" Lynnette continued to question while gripping her gun as tight as she could in her right hand.

Rather than answer her, Isaac boldly stepped past Lynnette on his way into the living room. Lynnette followed the man until she came face to face with him directly in front of the television.

"Isaac, you need to go!"

"Where's Isaiah at?" He asked bug-eyed.

"He's in the tub." Lynnette's heart skipped a beat. "I'm giving him a bath."

Isaac stood for a few moments before looking down the dimly lit hallway that led to the bathroom.

"Uh...I gotta go away for a while."

Lynnette's entire body began to quiver at that instant. All of the sudden, the only thing that she could see in front of her were her three sisters laughing hysterically at her.

"Go away, huh?" The young woman stammered, trying not to appear upset by the news. "And just where are you going to?"

"Someone told me to stay away from people, and that person was right. I got no business being around anyone right now, at least not until I get myself straight."

Lynnette rubbed her throbbing forehead and closed her eyes. "Get what straight, Isaac? What the fuck are you talking about?"

"I'm talking about no one will listen to what I have to say, and all that does is make things worse."

"Isaac, I've been trying to listen to you for the past few months, and all you do is just push me away!" She screamed in frustration. "What the fuck is the matter with you? And don't stand there and tell me that it's too hard to explain!"

"I can't even explain it to myself." Isaac shrugged.

Lynnette stared at Isaac before saying, "I bet you got

hooked onto some of Larry's shit, didn't you? You've done gone and got all fucked up on that heroin, and now you're all strung out!"

Isaac slipped his hands into his coat pockets and started to pace the floor until he eventually stopped at the mantle. He stood and fondly gazed upon a *Polaroid* picture of Isaiah as a newborn.

With his head still pointed at the child's picture, Isaac explained, "I got something inside of me, and it doesn't have anything to do with drugs." His voice began to break. "I thought my father could fix it, but all he could do was spit bible verses at me."

"What is this, Isaac?" Lynnette wearily moaned as if she were completely drained of energy. "What is going on? I mean, you're losing your mind. I'm hearing these little girls screaming all over the house like the place is haunted or something. Why now are things falling apart, dammit?" She yelled.

Isaac turned back to Lynnette with tears of his own streaming down his face. "I'm so sorry, baby girl!" He wailed out loud. "I never meant to hurt you!"

Lynnette dropped her gun to her side while tears fell from her tired face. "What were you doing with Isaiah this morning, Isaac?" Her voice faltered.

"Nothing that you think I was doing." He wiped his eyes. "It's not about that."

"What is it about then?" Lynnette stomped her foot on the floor. "Because when I walk into my house and see my man holding our son, completely naked in the middle of the floor, then it's about something, and I want answers!"

With his arms wide open, Isaac advanced towards Lynnette saying, "Lynn, you gotta listen to me!"

Lynnette raised her firearm and pointed it straight at Isaac's mortified face. It stunned even her to think that she could do such a heinous thing as point a deadly weapon at the only man she ever loved, or that even the notion of pulling the trigger would even enter her mind to begin with, but she was terrified of Isaac, more so at that moment than months earlier.

Immediately, the tears that Isaac was allowing to flow from his eyes dried up. He stood perfectly still in front of the playing television and calmly uttered, "You know what I told you a long time ago when I bought that thing for you. Never hesitate. When you get the chance, you pull the trigger...and never look back."

Lynnette covered her mouth with her left hand as she began to sob uncontrollably. Unable to hold the weapon any longer, she dropped the gun to the floor.

"I don't understand why you're doing this to me, Isaac!" She caught her breath. "All I ever wanted was for you to love me! And now, you're leaving us?" She relentlessly cried into her sweaty palms.

Lynnette removed her hands from her face and looked up to notice blood oozing from Isaac's right hand. Wiping her face dry, she stepped forward and asked, "Why...why is your hand bleeding, Isaac? What did you do to yourself?"

But Isaac wouldn't respond. Instead, he dropped his head to where Lynnette could not see his face.

"Isaac, answer me!" She screamed into Isaac's ear while placing her thumb over the open gushing wound. "How did you do this? Don't tell me that you've been bleeding like this all the way over here!"

Still, Isaac would not react. The man just stood with his head pointed to the carpet. Lynnette was in such a distressful state that paying attention to one thing at a time was virtually impossible. Isaac's hands, along with the rest of his body began to tremble all of the sudden. Out of the corner of her eye Lynnette could see the bathroom light flicker off and on as the baby began to whine; all the while the television was playing a commercial for *Palmolive* soap.

"You've lost a lot of blood, Isaac!" Lynnette anxiously pleaded while trying to remember just where she placed the bandages within the house. "Wait here while I go get—

But before she could finish her sentence or even take one step, Isaac abruptly raised his head and shined a pair of white eyes at her while hissing like a snake.

Shocked at the sight, the young woman jumped back, nearly falling to the floor in the process. That was when Isaac began to gnaw away at his own right hand with the sharp fangs that were steadily growing from out of his growling mouth.

Lynnette was horrified, so much so that she couldn't even budge while watching Isaac rip and tear at his own flesh right down to the bone. At the blink of an eye the woman reached down and snatched up the gun that was lying on the floor.

"Isaac!" She desperately yelled with all her might while pointing the weapon at his head.

But Isaac was gone; all that remained was a beastly existence within the home, a former lover. Lynnette stood and watched in stunned horror as Isaac stopped biting away at his hand before collapsing to his knees in a heap. His clothes began to shred right off of his body as his muscles expanded.

"llik eht tnuc!" *(Kill the cunt)* He snarled before thick, black fur started to sprout from out of his face.

Without waiting a second more, Lynnette pulled the trigger and fired three shots into Isaac's head, exposing parts of flesh that dropped to the floor. But it was those same loud, painful shots that only seemed to anger the creature all the more as its growling grew more animalistic. Soon, bones started to stretch, snap and break, forming both claws and hind legs in the process.

With her gun in hand, Lynnette raced like a madwoman straight for the bathroom. But before she could even reach the door, it suddenly slammed right in her face. The lights in the hallway flickered off and on while the shrieks of the little girls that she had been hearing for hours reverberated throughout the house, louder in its intensity.

Lynnette's crying eyes couldn't contain or believe all that was taking place, and as frightening as it was to hear a God awful brute in the living room, she was even more petrified that she was completely closed off from her child.

With every fiber of energy in her shaking body, Lynnette pushed, kicked and hollered at the bathroom door while watching the hallway lights continue to flash on and off.

From the bathroom door and back to the edge of the living room she ran to watch the growing beast stretch out a snout. That was all the motivation Lynnette required to sprint back to the bathroom door and scream at the top of her lungs, "God, please fucking help me!"

She could hear Isaiah on the other side of the door yell for his mommy, while behind her, what resembled a stampeding buffalo trampling across the floor, could be heard rounding the corner that led to the hallway.

Lynnette raised her gun, pointed it at the doorknob and fired. She used her right leg to kick open the door. She could feel the bones in her foot break, but that was perfectly meaningless at that point. Lynnette opened the door and slammed it shut behind her before snatching a naked Isaiah from out of the half empty tub that he was sitting in.

"Shh, baby!" Lynnette hysterically hollered before pointing her gun directly at the door.

There were no windows in the bathroom, which only meant that the young mother would have to make her final stand in the tiny room. She was determined to die before she let anything destroy her child.

To muffle the angry crying, Lynnette forced Isaiah's head into her sweat drenched blue blouse and waited for the creature to make some kind of appearance if any.

From the closed door to the flickering bulb above her head

she gawked, back and forth. It was a maddening experience to be trapped in. Her teeth chattered while her knees knocked together. She tried to stop crying, but the tears would not relent as the sweat that was saturating her face was also causing her to go blind momentarily. All Lynnette could see was Isaac's face stretch out and listen as he snarled at her like a mad dog. She wanted more than anything to die right then and there.

Then, just like that, the light stopped flashing, while the growling noises apparently ceased. Lynnette made sure to keep the baby's head stuffed into her chest while her own head bobbed up and down. The bathroom door stood still.

With her breathing erratic and out of sync, the young woman caught herself uttering a prayer, asking God to please take the beast away and allow her child to live.

Unbeknownst to her, she had popped a blood vessel in her left eye, which in turn caused blood to well up inside.

Just then, there was a bump at the door. Lynnette held what was left of her breath. Thanks to the busted lock, the door would never again close tight; instead it would only swing back and forth.

A sniffing racket could be heard on the other end. Lynnette attached to her prayer that Isaac would be there, back to normal again.

After so many gripping moments, ever so gradually, the door creaked open. The amber eyes of the beast appeared, along with the rest of its enormous, hairy body. Lynnette screamed as she fired two more shots at the thing before it stood to its feet and hovered over both her and Isaiah like a towering giant.

With only its right paw, the beast swiped the gun from out of the woman's hand, along with her right index finger which ended up landing in the sink behind her. Lynnette shrieked out in brutal agony before accidentally dropping the child to the floor.

With its left paw, the beast tossed Lynnette into the medicine cabinet, breaking the mirror and sending every item inside crashing to the floor.

Like something from out of a jungle, the beast growled and roared before picking Lynnette up and tossing her to the other end of the bathroom as though she were a doll baby.

She wanted to scream for help, but her throat was completely dry as she crawled about on the floor, trying with all her remaining might to reach Isaiah who himself was crawling towards his mother, crying a storm.

The beast then knelt down on all fours and used only its right paw to send Lynnette hurtling into the wall.

By then, her entire body was a bloody wreck. Her right eye was swollen shut and her right arm was broken, and yet, rather than wallow in the anguish of her own insufferable pain, she remained obstante in retrieving her screaming child.

The beast, noticing that the woman was still alive, simply snatched her up by her neck, opened wide its slobbering jaws and proceeded to devour her. Lynnette used her feeble hands to grab a hold of the thing's hairy snout long enough to where she could hopefully buy Isaiah some more time.

The beast, however, only shook her hands loose and roared with all its might while using its left paw to crack a hole in the floor.

But within the midst of the enormous hell that she was engulfed inside, Lynnette could sense something very odd. It was a beast that in all honesty could have wiped her out within the first few seconds of its rampage, but instead, it was toying with her. She crawled backwards until her backside met up with the tub. From where she was positioned, she could see tiny blood droplets trickle down from out of the beast's strange eyes and onto its snout.

She wanted to move, but just sitting on the floor watching such an atrocity before her only caused her soul to stiffen.

The beast drew close to Lynnette. It appeared aggravated, possibly by the baby's incessant crying. The thing grabbed Lynnette's limp body and carelessly threw it into the tub before turning around to face Isaiah.

Almost immediately, the boy stopped crying as he held up his tiny hands in defense.

Linus pulled his squad car up in front of Lynnette's house and got out. As the man nonchalantly approached the porch, right next door he took notice of an elderly black man and woman who were standing at their doorway, fearfully ogling the house that he himself was nearing.

Linus thought nothing of it, just nosey neighbors doing what they apparently do best, that is until he heard the beast's roar echo straight past the closed door.

Without giving much thought or consideration, Linus instantly recalled the Cummins' tape recording.

"Call the police!" Linus breathlessly yelled at the neighbors while reaching into his holster to pull out his piece. "There's a unit in the vicinity!"

But before he could even touch the butt of his gun, Linus heard yet another unearthly growl shoot out into the night. The man right away ran back to the car, unlocked the trunk and snatched out Fitzpatrick's twelve gage shotgun before taking off for the house.

"Isaac...stop!" Linus heard Lynnette feebly shout.

The detective kicked in the front door, and like a bolt of lightning rounded the corner to where the commotion was emanating.

The very second he reached the bathroom Linus saw the beast reach out for the Isaiah. Without a single hint of reluctance, the man pulled the trigger. The loud shot ricocheted off the walls of the bathroom like an explosion. The beast, however, only stood back up to its feet, and with one swift blow, knocked Linus to the side.

Linus could feel his left arm snap like a twig, but it wasn't painful enough for him to relinquish his own attack and pull the trigger once again while marveling at the beast's incredible size.

A third heavy slug ripped right through the creature's thick stomach before sending it crashing to its knees. A fourth round through its chest caused the brute to wail out a pitiful howl that resembled an ailing wolf rather than an unstoppable killing machine.

The thing laid on the floor, bleeding like a slaughtered pig and shaking violently. Horrified at what he was seeing, Linus managed to scoot himself from one end of the bathroom to the other, all the while keeping his distance from the beast and picking up Isaiah from off the floor.

Linus then caught sight of Lynnette's badly wounded body lying motionless in the tub. Her clothes were torn to shreds and she was coughing up blood onto her own face. Linus lunged over and anxiously tried to revive her while keeping a vigilant and frightened eye on the steadily dying beast behind him.

"Honey...honey, can you hear me?" Linus hysterically wept as his hands uncontrollably trembled.

"Isaac." Lynnette faintly whispered.

"Where's Isaac?" Linus looked from side to side. "Is he still in the house?"

But Lynnette could no longer answer, she could barely even move at that point. Linus held her hands in his while keeping his eyes tuned to the beast on the floor that was suddenly taking on a brand new form right before his very eyes.

"Just hold on, honey, the police are on their way." The man stammered.

The sounds of sirens could be heard blaring in the distant

background, but something was beginning to take shape within the bathroom. Fur, claws, muscles and even wolf-like facial features were slowly vanishing.

Every bone inside of Linus' body stood perfectly immobile. The beast's body quaked with such an aggressive fervor that one would believe that it was in the midst of a seizure.

It's so called growls were becoming more and more recognizable, like a person squirming in pain.

Its snout was deflating back to a nose. Bones and joints could be heard snapping back into place until what looked like clear liquid jostled from out of its mouth. Isaac's face, along with his eyes, had all reverted back to normal. There was no visible sign of swelling to be seen; it was as though the young man had never been cursed at all.

Soon, the shaking ceased. Isaac Mercer's bullet riddled body laid on the blood drenched bathroom floor. His eyes remained open until the right side of his face amazingly began to melt as though it were hot clay.

The entire bathroom was completely quiet and still as Linus, Lynnette and Isaiah all gazed upon the dead man in jolted silence. Linus and Lynnette's jaws hung wide open. Their words, if there were any to utter, were snatched right out of their throats.

From out of the corner of his eye, Linus could see two young officers rush into the bathroom with guns drawn. Both men carefully ventured into the bathroom looking as if they had just crossed another dimension.

"Holy Jesus," one of the officers choked at the sight of the naked man lying on the floor.

Slowly approaching Linus, the other officer steadily asked, "Detective Bruin, is that you?"

But Linus could say absolutely nothing. He held both Lynnette and Isaiah in his strong, right arm and would not let go.

"I'm...I'm gonna go call the meds." One officer stuttered before gladly exiting the bathroom.

Smoke from both Linus' shotgun and Isaac's mutilated body billowed into the air while the other officer knelt down to examine the dead man closer.

Suddenly, Mr. Mercer, from out of nowhere, stumbled into the bathroom, huffing and puffing as though he had been running a grueling marathon.

"Sir, I'm gonna ask that you step outside and—

But before the officer could get another word out, his hand was shoved aside by Mercer's sturdy shoulder. Then, with a pitiable expression upon his face, the man collapsed to his knees, took his son's malformed face into his hands and gently kissed him on the forehead.

Linus watched, and that was the extent of his actions for the time being. The man saw something that night.

The snow fell peacefully upon *Cypress* that cold, harsh evening.

CHAPTER 32

"GOOD MORNING. I'M BRAD *Wayne for Action Seven News. I am here on this cold, gloomy morning in front of 909 West Seventh Blvd, where a gruesome murder took place just last evening between eight o clock and eight-thirty. Twenty year old Isaac Mercer was gunned down in this house behind me after what one detective deemed a domestic violence dispute. Now, details are still sketchy at this hour. Apparently, authorities are keeping very tight-lipped on the situation, but I am here with a neighbor. Your name is, ma'am?"*

"My name is Mrs. Selma Godfrey."

"Okay, Mrs. Godfrey, are you able to tell our viewing audience at home just what exactly took place here last night? What was it you heard?"

"Well, at first, me and my husband saw Lynnette's boyfriend run into the house from the alley. He was out there talking to some man. I think they were out there foolin' around; up to no good. Then we heard them arguing. Next thing you know, we hear some kind of animal. Poor ole' Lynnette starts screaming like she's being killed. That's when some policeman ran up in there and shot the thing."

"Okay, ma'am, when you say policeman, are you referring to Detective Linus Bruin"

"I reckon that was his name."

"Now, Mrs. Godfrey, you mentioned that Detective Bruin shot

this animal that both you and your husband supposedly heard, is that right?"

"Yes it is."

"Did you see anyone carry the alleged animal out of the house, ma'am?"

"Well...no, but I sure heard something terrible in there. It sounded like a mad dog or something like that."

"Thank you, Mrs. Godfrey. As you can see there are various, wild stories from multiple sources. Once again, police are informing us that a domestic violence dispute inside is what led to Mercer's death. Right now as we speak, we are receiving information about both Isaac Mercer, as well as a very interesting bio on Detective Linus Bruin. It seems that Mercer had spent two and a half months at the Ashlandview Psychiatric Facility just north of here. We tried to contact Mercer's presiding physician, but he was unavailable for comments. From what we are receiving from Ashlandview, Mercer suffered from chronic blackouts which led to bouts of amnesia and paranoia. Now, if the name Isaac Mercer sounds familiar, that's because just three days earlier he was abducted by the late B.O.D. kidnapper, but managed to elude his captor. Detective Bruin was also involved in the case. From what we are still gathering, Detective Bruin himself spent four months in and out of a state psychiatric community, due to numerous mental breakdowns and domestic abuse."

"This is bull...t, man! How can a cop kill somebody for just domestic abuse? That cat just ran up in there and shot that man right in his own house for no reason whatsoever! Ain't nothin' changed a damn bit! Police are all pigs and they're all out to kill us blacks! Just one more dead n...a as far as they're concerned! And now they're runnin' up in people's homes and killing us now! None of us are safe!"

"Okay, um, we apologize for that disturbance, ladies and gentlemen. Anything can happen when you're doing live TV. As you can see behind me, tensions in this community are at an all-time high. Now, investigators are probing into this case as we speak, wondering just what cause of action, if any, led to Detective Bruin gunning down

Mercer. Besides a revolver that was owned by Ms. Glover, there was no other weapon in the house. As for this alleged animal that was heard inside the home, police were not able to ascertain such a detail, or any kind of forced entry on the part of Mercer for that matter."

"I hate the fuzz, man! I hate all pigs!"

"Once more, we apologize for the disturbance, ladies and gentlemen. Just to recap, twenty year old Isaac Mercer was shot dead last night here on West Seventh Blvd by Detective Linus Bruin. Mercer is survived by his fiancée, Lynnette Glover, their two year old son and Mercer's father. Stay tuned to Channel Seven for more late breaking news and reports as this bizarre and tragic story unfolds. I'm Brad Wayne."

CHAPTER 33

CAPTAIN BRICKMAN'S DISPOSITION WAS both low key and solemn as he stacked a series of papers all in a row while sitting quietly at his desk. From left to right, reports of the incident from the night before, along with a prostitution ring that was busted up around three a.m. were all gathered into his stiff hands and neatly placed to the side.

Staying busy was never a challenge for the besieged man; it was a natural way of life. But that morning lay heavy and hard upon him, like carrying a three hundred pound man on top of his shoulders for hours.

Purposely, he had managed to keep away from Linus so far that morning, even though seven o' clock hadn't even arrived yet. There was so much he wanted to say to his colleague and friend, but it wasn't the right time, not with the investigation underway. Instead, he chose to keep to himself, secluded to the safe confines of his office.

Every so often he would answer his phone to take angry complaints from those who found wrong with the police department, or he would come out to ask for another cup of coffee from one of the female officers, but all in all, the unobtrusive man remained stationery and out of the way.

A sudden knock at the door startled the captain to where he lost complete track of the filing detail that he was right in the middle of. Exasperated, he dropped the papers that were in his hands and looked up to see a silhouette stand on the other end of the stained glass door.

"Come in." He gently grimaced.

From behind the door appeared Fitzpatrick, who himself looked as if he hadn't slept a wink in two nights.

"Uh, sir, Mr. Mercer is here." Alan unenthusiastically stated.

Without saying a word, the captain groaned, gathered his papers and raised himself up and out of his creaky old wooden chair.

The man sailed past Alan on his way out of his office and through the main work area where phones were ringing off the hook every other second and officers were handing him the proverbial stare downs.

"He's downstairs in interrogation." Alan said while following right in behind Brickman.

Without stopping, Brickman replied, "I'm fully aware of where the gentleman is, Detective."

Both men carried on down the steps that led to the interrogation room. The captain was already an over boiling pot of unhinged nerves, having someone biting at his heels, at that time in the morning no less, only infused the man with even more ire.

Once they reached the correct floor Alan hurriedly and boldly stepped in front of Brickman and remarked, "Sir, any word on—

"Don't start with me, Fitz." The captain cantankerously ordered.

"Captain, he's up there with O'Dea." Alan pressed on. "You know just as well as I do that guy is gonna grill him like a criminal."

"What do you want me to do?" Brickman shrugged.

"Run upstairs, grab Linus and jump out the window with the man?"

"No...but if we could just get the D.A. on the phone, then—

"Look, I know O'Dea is a fucking prick of a guy. I also know that just a few doors down I have to explain to a father why his son was shot in cold blood last night."

Alan glanced behind him before slipping his hands inside his pants pockets and sighing, "You should see this Mercer fellow. He looks like he's about to go nuts at any moment. Officer Washington is right around the corner if you need any assistance."

The captain stared strangely back at Fitzpatrick as though he had lost his mental faculties before saying in a grunt, "Look, I've been up since nine last night. I'm high on *Sanka,* nicotine and cold medicine. Now, if I were you I wouldn't be concerned about my well-being as you are, because the question of why you left your piece in the trunk of that cruiser is gonna come up before the day is done, Detective. So what I suggest you do is head back upstairs, grab a cup of coffee and calm the fuck down. The day is just starting."

And with that the captain sidestepped Alan on his way past the interrogation room and directly to a tall, black officer who was standing against the wall like an on duty soldier.

The captain stopped, looked up at the officer and simply said, "Washington, we need you outside on crowd control."

Without blinking, the officer looked down at the captain and respectfully replied, "Yes, sir."

The captain stood and watched as the towering officer marched down the empty hallway before turning around and stepping just ten feet back to the interrogation room.

With an overwhelming sense of trepidation, the captain approached the door and paused. Through the blurry glass he could see Mercer's large profile seated at the table. Despite the fact that the early morning was already chock full of unbridled controversy and pain stricken calamity, Brickman had a pre-planned statement stored away in the furthest recesses of his brain, ready to send out at a moment's notice.

His sweaty right hand twisted the cold doorknob, beyond the door sat Mr. Mercer with his hands folded and his eyes closed to the world. The second Brickman shut the door behind him Mercer opened his red, sullen eyes and pointed them directly down at the brown table before him.

The captain could hear the protesters outside the window behind Mercer yell and chant for justice and an end to police brutality. They had been out there for the past two hours, and their incessant pleas were increasing as the morning tarried on.

"Uh, Mr. Mercer, my name is Captain Roy Brickman. Good morning." Brickman modestly broadcasted before sitting himself down on the other side of the table from Mercer.

Mercer's brooding face never parted from the table. It almost appeared as if he were either far away in another world or just studying the wood grain beneath his fingers.

"Sir, I, uh…I don't quite know what to say at this point." Brickman discreetly stammered as though he were trying to cough. "At this very moment, the department is conducting an extensive investigation into Detective Bruin's actions from last night. All we know for now is that Detective Bruin made his way over to see your son and bring him here for more questioning. And then, according to Bruin, everything after that went…black."

The more Brickman spoke the more he had hoped that Mercer would at least make eye to eye contact with him. But no matter how diligently the captain explained the situation, Mercer's face remained perfectly reserved.

"As of now, Detective Bruin is indefinitely suspended, without pay. Now, Mr. Mercer, we need to know—

At that very instant, a slight grunt cooed from out of

Mercer's throat before he slowly uttered, "Captain, can you imagine what it's like to look down upon your son and see his entire body opened up with bullets?" The man remarked without taking his eyes off the table still.

Brickman lunged forward a few inches in order to gain a more precise detail of the man's face and speech that he wanted so much to come to life.

"Something was wrong with my boy." Mercer continued on. "The young man I saw last night wasn't mine. The devil got to him, and I couldn't see it. The good Lord tried to warn me. He tried to open my eyes, but I was too blind. Rather than turning him over to Jesus, I sent my own son to a psychiatrist. A witch doctor," he bitterly snarled.

"Mr. Mercer, you say that you saw Isaac last night before he went over to his fiancée's house. What sort of condition was he in?"

"He wasn't well." Mercer sulked. "I've lived a bad life, Captain. I hurt a lot of people before God saved me. I figure this is Satan's way of getting back at me."

Captain Brickman leaned back in his chair while continually observing the misfortunate individual that sat across from him. The pre-planned words that he had stored away had all but been deleted; there was absolutely nothing else in the world that he could have said at that point that would have made any coherent sense to the father.

There were so many more questions that he wanted to ask the man pertaining to Isaac. Inquiries into the young man's personal life that only he could possibly be able to answer, but Mercer's face told the grim story of a man that was standing patiently at the throne of purgatory.

Just then, what resembled a whimper at first glance turned into something completely unexpected to Brickman. A compassionate smile came across Mercer's face at that second as he balled up his fists.

"Mr. Mercer, are you okay?" Brickman squared his eyes at the man.

It took a moment or two before Mercer eventually replied, "I remember when Isaac was little. That boy sure loved him some comic books. His mama didn't want for him to read them, but, every so often I would sneak one or two along his way. I knew I shouldn't have, but he was just a little guy. Little boys like those things I guess. Well, one day, I think he was about seven or eight, that little rascal tied one of his mama's red table clothes around his neck and jumped right off the back steps. He ended up landing on both knees. He cried and cried. I told him that if he kept on crying then his mother would find out that he was reading comics. Sure enough, that boy quit crying right then and there."

Brickman sat and envisioned a younger Isaac doing exactly what his father so fondly recalled him doing, leaping into the air and attempting to fly like a bird. For a very brief moment, Roy found himself smirking.

"It always seemed as though Isaac wasn't happy with who he was. He was always trying to be someone or something else. I remember, right before his mama went home to be with the Lord, she told him, 'Never change. Always stay the same good boy you are.'

The grin that was on Mercer's face suddenly vanished right before he deeply exhaled and got up from the table. From his chair he moseyed over to the window that overlooked Downtown *Cypress* and folded his hands behind his back.

From where Brickman was seated he could see nothing but clouds outside, even though Mr. Mercer could see so much more beyond what his own eyes would allow him to view.

CHAPTER 34

THERE WAS A SMALL, off to the side office that was located on the fourth floor of police headquarters. With his left arm wrapped in a sling, Detective Linus Bruin despondently sulked in his chair behind a clean and orderly desk.

The clothes that he was wearing just happened to be the same torn and bloody garments he wore from the night before. Not one detail on his entire body had been rearranged; from his unkempt hair, all the way down to his blood stained *Thom Mcan's*

His drooping face was a blank canvas from cheek to cheek. No sort of emotion whatsoever bothered to appear. Inside of him dwelt a teetering calm, like a cease fire in the midst of a hellacious battle. All night long the man had endured question after probing question, cameras flashing in his face and officers frantically rushing him to one end of the police station to the other as if he were a time bomb inside of a box.

His hands rested motionless in his lap while his face stayed poised on the desk in front of him. There was an itch on the bridge of his nose that the man didn't have the strength or will to scratch at.

A knock at the door disturbed the silence in the small office. From behind the door appeared Officer Donaldson who came in with a steaming cup of coffee. The woman quietly placed the cup down onto the desk before handing Linus a sympathetic smile.

"Thank you, officer." Inspector O'Dea delicately stated before blowing lightly on the rim of the hot mug. "That will be all for now."

The average looking man that was sitting across from Linus with his thin lips pressed tightly together was around the same age as the detective. He wanted to appear smart in his oversized, blue stripped tie and white shirt. The man's pepper-tinted hair was trimmed to perfection, with not one hint of an out of place sliver. His dubious looking white face supported a thick, grey mustache that was groomed to where a person could only see his bottom lip move up and down whenever he spoke.

O'Dea meticulously sipped on the edge of the cup before looking up at Linus and saying, "You must forgive me. I did not have the opportunity to savor my wife's delectable cooking this morning. The woman makes the best homemade sausage this side of the Ohio River. *Jimmy Dean* be dammed."

Linus sat and watched as the inspector placed his elbows on the table and folded his hands before glancing around the room and asking, "Are you cold?"

Linus only slightly shook his head from side to side. For him, and at that point, words were as hard to grasp as air in his hands.

"It's funny how thin the walls are in this building. Shows you just how old the place really is." O'Dea affectionately sighed. "My grandfather was an officer here back around the turn of the century. According to him, this place was falling apart back then, too."

Linus looked on as O'Dea turned his attention to the window to his immediate left. Both men could hear the protestors outside on the ground chant loud and clear.

"Boisterous, aren't they?" O'Dea looked back at Linus.

"Jesus, you look like you haven't slept in days, Detective," the man pointed. "Are you feeling alright? Well, that's a pretty stupid question." He flippantly grinned. "Look, I know you think I'm here to nail you to the wall, but that's not the case. I just want to know what took place last night."

All of the sudden, colors began appearing right before Linus' eyes as he sat there in his chair. It was a psychological disorder that seemed to occur at the perfect moment and in the perfect place.

"Now, you've been silent about the entire ordeal for the past few hours, Detective. Don't you think it's time to open up? I mean, you're gonna have to do a helluva lot better than domestic abuse with that mob out there, my friend." The inspector empathetically explained.

Linus batted his eyelashes in a rapid sequence before looking up at the man. He waited for O'Dea to ask even more questions.

O'Dea looked down and studied the papers that were lying in front of him. "How's your family?" He inquired with a straight face that never bothered to look Linus in the eye.

Linus sat for a moment or two before replying in a dry tone, "They're fine."

"How's Elizabeth?"

Linus contemptuously eyeballed the inspector before sternly answering, "Fine."

"That's good." O'Dea casually remarked with his eyes still staring at the papers. "I'm serious, that's very good." He adamantly reiterated. "Detective, in your statement, you mentioned that you went over to Ms. Glover's residence last evening to secure Mr. Mercer for more questioning. But what I'm curious about is, what more questions did you have for Mr. Mercer?"

Linus exhaled a long breath before muttering, "I was following up on a...hunch."

"A hunch," O'Dea spoke up. "What sort of hunch?"

"There were some loose ends that I had to wrap up, so to speak."

O'Dea studied Linus' face as if he were trying to drill into his wrinkled forehead. "Mr. Mercer, much like yourself, was spotted running from one end of town to the other yesterday. From Ms. Glover's home, to his shrink, to his father's church and eventually back to Ms. Glover's residence. What I want to know is, what kind of a hunch could you have come across?"

"I visited the Cohen girl last—

"The young lady that was kidnapped and raped by Cummins?" O'Dea hastily interrupted.

Taken off guard, Linus caught his breath and said, "Yes."

"Why were you visiting her?"

"I wanted to see how she was doing."

"How she was doing?" O'Dea frowned with his arms folded in a sanctimonious fashion. "Well, I guess we could call you a nice detective, if nothing else. But that still doesn't explain this so called hunch. What I'm curious about is why you didn't bring Mercer in two nights ago when you and Detective Fitzpatrick visited there?"

"He…he wasn't feeling well." Linus hesitated. "I decided to—

"Oh, I see, so you decided." O'Dea strongly emphasized at Linus. "So, not only are you a nice detective, but you're also the decision maker as well. That makes sense."

Linus sat and stared daggers at the inspector. The man was far from surprised at what was taking place before him; he expected every bit of O'Dea's smug treatment from the start.

"So last night you decided to pay a visit to Ms. Cohen in the hospital, to which afterwards, you decided to make your way over to Ms. Glover's residence to pick up Mercer. Now, when you arrived on the scene, what was taking place?"

Linus took his eyes away from the inspector and directed

them down at the desk. Right then, his body began to tremble all over again.

"Dammit, man!" O'Dea snapped, pounding his fists onto the table. "This is no joke, Detective!"

"I never said it was."

"Do you hear that out there? That is a medieval mob waiting for your blood to be shed! You shot a naked, weaponless, colored man with a twelve gage shotgun, a shotgun that was left in a cruiser by one Detective Fitzpatrick, whom we will be investigating next, and all you can do is just sit there and keep quiet!"

Completely unfazed by the inspector's tirade, Linus remained still and composed as though nothing were happening at all.

"What was the guy doing when you first busted your way into the house?" O'Dea anxiously inquired. "These are just some of the questions that the grand jury is going to throw your way."

Seemingly disturbed, O'Dea shot up from out of his seat and began to pace the room from front to back with his hands lodged inside his pants pockets.

"You say domestic abuse." The inspector shrugged. "Okay, maybe it was a domestic affair. It's no secret that those people can't keep a relationship together longer than a one night stand. But the guy didn't have a single weapon on him, and somehow, Ms. Glover's finger was sliced right off. Her entire body looked as though she were hit by a truck."

In vivid detail, Linus recalled holding Lynnette's wrecked and bloody body in his shivering arms. He could still smell her blood on his hands.

"There was a gun, but Mercer's fingerprints weren't found on the weapon. And yet, you decide to rampage into this house and blow this man away in a bathroom of all places. Jesus, I know you're fifty-three years old, Bruin, but do you mean to sit there and tell me that you can't overpower a naked man without shooting him dead?"

Crossing behind Linus every other second, O'Dea would stop to stare down into Linus' white hair as though he were admonishing a school boy.

"I wish we could work together on this one, Linus." The inspector rationally articulated. "I realize that you and I haven't gotten along too well over the years. I mean, we won't be exchanging Christmas cards anytime in the near future, but I've got both the D.A. and the Mayor breathing down my neck, and an entire town of colored hell-raisers wanting to burn down the city, all because you had a hunch."

O'Dea ceased his outburst momentarily while facing the caged window. It was all the better for Linus, he needed to come up for air before being waterlogged all over again.

"Did you happen to see some of the signs they got out there? One says, 'if it walks like a duck, and onks like a pig, then it's the fuzz.' The inspector sniggered, sounding tickled by the phrase. "They even managed to spell oinks wrong. Is any of this melting into that brain of yours?"

Linus clinched his entire body while listening to the man endlessly drill on and on. It was all melting inwards, just not through the proper conduits. There was no care left inside of him.

"It's been almost an entire year since your wife left you. The media found your file from when you went away. Christ, here I am trying to save not only this department's ass, but yours as well, and you just sit there." O'Dea then turned to the door and pointed, "Look out there, Linus. All those kids just waiting for one of us old farts to fall off of our perch. Hell, I've got a Mexican, or Chicano, or whatever they call themselves these days, drooling for my job. We're old men, Linus, too old to be chasing down kidnappers, rapists and murderers.

For God's sake, man, this is no way for an officer to go out, a broken down husk of flesh."

Linus suddenly raised his head back up and opened his mouth. At first, no words came out, but after seconds of silence, with a shaky voice he murmured, "I...I don't know what you want me to say."

O'Dea spun around in amazement and listened attentively at what else Linus was going to hopefully state.

"What I did...last night was, was all my fault."

The inspector stepped over, slammed his hands onto the desk and said, "It doesn't have to be all your fault, Linus. All you have to do is tell me what happened inside that house and we can go from there. What the hell makes you think I want to see an officer like yourself go down? Linus, you broke into a house and shot and killed an unarmed man. Something like this doesn't just up and go away overnight. Hell, it'll be on the *CBS Evening News* before you know it. This is all *Cronkite* needs to add yet another award to his already cluttered trophy chest. Unarmed black man shot dead in the buff, for no apparent reason other than he was beating his fiancée. Oh what a tragedy," O'Dea zealously satirized before nearing closer to Linus' face and yelling, "Help me help you!"

Linus wanted to look over at the loud inspector, he wanted to hand the same kind of treatment back to him, only worse, especially after the mention of his wife leaving him, but his stale body chose instead to remain immobile. It was as if he had lost any and all audacity to stand up for himself.

Inspector O'Dea pulled away from Linus and sipped on his warm cup of coffee. He then looked back at the window behind him before glancing down again at the detective.

"Stranger things have happened, I guess." O'Dea spoke under his breath as he loosened his tie and headed for the door. "Don't go anywhere, we still have a lot to iron out, you and I."

Linus heard the door slam behind him, he was all alone.

The man turned and gazed on at the shapes and sizes mill about in the busy office beyond the blurry glass in the door. Eventually, he would have to see all of those same shapes and sizes face to face; staying inside the room all day was improbable.

Linus sat and took a glimpse of his own blood stained fingers that he hadn't bothered to wash since before yesterday evening. The redness of his fingernails was beginning to turn a darker shade. For a second or two the man had to actually remind himself just where he was to begin with.

It took just about every ounce of energy, but Linus ultimately managed to get up from out of his warm seat and gingerly carry himself out of the room and towards his desk.

With just about every set of mournful eyes bearing down upon him, Linus began to empty the contents of his desk into a small, brown box that he had already seated underneath the desk.

Numerous pens and pads, a miniature U.S. flag and a framed picture of his daughters all found their way into the musty old box.

The detective could feel the enormous weight of every stare beam upon him. Besides the ringing of telephones, the entire room was quiet. A couple of typewriters could be heard in the background, along with the chanting protesters outside the building, beyond those annoyances, the fourth floor was a hushed tomb.

Linus could feel the tears begin to well up inside his eyes; he wanted more than anything to breakdown right there at his empty desk, but instead, he chose the restraint of pride to hold back the eventual emotion.

He swallowed his saliva and grunted while getting up from his seat. He put on his winter coat, loaded his box underneath his right armpit and without giving his co-workers a second glance he simply headed for the stairwell.

As Linus stepped down the stairs that led to the garage, his red eyes couldn't seem to tear themselves away from the grimy, discolored floor beneath his feet. He could hear perps hollering vile obscenities as he passed one floor after another; to him, they were just blurs in his head, like the buzzing of bees.

Linus took one more step, and before he knew it, he was at the final door. The man pushed open the door and right away caught sight of his own car parked just three yards ahead.

He briskly marched across the freezing cold parking lot while noticing his breath escaping with every step that he made. Linus' legs were becoming rubbery; his pace was uncoordinated. The weight of the box he was carrying was rapidly becoming heavier. His car appeared more like it was miles away rather than simple feet.

Nearly dropping his box to the ground, Linus, with one hand, feverishly reached into his pants pocket and pulled out his car keys, only to have the box and all the contents within crash to the cement.

Out of both frustration and fear, Linus kicked the box out of the way before kneeling to retrieve only his beloved frame. When he at last reached the car, he forcefully jammed the key into the lock so hard that it nearly broke in half. Just like that, he climbed in and slammed the door shut.

There alongside him inside the vehicle sat an ugly hush. It had been noiseless inside his head for the past few hours. He hadn't slept a single wink in two nights.

In his windshield Linus could see a young man shuddering and twisting about in his own pool of blood on a bathroom floor. In the rearview mirror he saw a creature seated in the backseat. Instead of being numb, Linus' body felt as though it were dipped inside a freezing cold tank of water; the sheer shock of it all repeatedly stabbed at every inch of his body.

The man couldn't even shake anymore. He was still, his hands were to the side and his eyes were adamantly pointed directly at the steering wheel in front of him. Linus' mouth hung slightly ajar, as if he were trying to speak a word. He no longer possessed any comprehension as to what day, month or year it was, all he seemed to be aware of at that point was the fact that it was daytime, and that reality was seen only through the open gate just a few feet away to his right.

All of the sudden, his eyes began to shift, from the steering wheel to the dashboard where his brand new *Peter Gabriel* eight track was lying. Ever so steadily his right hand reached over to the glove compartment. Inch by inch the tip of his fingers neared the latch until they ultimately made contact.

Without even looking, Linus reached inside and slowly pulled out a nine millimeter handgun. Just as many minutes as it took for his hands to reach the glove compartment, that was nearly as long as it took for him to pull it right back to his lap.

From his eight track, Linus' eyes progressed to the weapon that sat warm before him. By then, after only thirteen hours removed from the incident, Detective Bruin had managed to forget even the name of the young man that he had unsuspectingly put out of his own misery. As a matter of fact, everything that had taken place over the course of the past few days had all but been erased from his brain, everything that is expect the nameless young man that was lying on a bathroom floor.

Images of him convulsing while his face reverted back to the human form caused only a migraine as well as an elevated temperature. Within his shattered body he felt so much sorrow for the young man, so much so that he wanted to scream out his name.

Without thinking, Linus raised his gun, pointed it at his right temple and looked down at his daughters' smiling faces inside the frame.

"Linus," Alan knocked at the driver's side window.

Linus spun his head around to see his partner wearing

a serious and pitiable manifestation upon his face. Soon, the pride that Linus wore so gallantly back upstairs was beginning to dissipate.

Without speaking a word, Alan opened the door, and with little or no regard towards his own safety, he secured the gun from out of Linus' hand. From there he helped Linus out of the car and wrapped his arm around his shoulder while escorting his friend back into the building.

As they carried on, Linus' face grew even more anguished and deformed. The man wept; there was nothing else left for him to do but weep.

It was the one and only explanation he could ever hand the world.

CHAPTER 35

"THEY BOTH WILL FALL *to the ground. People will wail in agony at the feet of their god...but they will not find mercy.*" Isaac's grainy, wicked sounding voice droned on over Doctor Sanyupta's tape recorder.

"*I see, Isaac. And can you tell me when these buildings will fall? Do you have a specific date? A month, time or even a year,*" Sanyupta asked with a thoughtful composure in his tone.

"*Od ton kcom em, hctiw rotcod.*" (Do not mock me, witch doctor) Isaac hissed.

"*I assure you, Isaac, I am not mocking you. I am simply curious to know just when this harrowing event will occur, so I can warn others, that is.*"

"*Your time in this world is drawing to a close, mystic. Ruoy niart lliw eb ruoy tsal etaf. Deeh ym ylluferac.*" (Your train will be your last fate. Heed my words carefully)

"*I will do my best to be very careful, my friend.*" Sanyupta compassionately assured. "*On that note, let us conclude our session for the day. After lunch, you can go downstairs and help set up the Christmas decorations with the others.*"

Doctor Levin pressed the off button on the tape recorder before wiping his teary eyes dry. He wished that he had known about the recordings earlier, but like most of his so called "safe patients", he chose to shove Isaac off to the side, waiting to see if he would relapse back into his schizophrenic state once again.

Just one week earlier Isaac seemed perfectly well. From Jeremiah's point of view there were no apparent or visible signs that would have suggested the man required more time at *Ashlandview*.

But there was Jeremiah Levin, slumped over at his desk while the Thursday edition of the *Cypress Guardian* that was lying in front of him kept begging for the young doctor to take yet another glance down at Isaac Mercer's grinning black and white photo.

There was an overwhelming sentiment of shame that he was sinking in. Jeremiah felt like a failure not being able to fully diagnose Isaac's problem. There was that persistent pinching in the back of the man's throat that wanted to believe Isaac's despairing shape-shifting story, to a certain degree that is.

All alone in his office, Jeremiah sat and stared endlessly from the newspaper to his multiple degrees on the wall that in times past he cherished and fawned over so proudly. He has listened to the chilling taped sessions at least five times in the past hour, and not one of his precious diplomas had prepared him for any of what he had listened to in Sanyupta's meetings with Isaac.

A series of knocks at the door interrupted Jeremiah's penitent moment to himself. Discreetly and quickly, the man wiped his eyes with a *Kleenex* before shouting, "Come in!"

From behind the door appeared a young, bearded, well dressed white man. With a cordial smile wrapped around his face, the man strolled inside and announced, "It's almost noon, Jeri. How about some lunch? My treat."

Clearing his throat, Jeremiah swiped the newspaper from off his desk before slipping it inside one of the drawers. "Sure, Paul, I need to get out of here for a while anyways." He sighed.

"You know," Paul prudently uttered, "these cases usually

turn out like this most of the time. You let it get to you now you'll carry it forever."

Jeremiah stopped his every movement at that instant to look up at his colleague with a belligerent frown as if a mountain of anger was building inside.

"Paul, how many patients have you had die since you've been a resident here?" He pointed.

Paul blushed and turned away as to say that the question had embarrassed him. All Jeremiah could do was continue to stare on at the man.

"C'mon, how many," Jeremiah impatiently persisted.

"Look, Jeri, if you're worried about what you're parents are gonna say, then don't be. Paul shrugged. "You've got a helluva career still ahead of you. This is only a minor setback."

Wearing a deadpan expression on his pale face, Jeremiah got up from out of his seat, grabbed his coat from off the coat rack and stormed right past Paul on his way out the door.

"You forgot to close the door!" Paul shouted, following Jeremiah down the hallway.

The instant Jeremiah reached the elevator, an unrelenting sense of being closed in suddenly seized him. Even though he wasn't even remotely hungry, the very thought of remaining inside his office and waiting for his next appointment was about as appealing as listening to a two hour physics lecture.

"I hear Sanyupta is heading off to *Calcutta* next." Paul commented before pressing the button to call the elevator.

Sighing, Jeremiah replied, "Yeah, that's one city down, ten more to go."

"Can you imagine how long of a train ride that is from *Bombay* all the way to *Calcutta?*" Paul grinned before entering into the waiting elevator.

With a slight, thoughtless pause in his step, Jeremiah followed in suit. The man stuffed his hands into his coat pockets, looked up at the ceiling, and at the blink of an eye, he cleared his mind.

Karyn drove along the pot-holed layered road at speeds that barely reached 15 mph. Behind her were the sounds of angry cars and trucks honking their horns and yelling for her to move faster. One by one she watched as vehicles veered past her, cursing and giving hand vile gestures.

As soon as she saw the bridge just a few yards up ahead, Karyn began to press harder on the gas until both she and her car were right under the bridge's steel girders. To the side was a large enough walkway where she could park her car without obstructing traffic any further.

The withdrawn woman sat in her cold vehicle, sulking and feeling sorry for herself. Everything she did, from knowingly sleeping with an attached man, to handing down her curse only gripped her body with the kind of sweltering fear that wouldn't allow a person to breathe, let alone live in peace.

"Go home." She muttered with a trembling bottom lip. "Mama...I wanna go home."

Without allowing one more thought to enter into her head, Karyn began to slip off her clothes. From her hat, scarf, coat, sweater, pants and boots, all the way down to her underwear, every item went flying to and fro inside the car until she was completely naked.

Before long, the woman found herself crying. She was crying so hard that the tears were blinding her. Karyn then found herself looking up into the rearview mirror only to see that her eyes had turned completely white and fangs were gradually growing from out of her mouth.

Without even cutting off the ignition, Karyn got out and stepped onto the freezing cold pavement while drivers honked their horns and careened their vehicles from one side of the road to the other, gawking amazingly at the woman that was casually stumbling along the ice coated bridge.

Karyn could feel the fur begin to stalk out of her skin; that alone caused her pace to quicken towards the bridge's double ledge that led to the tip that overlooked *Lake Logan*.

It was well below ten degrees that afternoon. It was a possibility that people could see her change, but that jarring notion didn't seem to weigh heavily upon the fraught woman as she stepped up onto the first ledge and looked out over the sprawling, mighty lake.

Her nipples, along with just about every other portion of her body were near frostbite stage at that point. Her toes felt as though they were going to fall right off of her feet at any moment.

With every passing horn, Karyn found her shaking body nearing closer to the second and final ledge. Within the part of her brain that still held a remnant of common sense, she realized that it wouldn't be too long before someone would eventually pull over and try to coax her from off the bridge.

One final, fond memory crossed Karyn's mind at that instant. She recalled the past Sunday when she saw Isaac at the gas station. How her heart jumped from both fear and elation from just knowing that he was alright after the incident from November. He was the very first and only man that she truly cared for, even though she knew full well that he never held the same feelings for her in return.

And that was all she needed. Before her hands could even grow out into claws, Karyn shut her eyes and took one last look at winter before stepping out into the thin air and plunging herself into the inhumanly cold water below.

The woman let go, not once holding on for one closing gasp of air. As she went under, Karyn could feel the beast try to escape from out of her body one last time. She made sure to keep her demonic eyes open for the entire journey downwards into the abyss as more and more space came in between both her and the surface above.

With only her right hand extended outwards, she reached.

Lynnette laid motionless in her hospital bed with her body wrapped from head to toe in nothing but bandages. Her entire face had swollen to twice its own size, while her left eye had ballooned to the size of an egg, nearly protruding out of its socket. Her right eye was completely swollen shut. In order to keep the blood properly circulating she had to have her right arm elevated. She was hooked to a respirator; with blockage in her throat, breathing at that stage was unbearable.

She laid, watched and helplessly listened as her parents and three sisters who were all gathered around inside her room yelled, screamed, ranted and raved about how much of a bastard Isaac was for doing what he did to their beloved Lynnette. Their scorching words against the man were filled with all kinds of colorful cursing, some of which Lynnette had never even heard up until that point.

Every breath that the young woman could grab was sheer ecstasy. With her one eye, she could see where her finger used to be on her right hand. Writing poetry, going to school, even being a mother to her son were about as important as sailing around the world to her. The enraged human beings that surrounded her bed that afternoon were becoming more and more transparent, like mere distortions in time.

From left to right, her bulging left eye scanned the five grown images in front of her, hollering as though she weren't even in the room. Eventually, Lynnette learned to block them out of her head until all that was left were eyes. Two shining eyes that glowed in the dark. Nothing else but the two eyes stared back at her.

"You people are going to have to leave if you do not

keep your voices down!" A doctor impatiently bellowed as he stormed into the room.

Lynnette watched as her family turned their furious attention away from Isaac and to the hapless doctor that was only looking out for his patient's best interest. Then, something happened that Lynnette honestly hoped would not...she caught sight of Isaiah who was being held by one of her screaming sisters.

The child was sucking on his thumb while glaring back at his battered mother. In her one good eye, instead of seeing her baby, all Lynnette could spot was Isaac and his glowing eyes in the dark as they made love. She recalled the endearing story that he told back at *Jimmy's* roller rink, and the look of joy on his face when he arrived back from *Ashlandview*. Unlike in times past, the memories no longer left the fond effect upon her heart. Lynnette's soul had drowned the night before, and it would be an awfully long time before it ever dared to resurface again.

Isaiah reached out with his tiny right hand and playfully pointed it at his mother. Lynnette didn't move. She shut her eye as tight as she possibly could...wishing she could vanish away from the entire world.

CHAPTER 36

"YOU ALL BE CAREFUL going home." Mr. Mercer warmly greeted as he hugged two women that attended his church before sending them on their way out the front door.

Once he shut the door, the man turned to see Deacon Hawthorne taking a collection of pots and pans into the kitchen. Without even looking around at the empty living room, Charles followed the deacon and noticed him placing the heavy pots in the refrigerator.

"You don't have to do that, Brother." Charles smiled while going over and dipping dirty dishes into the already filled sink.

"Well, if it doesn't get done now, then it never will." Hawthorne modestly replied before shutting the refrigerator door.

Charles carried on in his washing duty as if his longtime friend not even there beside him at all. He scrubbed and scoured one dirty dish after another, even the ones that were already virtually spotless to begin with.

"Boy, that sure was some good macaroni and cheese Sister Rozell brought over." Hawthorne gaily commented from out of nowhere.

Sparking back to life, Charles chuckled without taking his eyes off the dishes he was cleaning, "Yes, sir, it was sure was."

There rested a tidal wave of silence in the kitchen. It was so encompassing that even Charles himself could feel the weight of it bearing upon him.

"Charles, why don't you stop that for now?" Hawthorne implored. "You can do that later."

Gradually, Charles took his hands out of the warm, soapy water and began to dry them off with a rag that was lying on the counter to his right.

With his hands clasped together, the deacon keenly asked, "When do you think the police will ever find out what made that man kill Isaac?"

Charles continued on drying his hands while taking unsettling glances back and forth from the deacon to the wet towel he was using.

"Brother," Charles reacted in a low tone, "there isn't a degree of investigating the police can do that will bring my boy back. I got folks all over telling me to sue this person and that person for millions and millions of dollars. Everyone wants to riot for my child, thinking that's the right thing to do. Believing that will bring Isaac back. They're only doing it for themselves because they're already mad at the world. They're searching for an outlet; something to fight for. Not one of them even knew my boy."

"Well," Hawthorne sighed, "at least he's in peace now. That's all that matters."

Charles slowly placed the wet towel back onto the counter before turning to a window and looking out at the dull, grey sky.

"What about Lynnette and Isaiah, Pastor? How can anyone explain to that little boy what happened to his father when he grows up? It's just a doggone shame." Hawthorne pitifully frowned.

Charles pulled himself away from the window and simply answered, "I guess we'll have to wait and see, Lord willing."

Deacon Hawthorne reached out and hugged Charles,

patting him on the back saying, "Are you gonna be alright, Brother?"

"I'm just fine." Charles grimaced from the other side of Hawthorne. "You tell Clara that her marble cake was darn good, as always."

"I sure will, Pastor." The deacon said as he walked into the living room and put on his coat. "Now, if you need anything, just call us. Clara and I are gonna be home for the rest of the day."

With a humble grin, Charles said, "I think I'll be just fine. You be careful out there." He added before opening the front door.

Charles watched with bated breath as the deacon carried on out to his maroon *Cadillac* before closing the door. Inside the house was a sudden, claustrophobic silence; not even the usual leaky faucet in the kitchen could be heard dripping.

With a pair of heavy, sluggish legs, the man began a solemn tour of his own home. Above the fireplace sat Isaac's picture that was placed next to his mother's. Gently, Charles positioned his son's frame to where it sat perfectly straight.

From the mantle he dragged on into his bedroom, dropped down to his knees and folded his hands together. But instead of closing his eyes, he kept them open and rotated his head slightly to the right to where all he could see was his closet door that was slightly ajar.

There was a prayer in the back of his throat waiting for the perfect opportunity to escape. It was just sitting and festering, like a dead animal on a searing hot day, not wanting to budge a single inch.

The man allowed only his thoughts to do all of his speaking for him. He was angry at himself for not taking his own son more seriously, but rather than explode into a vicious, house-wrecking tirade like he desired, he caged it all inside. The rage, the tears and even the prayer to God were locked up securely while his hands remained tightly clutched the longer he gazed endlessly on at the closet.

After five whole minutes of kneeling, Charles got to his feet and resumed his tour. As he exited his bedroom, the man captured a glimpse of the living room and the couch and recliner where both he and Isaac would sit every Sunday afternoon during football season. How the living room would come alive with the uproars of men whooping and hollering back and forth over who had the better team, *The Browns* or *The Raiders*.

Once the celebrated image melted away, Charles just happened to turn to his immediate left to find himself standing right in front of Isaac's bedroom. The man carefully shoved open the door to find the bed unmade, as usual. Along the walls were posters of *O.J. Simpson* and *Bruce Lee*.

Charles made his way inside and began to make the bed from top to bottom. As he fluffed the pillows, Charles couldn't help but to look over to the other side of the bed to notice Isaac's record collection lying next to the wall. Out of all the albums that were displayed, the man managed to catch sight of *Marvin Gaye's, I Want You,* and the album cover's artwork. For a brief moment, Charles squinted and cracked and very subtle grin before he laid the pillows down onto the bed.

Before he could even turn away, he glanced over at the nightstand to see a framed picture of Isaac, Lynnette and Isaiah that was placed next to the lamp.

With pouty lips, Charles picked up the frame and longingly stared at the three happy people. He affectionately recalled how proud he was of Isaac when he told him that he and Lynnette were getting married. How much Isaiah resembled his father; from the smile all the way to the hairstyle was like watching Isaac grow up all over again.

Without giving another glance, Charles placed the picture back down onto the nightstand and began for the doorway.

As carefully as he could, Charles shut the door behind him before standing perfectly still inside the hallway. By the position of the shadows he could sense that nightfall was drawing nigh. Much to his chagrin, twilight would arrive... in only a few hours' time.

CHAPTER 37

THE STYLISH LIVING ROOM was bathed in glorious, late summer afternoon sunlight. Beams shot off from just about every piece of furniture, from the couch and recliner, all the way to the mantle that was littered with nothing but frames of various family members.

There rested a demure and comfortable quiet inside the home that made it feel as though it was the safest, most gentle place on the face of the earth. The tranquility that permeated the compact dwelling was a seamless, almost untouchable slice of heaven that made each individual that resided within its walls content.

The locks at the front door were speedily being twisted and turned. From behind the door appeared a skinny little black boy who was dressed in a pair of black shorts, a stained white t-shirt and a pair of knickerbockers. The excited boy came rushing through the door and into the house as if he were being chased down.

The moment the child reached the living room he could hear a female from the kitchen humming an old gospel tune, while the clanging of dishes and the sloshing of water were a sort of backup for her tune.

The boy immediately tossed his school books onto the sofa and darted straight for the kitchen to find the humming woman standing over the sink washing dishes. The boy could only see the woman from the neck down. It was as if her entire face had been blurred out. She was wearing a purple silk dress with yellow flowers printed all over, and a pink apron with a pair of black, rubber soled shoes.

"Mama, you won't believe who I saw today in school!" The little boy breathlessly shouted while running to his mother's side.

The mother stopped washing dishes long enough to turn and see the orange stain all over the front of the child's shirt.

"Boy," the mother moaned as she knelt down to his size, "just how on earth did you get this on your shirt?"

Trying to catch his breath, the child proudly explained, "I was eating lunch and me and some of my friends were playing with our food."

"Child, you are twelve years old, you're too old to be playing with your food." The mother lightly scolded while trying to rub out the stubborn stain with her wet fingers.

"Mama, you won't believe who I met today at school!" The boy continuously ranted.

The mother sighed before saying, "Tell me who you met before you burst all over the place, little person."

"I met this girl, and her name is Lynnette." He beamed from ear to ear. "She's so pretty, mama."

Appearing indifferent to her son's found fortune, the mother replied, "You don't go to school to look at pretty girls, you go there to lean. You hear me?"

"Yes, ma'am," the boy unhappily sulked.

The mother stood back up and sighed once again before folding her arms and asking, "Okay, what is this girl like?"

Suddenly, the boy's glum demeanor was brought back to stunning life. He looked at his mother and eagerly responded in rapid succession, "She's got really pretty hair, she smiles really pretty and she smells nice!"

"So, she has pretty hair, a nice smile and a nice smell." The mother reacted in a more upbeat tone of her own, sounding as though she were interested in her son's story. "Would this young lady happen to go to church?"

"I don't know, mama, but she writes really good."

"I see." The mother said. "Well, perhaps as time goes by, you and this Lynnette person can get to know each other better. In the meantime, take off that shirt so I can wash it. Then you get in the living room so you can start on your books of the bible before your father gets home from work."

"Yes, ma'am," the boy gladly replied before taking off his shirt and handing it to his mother.

From the kitchen, the child raced into the living room, crashed himself onto the couch and set aside his school books. He then looked down at the white undershirt he was wearing to notice the striking scent of strawberries that was layered heavily upon it.

The very last thing that he wanted was to tell his mother that he and Lynnette kissed and hugged on the very first day of school, he knew full well that he would never hear the end of it. Instead, he got up from off the couch and made a direct bee-line for his bedroom where he reached up underneath his pillow for another shirt to wear.

"Where are you?" Mother called out.

"I'm coming, mama!" He answered before tucking his blue undershirt into his pants and running back out into the living room.

"And what have I and your father told you about running in this house, child? This is no playground." Mother said in a soft tenor before planting herself down onto the couch.

The boy sat himself down right next to her and said, "Hey, mama, can we invite Lynnette over for supper some time?"

"Well," mother hesitated, "we'll have to wait and see just

what kind of young lady this Lynnette is before we do such a thing. Right now, it's time for the bible."

"Yes, ma'am," the child said, still trying to catch up to his always fleeting breath. "Lynnette likes greens, just like daddy does, too."

"Is that right?"

"Yes, ma'am," the boy stated. "And she writes poetry and stuff like that, too."

"You found out everything about this girl on the first day of school." Mother questioned in a surprised manner.

"Yes, ma'am," the boy proclaimed, sounding as if he had accomplished a major feat. "I can't believe how pretty she is. I think I'm gonna marry her one day."

Mother paused for a few moments before saying, "Maybe one day, son. Right now, it's time to study. Where were we yesterday?"

"I was trying to remember the books of the bible." The boy groaned as though he were beginning a wearisome journey. "After I get through with the bible, can I read my comics?" He feverishly asked.

"After you get done with your bible lesson its homework time, then supper and then bed. So just forget about those silly comic books." Mother adamantly countered.

"Yes, ma'am," the child hopelessly bemoaned before opening his bible.

Suddenly, the boy's mother began to gently stroke his back before saying, "I'm sure that one day you and Lynnette will be happy together. With all the perversion that's going on in this world right now. War, *Doctor King* last year, riots here and there; it's nice to know that people, especially young people are talking about marriage. But you and this young lady have all the time in the world. I'm sure she's a very nice girl, just like you're a very nice boy. You make sure that you stay that way, and never go astray."

The boy's once dull body immediately lit up once his mother was done speaking. With a glowing smile, he said, "I will, mama. And when Lynnette and me get married, I'll never, ever hurt her or be mean to her. I'm gonna love her forever, just like daddy loves you."

"You make sure of that, young man." Mother patted the boy on top of his head. "And don't think for one moment that I didn't smell all that perfume all over your shirt earlier either."

The child began to blush at that instant before he happily diverted his focus back to the book that was lying in his lap.

"Genesis, Exodus, Leviticus, Numbers—

The boy recited before abruptly stopping midway to remember the next book. From the television set in front of him, to the calendar on the wall that read *September 2nd, 1969,* the boy rooted around in his brain for the correct answer.

When his overcrowded mind couldn't remember the next all important book, he dropped his hands onto the bible and looked forward with a blank appearance on his face, as though the very life had been inexplicably sucked right out of him.

With his mouth hanging wide open in a dumbfounded gaze, the child slowly turned to his mother's shaded face, and in a downcast stutter, he slowly asked, "Mama...where I am going?"

"It hate it when that happens." A young, curly-haired white man cringed through his facemask while watching Isaac's dead body slightly jolt on the table that it was lying on.

The man then cut off the switch to the circular tank that was filling the corpse with embalming fluid.

The rank and stifling stench of formaldehyde and ethanol was always hard to stomach, especially when the room that you were forced to do work inside had no ventilation to speak of.

The two purple tubes that were inserted into one of the corpse's right veins were carefully slipped out and placed onto the tank that was to the young man's side.

"So you mean to stand there and tell me that *Farrah Fawcett* is hotter than *Kristy McNichol?*" He quibbled.

"You betcha," an older, dark-haired white man answered back as he pulled off his mask and unscrewed a jar full of clear liquid that was sitting on a nearby shelf. "C'mon, Craig, you've seen *Kristy*. I've got bigger tits than she does, for crying out loud!" He laughed.

"You gotta be shitting me, Art!" Craig tenaciously objected, placing his hands on his hips. "Did you see her in that afterschool special last year? She was smoking hot!"

Laughing out loud, Art asked, "What do I look like, a thirteen year old? Don't tell me you still watch afterschool specials. How old are you again?"

"Okay, okay." Craig relented. "But you have to admit one thing."

"What's that, my friend?"

"At least *Kristy* doesn't have *Steve Austin* on her tail morning, noon and night."

Art, with his attention focused on the dead man's deformed face, said with a confident smile, "The guy's married to the most gorgeous woman on TV. I'd be around her all the time too if I were *Lee*. Grab the forceps and bring 'em over here."

Craig did as he was told and stepped over to a corner to retrieve a pair of silver forceps before handing them to his partner.

Struggling against the cadaver, Art said, "I'm gonna see if I can somehow...lift this fella's skin up to where he can look somewhat presentable at his viewing."

With strangeness in his eyes, Craig asked, "How do you think his face got that way to begin with?"

"Who knows?" Art shrugged. "Maybe his old lady tossed a bucket of hot water at him, which would explain why he beat the shit out of her." He explained while trying to smooth over the melted skin that was overlapping onto the gurney with the tips of his fingers.

Art stood over the corpse with a pale presence written all over his face, looking as if he were about to upload all over the floor. "Did you hear what he did to his fiancée?"

"I heard bits and pieces."

"He cut off her fingers and then tried to kill her in the bathroom, with the baby in there."

"Christ." Art murmured, shaking his head from left to right in a disgraceful manner. "What a fucking animal."

"Yeah, it looks like he got off scot free." Craig remarked, stepping backwards an inch or two to uncover Isaac's naked, bullet wounded body.

"Looks like he was in one helluva battle," Art examined. "Four shotgun wounds to the chest and stomach, and three pistols shots to the head. It makes you wonder who got it worse, the girl of him."

"Well, I'm sure that cop had a good reason for shooting him." Craig sighed.

"One of the neighbors, some old lady, said that she and her old man heard some dog or something up in there." Art said. "Crazy guy probably had some mutt tear the woman's fingers off."

"Yep," Craig lamented, "I guess some people are born that way."

Taking off his white apron, Art looked up at his partner and said, "I know one thing is for sure, we'd better find a way to make his face look respectable before the funeral, or else we're out of a job. You hungry," he asked while rubbing his stomach.

"I'm starved." Craig happily replied.

"C'mon, *McDonalds* on me," Art remarked while making his way towards the door.

"McDonalds, huh," Craig chuckled. "Moving up in the world, are we?"

Shaking his head, Art opened the door and quipped, "I just have to wonder how your parents ever found the will to put up with such a smart ass like yourself. But then again, this is coming from the same grown man who watches *ABC Afterschool Specials.*"

Craig laughed right back before turning and asking, "You gonna cover him up?"

Waving his hand, Art replied, "Forget about it, we're only gonna be gone for an hour. He'll hold."

Heading away for dinner, the two men left Isaac's shell alone inside the room before closing the door behind them.

Despite his disfigurement, there was a peaceful manifestation on Isaac Mercer's face, as though someone were speaking soft words of deliverance into his dead ears.

There was absolutely no way for anyone to possibly comprehend the pains of the mutation the young man endured whenever the beast chose to emerge, or the mental trauma that such an occurrence carried along with it. The battle had at least ceased; the war was brought to an abrupt, if not merciful end.

There was so much more Isaac wanted to do before leaving his family, before having an affair, before letting his mother go. Twenty years was far too little time.

Seconds passed before the white sheet that was once covering Isaac James Mercer's midsection was mysteriously pulled back onto his cold body to the point where it covered his distressed face.

The bright light above suddenly went off all by itself... leaving Isaac alone in the dark.

A FINAL WORD

A POEM FROM GRANDMA, MRS. GLADYS GLOVER

COMING BACK

I SAW MY MAN *run away, run away, run away, into the valley of lilies. He ran so far that after a while, I lost sight of him.*

I began to chase after him. I ran, and I ran; I ran like the wind towards him, until he was no longer in sight. I looked up at the heavens and asked God, why? Why did my man run away from me, so far? God simply said, because he loves you so much.

I asked Gog again, why did my man run away? And God gave another answer, but this time, his answer was more cold and ugly. He said, sometimes people run off because they're not happy with the ones there with.

God had hurt me when he said that, he hurt me so bad, so bad that I spat into the air at God and ran away from him. But God told me to stop. I stopped, turned around and faced God again. God then said, just because they're not happy now, doesn't mean they won't be happy another day. If your man wants to come back, then he will, and it will be even better than before.

I asked God if he would promise me that, and he said that he would. So I waited, and I waited and I waited some more. Here he comes. His beautiful face shining in the sunlight. His strong, loving arms stretched out to me, wanting to hold me like a baby. His gracious and warm smile beaming like the sun's rays. It was my man, coming back again. It was the man that I once knew, from a long time ago. The man I fell so deep in love with in another place, in another time. How my heart and my soul cry out in joy.

Please, God...don't let Isaac come back home...ever again.

Printed in the United States
By Bookmasters